The Iron Angel

The Iron Angel
by
David Fulmer

A Bang Bang Lulu Edition

First Print Edition

Bang Bang Lulu Editions
www.bang-bang-lulu.com

Fulmer, David.
The Iron Angel / David Fulmer. — 1st ed.
1. Saint Cyr, Valentin (Fictitious character) -- Fiction.
2. Police -- Louisiana -- New Orleans -- Fiction.
3. Prostitutes -- Fiction. 4. Creoles -- Fiction.
5. New Orleans (La.) -- Fiction.
ISBN-10: 0-9886105-3-1
ISBN-13: 978-0-9886105-3-8

Author Photograph by Bryanna Brown

Published in the United States of America

To the women who
define my life.

My mother, Flora Prizzi Fulmer.
My daughter, Italia Fulmer.
And my wife, Sansanee Sermprungsuk.
You are always with me.

CHAPTER ONE

The cribs of unpainted clapboard lined both sides of Robertson Street like horse stalls, with barely enough room for a bed with a dirty mattress and a washstand. The hovels rented for a dollar a day and women charged a quarter for the pleasure they could offer. Some featured a wooden panel that could be opened and lowered from above so the strumpet could lie in view of the street the way a slab of meat might be laid out in the grocer's window. The only sounds were catcalls, curses, the breaking of glass, and the occasional screech of rusty hinges or dry bedsprings. Faint music drifted from a saloon a block over on Villere, where a small dance band played for the drunkards and their hussies.

The new electric lamps barely illuminated what appeared to be a convention of stumbling cadavers and furtive rodents. Men who either could not afford a clean woman or chose to traffic in foul flesh wandered or scurried about. Few lingered, preferring to get what they came for and then disappear back into the night. Those who arrived too drunk to navigate might wake to find themselves stripped down to their union suits. Now and then, one didn't rise at all and they'd call for a wagon. The coppers patrolled in pairs when they bothered to pay a visit.

The man who called himself Gregory stopped to catch his breath. The warren that cut along the back end of Storyville all the way to the walls of St. Louis No. 2 was cast in shadows and there was no mistaking the sour stench. The open privies, the garbage that filled the gutters, and the random foul airs had him drawing his silk scarf over his nose and mouth.

Gregory found a spot down a narrow walkway that led off Conti Street into a courtyard. He settled in this cavern to watch and wait. Out on the street, filthy harlots with their brains burnt to cinders on whiskey, hop, or disease staggered about, calling out to any man who happened to pass. Most were trash white, others were darker-skinned, and a few fell into a muddled middle.

"Come get some of this here," one pale creature shouted in a broken flute of a voice, as she lifted her skirts to expose her bare crotch. "Who wants some? Ten cents! Ten cents!"

Another dropped to her knees in a doorway, one hand held out as she waited for a man to pay for the service she offered. Several more ambled along with small mattress pads folded under their arms, ready to lie down in any dark place that would serve. And a trio hung like buzzards on a corner, their flat eyes flicking in sharp twitches and fingers stroking leather saps and wooden bats as they scanned the banquettes for drunks to roll. All of the women wore Mother Hubbards that had once been white but were mostly splattered with patterns of spilled whiskey, dried blood, and God knew what else. To Gregory's eye, not a single one was comely.

Presently, he heard a voice in the courtyard and turned to watch a man bend a woman over a trashcan and toss up the hem of her dress. After a rough half-minute, the fellow let out a hoarse cry. He lurched back, buttoning his trousers, then stumbled off. The harlot straightened, hitched her petticoats, and spread her legs to allow what her customer had deposited to dribble onto the cobblestones. She dropped the skirts and shuffled away. Gregory knew he could be on her and done with it in a matter of seconds, but that would be too easy and not worthy of his craft. So he returned his attention to the street.

The bells had just struck eleven when the door to a crib across the way slapped open and a tall stick of a man reeled out. A woman appeared, leaning against the frame, yawning, a pint bottle in her hand. Gregory studied her. Cast in the feeble glow of the streetlamp, her chin and cheeks were stark, her nose rounded enough to mark her as some brand of Creole. She was thin but still young enough that her flesh had not yet begun to sag. Though she was as decent as a whore on this street came, she displayed signs of the curses that had brought her there. The way she swilled the bottle, for one thing, downing it by fast inches until it was empty and she could pitch it into the gutter.

Gregory watched her lick her lips of the last drops of whiskey and rouse herself to scan the banquette for a fellow who would pay her enough to buy a fresh bottle. And so it would go through the night. He knew that the work would be simpler later, but he wanted this next one fresh. So he moved to the banquette and stood waiting until her eye fell upon him. She lifted her chin, offering a welcoming smile of gray teeth as she allowed her kimono to fall open to the chippie underneath. He crossed the narrow street and opened his hand to reveal two gold dollars.

The woman's grin widened in a ghastly way. "What's your name, sweetheart?" she said, and stepped back to allow him inside.

It was only after he had closed the door that she saw the harsh and brittle light in his eyes and her smile sank by degrees into a hopeless mask, as if she had known all along that one night such a visitor would come for her.

Four blocks over, Basin Street was a dazzle of artificial light that began at the open doors of Anderson's Café and Annex on the corner of Iberville and radiated down the line. The banquettes were crowded but not overflowing as the traffic from the trains at Union

Station had slowed to a trickle. Pickpockets, pimps, and street rats darted amongst the gentlemen in their Saturday night suits like Mississippi eels.

Inside Anderson's big room, the tables were full, the drinks were flowing, and the band was playing bubbly brass, all under a small galaxy of golden stars hanging from the two dozen chandeliers. The bar that occupied most of the south wall was doing only fair business, as the tenders in their brocade vests and short ties poured champagne and rye. The few men who had brought women deposited their ladies in the salon room in back.

In the heydays, twenty-thousand dollars might float across the table as a selection of the slickest gamblers in the country would be on hand. Now a wise eye would pick out the odd uptown rounder plucking the green feathers off some gentleman who was pleased to lose his money just to say he had sat down over cards with a genuine Storyville sharp.

For almost twenty years, the establishment had stood as the most famous address in the most famous red light district in the country; and in fact, the only legally-sanctioned district. That by way of the 1897 ordinance created by one Sidney Story, a pious gentleman who had to leave the city to escape the shame of having his name forever affixed to a twenty-block square dedicated to the commerce of sin.

It had not been Story's legal decree but Tom Anderson's deft hand that had driven the District. It could be rightly stated that between his role as the "King of Storyville" and his terms as a state senator, the man was legend in New Orleans and beyond. He had earned the title.

Four decades earlier, he and a partner opened a modest cafe and he used his special gifts to nuzzle close to the police on one side of the street and the criminal element on the other, playing the middle in such a masterful way that he managed to build an empire. He had outlasted mayors and police chiefs and city councilmen, priests and cardinals, an assortment of business magnates, and various crime lords. The years passed and some of his peers went into retirement, others into their graves. Still, Tom Anderson remained. Weary or not, he remained.

Sporting men around the world knew the great room of the Café and Annex, with its fifty-foot bar, tapestried walls, dazzling chandeliers, and rings of tables. On busy nights, the drinks flowed, the waiters rushed about, and the jass music went on until all hours of the night. In a small stroke of genius, the creator of this palace had added a private salon for ladies, so that a well-heeled fellow squiring an octoroon beauty out of one of the houses had a place for the damsel to tarry while he drank and gambled. There was not another establishment like it anywhere on earth; and yet it no longer brought much pleasure to the man who had imagined and then built it, and had so become a local legend.

At this moment, the legend was emerging onto the banquette, having had his fill of handshakes and backslaps. He now stood in the shadow to one side of the doors, waiting for his driver to arrive. It was not even ten o'clock and he was ready to go home.

He gazed down Basin Street, musing on how it had changed. The rounders who had frequented the District since before the ordinance loved to spend the lazy afternoon hours in some saloon or other regaling the other layabouts with their tales of times when it was good. How every sporting house along Basin Street had been a mansion and even the most modest address was clean and safe all the way back to Villere Street. These characters would swear that the beauty of the octoroons and quadroons who staffed the bordellos "down-the-line" would take a fellow's breath away and the arts of love the doves employed brought kings and ministers and titans of business from around the world to their gilded doors.

These same loose-tongued sports now bemoaned the fact that a good number of the storied madams had gone away. Some had made small fortunes which they carried on to their lives as rich matrons. Others had sensed the District fading like a wilted rose and traveled on to the greener pastures of St. Louis, Denver, and beyond. Still others had sworn off their evil ways, accepted Jesus into their hearts, and sought comfort in the embrace of the church. Two in succession had married Mister Tom, both exchanging their bordellos for fine homes with trellised gardens which they got to keep when he divorced them. On this September night, he wondered if it was true that Storyville truly was in a slow descent as those fools claimed or if it was just his tired eyes.

Lulu White leaving the city for an indefinite stay in California had struck the first ominous note. That grand lady, the most notorious madam in New Orleans for a dozen years, was seeking brighter lights. She was rumored by some to be after a place in moving pictures; others opined that she was on the trail of George Killshaw, the fancy man who had run west with over fifty-thousand dollars of her money and then disappeared.

Her mansion, Mahogany Hall, remained open, still with the loveliest women in Storyville and the elegant service to boot. But who knew when suddenly those heavy doors might close for good? And then others would begin to tumble, one address after the next?

For the hundredth time, he paused to muse on the coincidence of the District beginning its decline right around the time that Valentin St. Cyr took his new wife and escaped the scarlet streets. Though he knew there was no connection between the two, he also couldn't shake the notion that things would be different — as in better — if the Creole detective had remained there.

~

After she finished her bath, Justine wrapped herself in a kimono and stepped along the hall to the doorway. Valentin sat at the dining room table with his head bent over a book and a glass of brandy resting at his elbow.

In the lamplight, he looked much the way he had when she had first laid eyes on him as she stepped into the parlor at Miss Antonia's house on Basin Street eight years before: a curious Creole of Sicilian from his father and African, French, and Indian from his mother. Depending on the way he turned, he could pass as any of these and for white, too, which was how he had lasted so long as Tom Anderson's right-hand man.

In the light of day, she could see flecks of gray in his hair and certain lines around his eyes. Still, she knew that society women and Storyville strumpets alike would regard him as a fine-looking man and even though he had placed a ring on her finger at long last, she did not take him for granted. He was a fellow with a history of prowling, after all, and she knew that time hadn't erased the old urge from his bones.

Sensing her there, he stopped his reading and looked up. She took the chair next to him. "Quiet night," she said.

"They're all quiet," he said.

She began running an ivory pick through her curls. "And you don't miss it at all."

He heard the mocking note in her voice and returned her smile. He closed his book and took a sip from his glass. "They get along fine without me," he murmured. "Anyway, it's Each's problem now. I'll leave it at that."

"All right, then." She saw the way he was looking at her as she laid the pick aside and said, "What is it?"

He raised a hand to touch her check. It was his turn to consider

7

his good luck. He had almost lost her three times. It was after the last that he decided he wanted them to make a new life.

She said, "Valentin?"

"It's nothing," he said, and poured a glass of brandy for her.

The windows were open and a soft night breeze curled from the southwest and along Lesseps Street like a gentle wave of smoke. She sipped from her glass and he gazed out into the night that draped Louisiana to the south.

Beyond the lights of the city, the sky was dark wine in which distant stars floated like a smattering of glass beads. The further from New Orleans, the richer the shade grew, until it was a kind blanket laying upon the curvature of the earth. Over the bayous to the west, the darkness was complete and the silence had a substance that was strange to the ear.

When Sister Rosalie came on her rounds and found the corner bed empty, she first searched the ward, then hurried outside and started across the grounds to rouse the caretaker. She dreaded his grousing at being awakened from a sound sleep, but she wasn't about to wander half the night. The front gate was locked, but a determined patient could find a way out. She recalled a few years before when a woman had walked all the way to Lake Misere and then waded into the cold water. Her body was found the next morning by a Cajun out setting his traps. The last thing a poor convent needed was another such tragedy.

The sister stepped into the garden and felt the shadows wrap around her. She could smell the gardenia and oleander planted along the stone wall and the wild scents of lush earth and flowering vines carried on a night breeze from the banks of Sweet Lake.

She had proceeded only a dozen paces when she had cause to stop and stare for an astonished moment, imagining that one of the statues of the saints had come to life. Though she had been a bride of Christ for twenty-seven years, she had never seen a true miracle, and had come to count only on small blessings.

She wasn't witnessing one now. It was no stone saint transformed into flesh and blood, but the woman who belonged in the bed on the second floor of the ward, the one they called Evangeline because no one knew her true name. She had come from nowhere with nothing save what she wore and a small leather-bound book, another of the Lord's lost souls. In the three weeks since she appeared, she had displayed more penitence than many of the sisters, her hours spent silently gazing into the skies, as if searching for God in that indigo expanse, and murmuring her prayers as if she knew He was listening.

Sister Rosalie had begun to wonder if Evangeline was a true angel, like the iron casting over the arched front gate, but come to life. She prayed that this was true, if for no other reason than to end her doubts. Moving along the path of pebbles that wound through the stunted trees and cold marble sculptures, she approached so as not to startle the poor woman. When she was a dozen paces away, she said, "Evangeline?" keeping her voice low.

Evangeline stopped and turned. "Sister Rosalie?"

She smiled a faraway smile and the sister mused on how the peace of Our Lady of Sorrows had settled upon the mysterious woman. She was handsome, a Creole with the high cheekbones and slanted eyes of the Cherokee, full lips and an aquiline nose that harkened East Africa, and an *au lait* cast to her flesh. Her hair, gone a dark gray, was parted in the middle and pulled into a long braid. The sisters had guessed her age to be well into the sixties, yet her health was good, especially for one who appeared to have roamed the land for years.

"Why did you leave your bed?" Sister Rosalie said.

"I couldn't sleep." Evangeline waved a vague hand. "I had a dream."

"A nightmare?" The sister stepped closer.

Evangeline shook her head and stared down at the ground, her brow stitching. "I was in a little house," she said. "The sun was fading. I could hear voices of children playing in the street. My husband came in the door, home from work. I heard music. And someone was calling to me. Someone I couldn't see." She raised her eyes again. "Then I woke up."

Sister Rosalie, sensing something, said, "The man who was calling you, did he speak your name?"

"I don't remember."

The sister placed a gentle hand on her arm. "Let me take you to your bed. It's almost midnight. And it's getting chilly out here."

Evangeline fixed her gaze as if preparing to argue. Then she bent her head and let herself be led along the path through the stone garden.

The rest of the Storyville night passed calmly. By three o'clock, Anderson's Café was almost empty and some of the other saloons had sent the stragglers away and locked their doors.

When Black Jimmy and Jake arrived at the corner of Basin and Iberville for the hourly meet, Each told them the action was winding down and that they were done for the night. As usual, Jimmy tried to milk another hour's pay by turning nothing into something, this time a minor spat in a bordello on Franklin Street. Under questioning, he admitted that it was over and the house was quiet again. So Each sent both of them home.

As he walked the blocks to his rooming house, he wondered if it was time to let one of the men go. Except for the occasional row, the District was now bordering on sedate. This would suit the do-gooders quite nicely, but it did not bode well for the madams, the rounders, the sporting girls, the saloon-keepers, and all those who paid them visits.

Turning the corner onto Canal Street, he tried to imagine where he would go and what he would do if one day Storyville simply ceased to be.

Chapter Two

The body was discovered at noon by Elva Coy, a street whore who had gone around to the storefront at the end of Claiborne to pay the fat landlord her dollar and now wanted into the crib with the number 17 painted over the door.

Robertson Street had barely lurched to life. Empty bottles cobbled the gutters in shiny glass that reflected the hazy sun that had come up over the river. All that moved was the crew of four Negroes tasked with shoveling what they could of the four-block mess into the bed of a hack and moving on before the harlots appeared and another day of mayhem began.

Elva knocked a second time, waited, then smacked the door with an impatient palm. She wanted an early start, snatching the first arrivals and finishing her day's work while the other floozies were barely shuffling onto the banquettes.

"Hey, you in there," she called out. "Open up, goddamnit. I paid the man. You're out." She waited another few seconds before lifting the latch and pushing the door open. Her eyes required a moment to adjust to the gray light. She thought the woman on the bed had fallen asleep or had passed out in a bizarre posture. Then she saw the rest and let out a hoarse shout.

Captain J. Picot was alerted to the news of the body in the crib on Robertson Street when he arrived at the Detectives section at Orleans Parish precinct. He listened to the report, fixing the desk clerk who had delivered it a hard stare of muddy brown eyes. "Why is this important to me?" he said.

The clerk, whose name was Cassidy, was new to the job and not yet accustomed to Picot's humors. He sputtered something about being told to bring anything having to do with Storyville to the captain's attention.

Picot waved him quiet and made a sour face. "You ain't ever been down there, have you? Robertson and Claiborne don't count. I don't give a goddamn how many of those whores turn up dead." He started to stalk away, then stopped at the doorway and snapped his fingers at Sergeant O'Dell. His mouth stretched in a rubbery grin. "Send this boy on a patrol back there, Sergeant. It will be a boon to his training." With a snicker, he walked into his office.

The clerk's cheeks had gone pale. Sergeant O'Dell waited until the captain was out of earshot before saying, "Don't worry, son. You're not going near that place. The captain can fuck himself."

Picot had barely settled into his leather-padded chair when his telephone rang. The party on the line, one of his score of street spies, spoke a quick dozen words. The captain dropped the receiver and pushed the telephone box aside. He called out and a detective named Salliers poked his head into the doorway.

"Who's out there this morning, besides you?" the captain said.

"Just McKinney," Salliers said.

Picot mulled for a second, then said, "You and him get down to Robertson. Someone found a body in a crib." He noticed the detective's puzzlement and said, "I know. Just go. But don't waste the whole morning. See what's what and report back."

The stairs to the second-floor office had become too vexing a climb for a man of Tom Anderson's age and girth, so for the past two years he had conducted his daily business from the round table situated near the end of the bar and facing the brass-plated double doors that opened onto Basin Street.

As soon as he stepped inside, the day bartender laid down the rag he had been using to polish the copper and poured a small glass of brandy to go with the coffee that was already steaming on the bar. Anderson sipped the liquor as he studied the face in the broad mirror. What was once the most renowned visage in New Orleans had gone wide and sallow. The grand handlebar mustache that he had waxed every morning with such care now drooped in a listless way. The blue eyes that were known to dance with bright pleasure and flash with dark anger were a weary, bloodshot red that peered through the wire-rimmed spectacles perched on a broad nose.

After he finished his brandy, he moved to the table, feeling his bones creak. The physical ailments he could accept. Such was the way of world. No one grew younger. The way his spirit had been troubled of late concerned him far more. Late at night and deep into the morning, he found himself awake, standing on the back gallery of his house on Marengo Street and gazing into the garden as he pondered mysteries that had never before crossed his mind. Why were these thoughts coming to him now, on the cusp of his seventieth year on earth? Was it the better part of a lifetime devoted to the commerce of sin?

He felt the doubt and confusion rising again this morning. The brandy hadn't helped, clouding his mind so that he had to spend a few moments remembering what he had been doing. His copy of *The Times-Picayune* lay open on the table and he paused to check the date: September eighth. Yes, that was it: Tuesday, September eighth, the year of nineteen-hundred-and-fourteen, and his eyes were resting on an article about the Germans marching to within ten miles of Paris. Along other fronts, the Huns' creation of a new way to do battle using trenches. Meanwhile, thousands continued to murder each other. And they screamed about Storyville's little bit of wickedness.

He was mulling this absurdity when the front door opened and a thin figure appeared, the features lost in the light from the street. Only when the door closed again did he recognize the young fellow who worked the streets for him. The day bartender, wise to his employer's poor memory, called out: "Hello, Each!" in a loud voice.

Each approached the table. "Good morning, Mister Tom." He performed a quick, clumsy bow.

"How did the night go?" Anderson inquired.

"Went fine, no trouble," Each said. "But in case you ain't heard…they found a woman dead in a crib on Robertson this morning."

A dead crib girl was not news and the King of Storyville waited for more. When Each didn't continue, he said, "Were the police notified?"

"Oh, yes, sir."

"Well, it's being handled, that's what matters." Anderson said. "Anything else?"

Each cleared his throat. "It ain't that the girl died, Mister Tom. She was murdered. It's the way it happened."

Anderson laid his pen aside. He was aware of the day man stopping to perk an ear. "What's that?"

Each said, "You heard about them two gals they found, one in the middle of the summer and another one about a month ago? They was mattress whores."

Anderson said, "Yes, I remember something about that."

"This one this morning was done just like them two. Except that she was in a crib."

He went on to describe what he knew as his employer's frown

shifted from impatient to appalled. When he finished, the King of Storyville raised a finger. "The telephone, please."

The bartender placed the candlestick set of wood and polished brass on the bar and Each stretched the line to the table. Anderson lifted the handset, clicked the armature, and waited. He spoke gruffly and waited some more. Then he said, "Chief? Tom Anderson." He listened. "She's well, sir. I'll tell her you asked. I just now heard about the woman in the crib on Robertson Street." A blur of words squawked from the tiny earpiece. "I understand. Could I ask that they not move the body. Just until I can get someone back there to have a look."

He stared at the wall during the gap of silence that followed. The chatter resumed. With a roll of his eyes, he muttered a *thank you* and dropped the handset back into the cradle. "The detective in charge is named Salliers," he said, and waved Each away.

After breakfast, Valentin helped Justine clear the table, then took a quiet stroll to the corner grocery for the morning *Times-Picayune*. On his return, he carried the newspaper and a cup of coffee brewed with chicory to the back gallery.

The day had dawned hazy bright and warm and the sun was casting shadows around the fig trees and hydrangeas that he had planted with no small effort. Those fellows he knew from the saloons and sporting houses would hoot with laughter at the thought of Valentin St. Cyr, gentleman gardener. Or the notion that he spent hours every day reading books of history and sometimes religion from the small library he had built over the years. Another strange departure from Storyville.

He perused the papers to the twittering of the birds, noting another item about the opening of Xavier University as the first Negro college in the United States. If he turned to the editorials page, he'd find furious screeds claiming the school was an abomination, that God did not intend for people of color to be educated. These were absurd arguments for a place like New Orleans, with its jumble of bloodlines and palette of colors, but some folks wouldn't let the world change, as it was bound to do. He tossed the grounds from his cup, folded his paper, and went back inside.

When Justine appeared, she found her husband standing at the kitchen sink, gazing out the window. She never knew what to say when she found him that way.

Though he had told her more times than she could count that they had left Storyville behind, she knew he missed the wild nights, the music and lights, the fast action and edge of danger. Yet she sensed that he was at peace in their little house and wasn't about to run back there. That they had escaped was enough; or so she hoped.

She moved from the doorway and passed through to the bedroom to dress. When she came out, ready for her day, she kissed his cheek and left the house to catch the St. Claude streetcar on her way to the French Market. Valentin watched as she walked off, feeling lucky to have claimed her. Lucky to have her alive and not encased in a stone bier for him to grieve over until he could join her. It had been that close.

She had not been gone a minute when the telephone clattered. He let it ring until it stopped.

Each arrived at the corner of Robertson and Bienville streets to find a wooden barrier had been placed there and another at the south end of the block. A Ford touring car with New Orleans police emblems on the doors was parked in the middle of the narrow street. Two uniformed coppers stood on either side of the open door of a crib.

One of the officers raised a hand at his approach and said, "Crime scene here."

Each said, "Mr. Anderson sent me. He spoke with Chief Reynolds. I'm to see Detective Salliers."

The policeman took a moment to study him up and down before stepping through the doorway. Each was aware of shapes moving about in the close space and voices talking back and forth. The copper reappeared to resume his post. A thick-bodied man leaned out. He had removed his jacket and sweat stains darkened his shirt. With a bristling blond mustache and light blue eyes over round cheeks, he might have been a jolly sort. At the moment, however, the expression he wore was annoyed.

"You Anderson's man?" Each nodded. "All right. You can come on in and have a look. But don't touch nothing, understand?"

"Yes, sir," Each said.

The detective waved him inside.

Though Each was used to the sour filth of the cribs and the lowdown women who used them, he wasn't quite ready for the sight he beheld once his eyes adjusted to the low light. He felt his stomach heave and shifted his gaze, praying that he would not lose his breakfast in front of the copper. Mr. Valentin had told him how to breathe at such times. As he went about settling himself, he noticed another man leaning in the corner with his arms crossed. It took a moment for him to recognize a detective named McKinney. The policeman gave a slight smile and hiked an eyebrow. Each nodded, took a breath, and turned back to the narrow bed.

The body was splayed in four directions, naked save for the pieces of white cord that bound the wrists and ankles to the corners of the iron bed frame. The woman was paper pale and bone thin. The hair on her head and that between her legs was black and oily. Her eyes and her mouth were opened wide, as if witnessing

18

something that horrified her. At first Each thought the red cross that extended from her chin to down below her navel and then from the aureole of one sagging breast to the other was lipstick. He stared more closely and realized that it was flayed flesh.

He heard Detective Salliers say, "So? Seen enough?"

Each swallowed and gave a numb nod. "Mister Tom is going to want to hear back whatever you can tell me."

Salliers huffed. "Ain't a lot to tell," he said. "We think her name's Alice Carton. That's what one of the other whores said. She ain't a regular around here, so we don't know nothing about her. We'll check her records when we get back downtown." He waved a pudgy hand. "Anyway, the cause of death is suffocation. The first officers on the scene still could smell ether."

"That's how he put her out?

"And after that, she was smothered, probably with that pillow there. Then she was tied up. Then he cut her."

"Is that all?" Each said.

"Is that *all*?" Now the detective guffawed. "What else did you have in mind?"

Each felt his face flush. He knew from following Mr. Valentin that he was supposed to ask questions. There would be clues and such on the body and around the crib. He might find a street whore who would never dream of talking to a copper, but would tell a private detective anything she knew for the price of a pint bottle. It was one of the reasons that the New Orleans police had despised St. Cyr. Too often, he got what they missed.

"All right, you done here?" Salliers said. "Because this young lady has an appointment at the morgue."

Each glanced at McKinney, mumbled his thanks, and backed out the doorway and onto the banquette. A hack from the city morgue had arrived and was standing by. Within another half-hour, the body would be laid out on a cooling board and not long after that, on her way to a pauper's grave in Metairie or beyond.

He saw a few harlots who were out at this early hour watching the scene at the crib with flat eyes. No one was edging closer. They were a superstitious lot, and even the most devout paid heed to the *voudun*. No one would want to wander any closer to the evil that had been visited on that filthy room.

With a last glance, Each began the walk back to the Café. He had just reached the other side of the street when he felt a tap on his shoulder and turned to find McKinney with his jacket slung over his shoulder. The detective was a tall, broad-shouldered Irishman, his face still young in spite of a beard that was showing strands of gray among the ginger and his brown eyes were bright and calm.

He didn't speak right away, instead reaching into his trouser pocket for his Omars. He shook the pack and offered a cigarette to Each, then stuck a second one between his lips. Each produced a box of lucifers and snapped a flame. McKinney breathed a long plume of smoke. They watched the morgue attendants step into the crib.

"Hell of a thing to see in the morning," the detective said.

"Hell of a thing anytime," Each said with a nervous laugh.

"Bet you wish Mr. Valentin was around," the detective said.

"Just about every day," Each said.

"How's he faring?"

Each would have been wary had any other copper engaged him, but McKinney and Mr. Valentin had forged a friendship during the investigation of the murder of a wealthy man at the dirty end of Rampart Street and had stayed in touch ever since. In any case, Each was relieved to have something in common to discuss. Something other than the mutilated body of a crib whore.

"I suppose he's doing all right," he said. "He pretty much spends his nights at home with his wife. He works for those lawyers, you know. So the only time we see him is when some rich fool gets himself into trouble over here."

The detective snapped his fingers. "And he's in and out like that."

"That's correct." Each smoked in silence for a moment before saying, "What happened back there?"

"What happened was some poor crib whore let in the wrong customer," McKinney said. "It's a wonder more don't end up like her." He paused to tap an ash into the gutter. "You know about those others?"

"I heard about them. They was done the same way?"

"I saw the one who got done during the summer. It was just like her. Another detective told me it was the same with the other one. Except the first body was left in an empty lot below Tchoupitoulas and the second one in that alley that runs between St. James and Celeste.

"So it's the same fellow?"

"Ain't no doubt about it. Not one bit." He finished his cigarette and flicked the burning butt into the gutter.

The attendants had begun maneuvering the stretcher with the woman's corpse, now wrapped in a linen sheet, out the door. They hoisted the body onto the bed of the hack and climbed up into the seat. The driver snapped the reins and the two white horses began a slow clop toward Canal Street.

Each was aware of the motion about the intersection coming to a stop. He knew there was a good chance that this was all the funeral that Miss Carton was going to get. There would be no first or second line for her, no grieving family, nary a tear shed. A few of her sister whores might pause for a moment to ponder her demise before the next man with a few coins on his person came into range. Her bier might bear her name and "Died Sept. 1914" in crude letters. But she would be forgotten for all time.

McKinney poked into these bleak thoughts. "Tell Mr. Valentin I said hello and that I hope he's doing well," he said before walking off.

Valentin stared into the closet before choosing a light cotton shirt and his pale gray linen suit. He was annoyed that he had to wear a tie, but he knew his clients expected a certain decorum, and so he pick his charcoal gray. As he dressed, he passed a brief glance over the bottom drawer of the chest, where a whalebone sap, stiletto in a sheath, and Iver Johnson revolver lay tucked inside a cloth. For years, strapping the stiletto around his ankle, slipping the sap into a back pocket, and dropping the pistol into an inside pocket had been part of his ritual and he had never wandered onto the New Orleans streets without his weapons. Now it had been months since he had so much as peeked inside the cloth.

He stood before the mirror. He knew his particular Creole was so curious – Sicilian father and African, Cherokee, and French mother – that he could pass in any direction. And yet on this morning, in business clothes, to his eye he looked ordinary, befitting his life and work of late. In a few minutes, he would walk to the streetcar stop, then ride to an office on St. Charles to deliver weekly reports to three attorneys. If he concentrated, he might be able to stay awake.

The doors of the Crescent Saloon stood open to the morning breeze. The bartender in his white apron was sweeping the banquette. Each walked past him and stepped into the cool and dark. The barkeep, a thick-bodied, thick-armed Italian who sported a sweep of a mustache, leaned his broom against the door frame and followed him inside. "What'll it be, friend?"

"A whiskey would do just fine." He laid a dime on the bar.

"Let me get that."

Each turned his head to see a fellow in a worn suit, dusty shoes, and riding cap standing by with his hands stuffed in his pockets. He appeared to be in his thirties, with thin blond hair and a thinner blond mustache. He regarded Each from behind his spectacles with a gaze of friendly blue eyes. The barkeep poured a second whiskey.

"That was one hell of a thing on Robertson," the fellow said as he raised his glass. "You get inside, did you?"

Each peered closer. "I know you."

"Reynard Vernel. I'm a reporter."

Each grasped the proffered hand. "That's right. It was..."

"During the John Benedict murder." He smiled. "Mr. St. Cyr let me tag along."

Each took a sip from his glass and pondered the happenstance of crossing paths with two men who had been around for the same seven-year-old case, both in the space of an hour.

"You were just a kid back then," Vernel was saying. "And now you've taken Mr. Valentin's place."

"Oh, no, it's nothing like that." Each said.

"Well, I'm guessing you weren't inside that crib for pleasure," Vernel said with a tilt of his head.

"Mr. Anderson asked me to have a look, that's all," Each said. "So, are you still with *The Sun?*"

"I work for the *Picayune* these days," Vernel said. "I mean *Times-Picayune*. Old habit." He drank off his whiskey and tapped a finger on the bar. The saloonkeeper stepped up to refill both glasses. After he moved off, the reporter said, "So what about her?"

"Who?" Each said.

"The woman in the crib. They say how she died?"

Each was puzzled. "Shouldn't you be asking them about it?"

"They won't talk to me," Vernel said. "You don't know? That goddamn Captain Picot put out orders that no one but him is to speak to any of the papers. And he won't give us anything." He smiled as he raised his glass. "So you're my only hope."

When Each arrived back at the Café, he found that Mister Tom had already called for his car and had gone home to Marengo Street. He asked the day man for a glass of water and the telephone. The bartender found something in the general vicinity to occupy himself while he bent an ear.

Anderson's Negro maid took the call and beckoned the King of Storyville to the phone. The voice was gruff. "All right, let's hear it," he said.

"She was tied to the bed," Each began. "The detective said she was probably knocked out with ether. Then smothered with a pillow." The scene in the crib reappeared, and he swallowed and made a gesture to the bartender, who quickly poured a shot of rye, his third of the day.

"You there?" Anderson said.

"Yes, sir." Each drank off half the liquor. "She was cut open. Started at her chin and went all the way down her body to her... her part down there, you know..."

"Good lord."

"Then she was cut from one tit to the other. Like a cross." He finished the whiskey. The wide-eyed barman lifted the bottle again. Each shook his head.

Anderson said, "So it was the same as those other two."

"Except that they was found outdoors and she was in the crib," Each said.

After a troubled silence, Anderson said, "Anything else?"

Each said, "You know a reporter named Vernel?"

"I believe I've seen his name. He with *The Sun*?"

"He was. *Times-Picayune* now. Well, he was down there, and he

24

followed me and asked what I saw."

"Did you tell him?"

Each had a sudden change of mind and waved for another whiskey. "Yes, sir, but not all of it. I didn't think..." He waited for the explosion.

But the King of Storyville surprised him. "Didn't St. Cyr teach you anything?"

"Sir?"

"Don't ever talk to a reporter unless *you've* got something you want in the paper. Understand?"

Each heard the crack of the handset dropping into the cradle and considered that the King of Storyville and Captain Picot treated newsmen exactly the same way.

CHAPTER THREE

Sister Rosalie did not see Evangeline at breakfast. Once the tables were cleared, she had one of the cooks put a slice of ham and a scrambled egg on a small baguette and wrap it in waxed paper. She filled a tin with tea and walked across the grounds to the dormitory, only to find the bed empty. The mute woman who was mopping the floor pointed vaguely to the south.

The sister found her sitting on a marble bench in the shadow of the plastered wall, holding her bible open in her hands. A few leaves had fallen on the cold stone on either side of her. When Sister Rosalie spoke her name, she looked up and offered a faraway smile. The sister held out the roll and the tea. "This is for you."

Evangeline cocked her head, befuddled. "Communion?"

Sister Rosalie laughed. "No, breakfast. Aren't you hungry?" When Evangeline made no move to accept the food, the sister brushed away the leaves and sat down. "What are you reading this morning?"

"A psalm." She ran a finger over the thin paper with its black and red print.

"Which one?"

"Thirteen."

Sister Rosalie squinched her eyes. "'How long, Lord? How long will you forget me? How long will you hide your face?'"

She paused. Evangeline continued in a soft voice, gazing at a patch of sky above the trees as if the words were written there. "'How long must I carry sorrow in my soul, grief in my heart?'" Sister Rosalie smiled. "'Look upon and answer me, Lord,'" Evangeline went on. "'Give me sight, lest I sleep in death, lest my enemies prevail, lest my foes rejoice at my downfall. Grant my heart joy, that I may sing your praise.'" She looked away, shy as a girl.

"How many others do you remember?" Sister Rosalie said.

"I don't know exactly. Many." She closed the bible.

"Where did you learn them?"

"In church."

"Which church? Maybe I know it."

Evangeline turned to her with vexed eyes, as if she didn't understand the question. Sister Rosalie waited a moment, then handed her the tin and watched as she took a small sip. "Honey." She sighed with pleasure. "I always loved honey in my tea."

The sister placed the wrapped sandwich on the bench. "I'll leave you to enjoy this in peace," she said and stood up.

"Thank you for your kindness, sister," Evangeline said.

"May God bless you this morning," Sister Rosalie said.

She had gone a half-dozen steps when she heard Evangeline say, "Thomas." She stopped and turned around, tilting her head uncertainly. "The disciple?"

"The priest," Evangeline said. "It was Father Thomas."

With that, she opened her bible and passed a hand over the delicate page. Sister Rosalie watched her for another moment before slipping away.

Captain Picot was standing in his office doorway when Detectives Salliers and McKinney returned. Both were moving to their desks when he called to them and crooked a thick finger.

Picot moved to his heavy leather chair as the detectives stepped into the office. "So?"

"The woman was a crib whore, but not one of the regulars down there," Salliers said. "She was knocked out with ether and then smothered. Probably with a pillow. The perpetrator stripped her naked and tied her spread-eagle to the bed frame. After that, he cut her." The detective used his index finger to trace the wounds. "Just deep enough to open up the skin. And just shy of the mouth and all the way down to her, uh, pubic bone. From one tit to the other, but not the nipples." He paused to shake his head. "Fucking peculiar is what it is, Captain. I think maybe we got a—"

"What we got is some sick individuals in this city. Else, there wouldn't be a Storyville to begin with."

Salliers reserved comment on that point. "Do you want a report?"

The captain flipped a dismissive hand. "Just your notes will do fine." He barely glanced at McKinney. "Same goes for you. Then both of you get back to your cases." He saw the two detectives exchange a look and said, "What?"

Salliers said, "The other women. The two from before. They were done the same way."

"Oh? Is that right. Did you see both bodies?"

Salliers said, "No, sir. Just one. I heard about the other."

"Same for me," McKinney said.

"What I thought," Picot said. "It doesn't matter. These are street whores we're talking about. We have better things to do." With a last hard look, the captain swiveled in his chair to stare out the window as the swath of late morning sun that was breaking through the clouds.

Valentin stepped into the small office off the dining room to select a book from the shelf. He locked the house and walked to the corner of North Claiborne to catch the streetcar.

Rather than take the direct route, he rode three cars, the first on the Esplanade line, then on the Decatur Street looping along the river below the Vieux Carre, and last onto the St. Charles. He kept his head bent over his book as the blocks passed, and after a half-hour of stops and starts, stepped down at the corner of Julia Street and waited for the traffic to clear before crossing over.

The gold-burnished placard next to the double doors announced the law firm of Mansell, Maines, and Velline. The building always reminded Valentin of a grand mausoleum. A sepulchral silence greeted visitors stepping from the foyer into the lobby, with the slightest footfall echoing off the marble floors, along the walnut-paneled walls, and up to the high arch of the ceiling. It was a hushed and somber place where the majesty of the Napoleonic Code reigned.

At the precise center of this cavern sat a desk and behind the desk was a severe woman named Mrs. DeCourt. Blade thin and fox-faced, in a shirtwaist a decade out of style, she was the grim-eyed gatekeeper. Valentin had been in the employ of the firm for almost three years, and yet every time he arrived, she greeted him as a stranger and a threat, perhaps a miscreant who might lunge at her with a deadly weapon or toss a bomb into a partner's office.

The regimen never changed. He would announce himself and she would take a long moment to consult the ledger. Then, in a tone so deliberate that she might have been addressing a child or a dimwit, she would instruct him to take a seat and wait. He would instead make a point of pacing the lobby, hoping to irk her.

This time, the wait was short and instead of the attorney Sam Ross, a courteous but blank young law clerk appeared to explain that he would be escorting him to the conference room on the sixth floor. Valentin was puzzled; his meetings had always taken place in one of the street-level offices.

When they exited the elevator, the clerk showed him to the

double doors at the end of the plush-carpeted corridor, then retreated. Valentin stepped into a room that occupied the lakeside corner of the building and featured wide windows on the two outside walls. At its center was a solid oak table, twelve feet long with leather-upholstered chairs placed at exact intervals.

A tall Negro in waiter's garb and with pronounced African features was standing next to a cart upon which were arranged a silver coffee pot, cups and saucers, and a tray of fruit and pastries. When Valentin placed his valise on the table, he said, "Good morning, sir. May I serve you something?"

The detective stepped to the cart. "All right if I get my own?" He saw the Negro's brow hike and said, "I prefer it that way."

As he set about pouring a cup of coffee from the silver pot, he sensed the waiter's curiosity as the man thought he recognized something familiar in the Creole detective's features. He was used to the looks. Now he turned to survey the room. "Why all the arrangements?"

"Don't know for sure, sir," the waiter said, keeping his voice low. "Usually when they do like this, it's because one of them senior partners is going to be in the room. Mr. Mansell in particular. He likes to call meetings so he can hear himself talk."

Valentin laughed at the comment and crossed to the window to gaze over downtown New Orleans. He could spot a section of the French Quarter between the buildings, but none of the red light district, as if that blight had been conveniently removed from view. What he surveyed was indeed a regal view of the city and the idea that he would end up in such an elegant venue would have not so long ago been preposterous. And yet there he was, sipping excellent coffee from fine china.

For this, he could thank Anne Marie Roget, née Benedict. Seven years earlier, his investigation of her father's Rampart Street murder had led him to her and an afternoon that left her silk sheets bloody. After the case ended and the heat between them cooled, Valentin returned to his life in Uptown and she moved on to marry a gentleman of her social caste. Before her nuptials, she passed along a request that the Creole detective be kept on retainer with the family law firm for as long as he so desired.

The attorneys had been frankly irked at the intrusion of an operative whose resumé featured a decade in the Tenderloin. Until they discovered what an able agent they had acquired. The Mansell, Maines, and Velline assignment led to two others, and he was able to walk away from Storyville at long last.

Though Justine was delighted at this turn of fortune, she kept a cool eye cast in Miss Benedict's direction, suspecting that the young lady would want something in return for the favor. Like another frolic on the four-poster bed in the fine house on Esplanade Ridge.

His fond memory of her cross-armed suspicion was interrupted by the sound of voices in the corridor. He looked over at the waiter, who murmured, "So you know, if they send me away, it's serious business."

Valentin stood by as three men entered. First through the doorway was the attorney Samuel Ross, his prime contact for the firm's business. That he had grown shorter since Valentin had begun working for the firm was an illusion; that he had grown rounder was not. Red-faced, button-nosed, and bright-eyed, he remained jolly. Though with all his soft edges, he was strictly business when it came to clients' interests.

Valentin could see that this was such an occasion. The senior attorney's visage was stiff and his hands twitchy as he turned to one side, gestured toward the man next to him, and said, "Mr. St. Cyr, I'd like to introduce you to Mr. Louis Velline, one of our senior partners."

Valentin took the delicate hand of the craggy old bird with snow-white hair and jutting brows over eyes of dull blue. The patrician nose was so thin as to barely accommodate the nostrils, the lips were a shade of purple and drawn thin, and the pale flesh dotted with liver spots.

"I've heard of the good work you've been doing on behalf of our clients," he said. "The *discreet* work. We are grateful." He tilted his head in the direction of the man standing just behind him and to his left. "This is Mr. George Alberton. George, Mr. St. Cyr."

Valentin recognized the name of the patriarch of one of the New Orleans families who had come into wealth after the British had left and managed to keep it even through the blockade, when so many had lost their fortunes. The detective could not say what Alberton and his peers did for their money, other than to move it around. He did know that the man was reputed to be much of the power behind the current mayor. A Tom Anderson of the straight world, in other words.

For all that, Alberton was not impressive in features or bearing and would be difficult to pick out of a crowd. While his thin gray hair, spectacles, and the dry planes of his face rendered him as bland as American bread, his tan eyes held the arrogance that Valentin often observed in members of the moneyed class. He did not offer the detective his hand, instead moving to a chair at the table. The two attorneys flanked him and Valentin took a seat opposite, returning the searching stare and feeling a flicker of heat rising from his gut.

Alberton made it all the worse by addressing him in the clipped monotone of a superior to a servant. "Before we speak of this matter, I'm going to insist on complete secrecy," he said. "You let a single word of what we discuss leave this room, you'll regret it. Are we clear on that?"

Valentin held the gaze for a quiet few seconds, then said, "And if you threaten me again, you'll regret it. Are we clear on *that*?"

Except for the soft groan that rose from Sam Ross's throat, the silence was leaden. Louis Velline gaped, his old eyes hardening. The detective drew himself up and buttoned his jacket in preparation of being tossed out the door, right along with his employment with the firm. He could not say why he had gone so rude with this rich man, but it was too late. The words had left his mouth.

He was wondering if Justine would murder him now or later when he heard a snicker from across the table. George Alberton's lips were curling. "That's just what I would have said."

The moment passed. Sam Ross's face reclaimed some of its color and he let out a shaky breath. Alberton glanced his way. "It's quite all right. Anyone who worked for Tom Anderson for all those years certainly knows how to keep a confidence." He saw the Creole detective smile and said, "You wouldn't be sitting here if I didn't know all about you."

With the air now back in the room, the younger attorney spoke up quickly. "Coffee, Mr. Alberton? Mr. Velline?"

The senior attorney and his client declined. Ross made a nodded to the waiter and the Negro left his post and moved into the hallway with a last sidelong glance at Valentin.

Once the door had closed, Alberton said, "We employ a maid named Belle Baptiste at our home. A mulatto woman. She's been with us for thirteen years. She and her daughter Emelie have rooms of their own in the house. They're like family. I've paid for the girl's schooling, just as I have for my own children." He paused, then said, "On Saturday, Emelie disappeared. She left in the early afternoon. When she didn't come home, I called the police. They were of no help. We were up all night and all through Sunday. Belle was frantic." He paused. "Someone has taken her."

33

"What makes you think that?"

"Because on Monday morning, she telephoned the house. She wouldn't say where she was or why she had gone off. Only that she was safe."

"Have there been any demands?"

"No, nothing."

"Then why do you think she was taken?"

"Because when I spoke to her, I heard a voice in the background."

"Perhaps she just ran off."

"She wouldn't. She's not a foolish girl."

"How old is she?"

"Sixteen."

Valentin couldn't imagine a girl that age who was not foolish in some way, but he kept this thought to himself.

George Alberton folded his hands before him and said, "It's my understanding that you're able to travel in, uh...*Colored* circles."

The detective had never heard it put quite this way and enjoyed a private smile. His outward reaction was a shrug.

"We want to find her," Alberton continued. "Can you help?"

"I'll see what I can do," Valentin said. "But I won't make guarantees."

"Why not?"

The detective wanted to say, *Because I don't know what you're hiding yet*; instead, he said, "Because what you describe is an unusual situation."

"We just want to locate her and make sure she's not harmed."

"If she has been taken, you'll be asked for ransom money."

"I don't care. I'll pay."

Valentin said, "All right, then. I can look into it."

A signal passed and Velline turned to Sam Ross and said, "What do you have Mr. St. Cyr working on?"

"A few small matters," Ross said. "Nothing that requires a great deal of his time." He looked at Valentin and raised an eyebrow. "Correct?"

"That's correct," Valentin said.

Mr. Velline said, "Then you're to devote whatever time it takes to locate the young lady."

"I understand," Valentin said. He took a sip of coffee and said, "I'd like to get started now, if we could."

The senior partner got the message and he and Ross rose from the table and left the room. Valentin opened his portfolio for a writing tablet and a pen. "All right, sir," he said. "Tell me about Emelie."

Chapter Four

The afternoon edition of *The Times-Picayune* hit the streets at two o'clock. The pages were posted on a board on the side of the building on the corner of Poydras and Carondolet ten minutes before the young boys were cut loose over downtown and the trucks were sent on their way across the city.

The item was tucked on page ten, below the fold.

Woman Found Slain

3rd Terrible Killing
in As Many Months

~

Bodies Reportedly Mutilated
by Reynard Vernel

The mutilated body of a young woman of ill-repute was discovered early this morning in a crib on Robertson Street.

The body was mutilated by a specific cut in the form of a cross, according to one witness. Other witnesses stated that the victim was the third to be butchered in such a manner this year. Two others were murdered and their bodies left outside, according to police sources.

The sound of Captain Picot's table lamp crashing to the floor caused the detectives in the section to come alert in a quick instant. Two of them, expecting the worst, left their chairs and began edging toward the door. They stopped when they heard Picot yell, "Salliers and McKinney, in here now!"

The detectives stood up to make the long walk. "And someone out there go get me another newspaper," the captain barked.

They stepped into the office to find the captain standing with his left hand on his hip. In the right was the section of *The Times-Picayune* he had used to swat the telephone set off his desk. The rest of the pages were scattered about the carpet, waving this way and that in the breeze from the ceiling fan.

"You know what's in here?" he said, shaking the newsprint in the air. "A story about the tart in that crib." He swung the paper between the two. "Who talked to a reporter, goddamnit?"

"Nobody," Salliers sputtered. "There wasn't any around. Just that kid from Tom Anderson."

Picot glared at McKinney, who said, "There were no reporters when we were there."

"The name on the story is Reynard Vernel."

McKinney said, "I know him." Picot's gaze went sharp and he said, "Know the name, I mean."

"I know him, too," the captain said. "He and all the others were told if it involves this precinct, they come talk to me. Nobody else."

"Does he use someone's words?" Salliers said.

Picot stopped to glare at the page in his hand, his lips pursing. "He says…'witnesses' and 'police sources.'"

McKinney said, "He probably means the records. On those two other women who were killed."

"So, what, the sonofabitch looked at the incident reports and talked to some of the whores and comes up with this?"

The two detectives exchanged a glance and Salliers said, "Anderson's man, what's his name?"

37

"Each," McKinney said.

"Yeah, him. He was in the crib. He saw the body. Maybe Vernel talked to him."

"Shit," Picot said and then gave a doleful shake of his head. "That's it. That's exactly what happened."

"May I, Captain?" Salliers gestured to the paper.

Picot handed it over, then stepped through the scattered pages and dropped into his chair. "I dream of the day when that old fool is gone," he muttered.

Salliers read the story, with McKinney peeking over his shoulder. When he finished, he said, "It's way in the back, captain. Most people won't even see it."

Picot gave him a cool look. "Is that so? You know who *will* see it? Because I do."

Tom Anderson paid the kid an extra dime to run a copy of the afternoon edition to his front door before he went off to cover the rest of his route. So when the King of Storyville heard the slap of the paper landing on the gallery, he ambled out into the breezy end-of-summer day. Once he managed to bend down and pick up the paper, he settled with a grunt into the gallery swing and flipped the pages until his eyes landed on the small item about the woman in the crib.

It conjured images of sad women and their horrible last seconds. After he muttered a quiet Catholic prayer for their departed souls, his thoughts shifted to the damage. He guessed it would be slight. The latest victim was the only one of the three found in the District. The madman perpetrating the acts was moving from place to place, likely to stay ahead of the police. Maybe he would take his next one in Marigny. Maybe on Lesseps Street. Maybe in Valentin St. Cyr's back garden, the one Each had told him about. As he

38

turned to the business pages, he mused on how a killer on the loose once would have set the Creole detective into forward motion.

Justine was slathering oil and rosemary on a chicken and humming a tune she remembered a professor playing when she heard the rattle of an automobile turning the corner from Marais Street. The engine noise drew closer, but instead of passing by, the Ford stopped in the street outside the house. She waited for it to move along so she could resume her song. When it didn't, she walked through the house to stand at the screen, wiping the oil from her hands with a kitchen towel. She pushed the door open to see Valentin sitting at the wheel of the brick-red roadster.

She poured the coffee, added brandy to both cups, and carried the tray to the front gallery. He was leaning at the railing, admiring the machine. She placed the tray on the little wicker table and sat down. "So explain this to me," she said.

He picked up his cup, took a sip, and then told her about the meeting at the law firm, leaving out his sniping with George Alberton. He had no qualms about sharing the details of the young girl's disappearance. Justine would never speak a word of it to anyone, no matter how much a female love of gossip itched her tongue. And she possessed a sharp wit that might catch something that he missed.

He went on to what Alberton had told him after the attorneys had left the room. "The young lady — her name is Emelie — took the family dog for a walk in Audubon Park. An hour went by and the dog came back. No trace of her. The next morning and every morning since, at eleven o'clock, she calls the house. She says she has not been molested. But she's not saying anything more."

"And she doesn't know who's holding her? *If* she's been taken."

"Not from anything she's said."

"And no demands?"

"Not so far," Valentin said.

Justine sipped her coffee. "She's a young girl. Maybe she just ran off."

Valentin said, "That was the first thing I thought of. I asked Alberton and he said she wouldn't do that. The mother said the same, but..."

"You don't believe her?"

"I don't know yet."

Justine said, "You said he has two daughters of his own?"

"One's in Baton Rouge," Valentin said. "She's twenty-two and engaged to be married. The other is seventeen. She's at home. She attends a finishing school."

"He must have had those girls late."

"When he was in his forties."

"How old is Mrs. Alberton?"

"I haven't had the pleasure." He noticed his wife's pretty brow furrow and said, "Are you wondering why they didn't target her? Or the younger daughter?"

Justine said, "He'd be even more likely to pay."

They sat mulling this for a few moments. Valentin placed his cup on the railing and dug into his jacket pocket. "Speaking of paying, I got this." He drew a bank check in the amount of a twenty-five dollars from his pocket, handed it to her, and turned a thumb toward the roadster parked at the curb. "And that."

Her eyes went wide. "He gave you an automobile?"

Valentin laughed. "Oh, no. He asked how I made my way around the city and when I told him mostly streetcars, he said that wouldn't do. Not with a case that involves someone under his roof. The Ford had been sitting in a garage. It's mine to use until I settle this."

Justine studied the roadster for a moment before saying, "Then take your time."

Reynard Vernel stepped out the front doors of the building to find the two detectives who had been at the Robertson Street crib the day before lounging against the police car that was parked at the curb. Salliers was smoking a cigarette and regarding him with dim eyes. McKinney was wearing a faintly vexed expression, as if something troubling was on his mind.

Salliers tossed his butt into the gutter. "Good evening, Mr. Vernel."

"Officers," Vernel said.

"Heading for home?" The reporter nodded. "How about we give you a ride? But first we need to take a detour. Captain Picot wants a word with you."

"This late?" Vernel said. "Can't it wait until the morning?"

"No, it can't." Sallier's tone had switched abruptly. He grabbed the handle and swung the back door open. "Get in."

The reporter turned to McKinney with a question in his eyes. The detective shrugged. Vernel climbed into the seat.

Valentin stopped admiring the machine when the boy came up the street with his bag of newspapers slung across his shoulder. He carried the paper onto the gallery and spent a half-hour reading as the day wound down. He was idling through the back sections when the item caught his eye.

A dead body in a crib was not news and a murder wouldn't draw much notice, as the slatterns died with regularity from violence and various grim ailments. The words "butchered in the same manner" did hold his attention.

41

His gaze went blank and he felt a surge in his gut. He had read not a word about the other two victims whose corpses had been left lying where they fell. They were worth neither attention nor ink. But one had been taken in Storyville, though in the last filthy corner of the quarter. He stared over the top of the page. At that moment, the miscreant might be planning a—

"Valentin?"

She spoke his name a second time. He looked up, blinking, and the cast of his features held her. She had seen that distant look before.

In the next second, it was gone. He said, "I'm sorry, what?"

"I'm ready."

She had changed from her day dress into a gray pleated skirt, a white shirtwaist, and black cotton vest. The brim of her hat held a veil that was at the moment turned up. She was regarding him with bright eyes.

"Ready..."

"To go motoring," she said. "Before dark, please."

He got to his feet and hurried into the house. She saw the newspaper open on the wicker table and bent to the page he had been reading. The item at the center caught her eye and she whispered under her breath. When she heard him returning, she straightened. He appeared on the porch, snapping the must from the driving hat that had been hanging in the closet for months. He doffed it and bowed with a hand toward the street. After she started down the steps, he noticed the paper laying open on the little table, with the story about the Storyville killing in plain view.

~

Gregory retired to the attic with his tools and the afternoon edition of *The Times-Picayune*. He did not expect a front page item, not for a crime that involved a lowdown trollop, but as he plowed deeper and found nothing, his felt his forehead begin to burn. Then, at last, there it was, on page ten.

He paced the boards from one end to the other, reading over the black print a half-dozen times, searching for any deeper meaning. There was nothing he could detect. He laid the newspaper aside and walked to the round window to look out on the city and think of the thousands who were reading the words about the woman on Robertson Street – and the two who had come before.

He turned to study his face in the cheval mirror, looking past the bubble eyes and puffed cheeks, the squashed nose and flabby lips to see the watchman come to life in his sinister glory.

His wicked acts were now a matter of record, never to be erased. A century from this night, someone might be rifling through dusty stacks and read the words on a yellowed page and know that he had made a mark. And that it had not been some foolish trifle, like news of his father sitting on some board of directors or his mother being honored at a flower show. This was the death of a human being, the greatest drama of all.

It was something he would relish in a delicious secrecy as his mother prattled on about this or that, his sister twittered over her beau, and his father harrumphed about the world going to hell. And they would never dream what lurked in their midst.

Gazing out the window, he gave a start when he saw an automobile hurtling along St. Charles Avenue and imagined a police car heading for his address, the siren wailing. Then he saw it was only a runabout speeding in the direction of Audubon Park.

~

The night was clear and warm, so Valentin had left the top down. He was still getting used to the automobile, and it had required a clumsy minute for him to turn the crank, get the engine popping, and adjust the idler. He used the throttle handle that was

43

located under the steering wheel rather than the pedals and after several stops and starts, managed a smooth drive to Jackson Street. He turned south, following the curve of the river.

Justine forgot about the newspaper on the gallery and settled back to enjoy the ride. She had ridden in fine automobiles owned by certain well-to-do customers. Miss Antonia had kept a Packard touring car parked in the alley behind the bordello. But Justine and the other girls had been paid passengers, carried off to entertain some rich man or other. This was better. And faster; Valentin pushed the Ford along at a lively pace, the engine gurgling and tires humming as they swung onto Canal Street.

The dazzle of downtown lights passed in a blur. When they made the left onto St. Charles and reached Girod, Valentin pointed out the law offices. They followed the streetcar line and once they rounded Lee Circle, the machines they saw were mostly shiny new models that belonged to the grand Garden District mansions.

As they drew near Audubon Park, Justine remembered what Valentin told her about the young girl going missing while walking the family dog. As if sharing the thought, he slowed the car and they crawled along the edge of the green. He switched on the two brass headlamps against the falling darkness. It was true that he was thinking about Emelie. But the thought that had been nagging him all through the drive was that the one who murdered the poor woman on Robertson Street was lurking somewhere in the shadows of the city. He drove on.

When they rounded the corner at the end of St. Charles, they found Carrollton Avenue clear. He pushed the accelerator handle and the roadster leaped ahead. After a few blocks he glanced at the speedometer and called out, "Forty!" The wind was whipping her scarf and bringing tears to her eyes.

The tour took them past the Fairgrounds and City Park to the lake, where the lights of the hotels and dance halls were aglitter. He turned south at Elysian Fields and they rode it all the way down Josephine to Lesseps. It was just after seven o'clock when he pulled to the curb, doused the lamps, and flipped the ignition switch. The engine rattled into silence.

Justine lifted her veil. "Well," she said.

Valentin ran his hands over the wooden wheel. "So, you like it?"

"I do," she said. "I'd like it more if I could drive."

Sister Rosalie walked from the chapel to the ward as a half-moon rose over the trees, then climbed the steps to stand in the doorway. Evangeline was sitting on her bed, staring out the window, her bible open on her lap. Her face was cast in silver light and she looked quietly beatific, as if hearing God's voice. The sister longed for such serenity. She had come to say goodnight, a small deception, since her true purpose was hope for another piece of the puzzle. Now she decided to leave Evangeline alone with her prayers.

On her way across the grounds to her own bed, she saw the silhouette of the Mother Superior behind the amber glass of her chancery office.

She knocked and opened the heavy oak door. The Mother Superior, who considered the role the bishop had foisted on her a burden laden with pretense, preferred to be called Sister Antoinette. Her kind heart was tucked inside a small body that radiated energy and the sisters joked that when she moved about the grounds, she outran the squirrels.

Even so, she looked tired as she waved Sister Rosalie into the room. The desk, the chair, the thick carpets, and the dark walnut moldings seemed to press down on the modest woman who sat nursing a glass of wine. Without asking, she leaned forward to pour a second glass for her visitor. Sister Rosalie settled in one of the chairs on the opposite side of the desk, moved her rosary to one hand, and lifted the glass with the other.

They exchanged pleasantries, then sipped in silence for several moments. The Mother Superior said, "What is it, Sister?"

"Do you by chance know a Father Thomas?"

The Mother Superior mulled the name. "There was a Father Thomas in St. Tammany years ago, as I recall. But that was long ago. He's dead now. He's the only one I know. Why do you ask?"

"Evangeline mentioned the name." Sister Rosalie described finding the woman in the garden. "She told me about a dream she had. With a husband and children. And I was wondering if there might be someone looking for her." She took a sip of her wine. "I'd like your permission to speak to Sheriff Lasser about her. To see if there have been any reports."

Sister Antoinette smiled in a sly way. "Oh, I'm sure the sheriff will be happy to assist you." It was a small joke around the convent that the officer held a certain affection for the sister. Now the Mother Superior watched her charge blush beneath her habit.

"You have my permission," she said. "Someone might be missing the poor woman. And we'd all like to solve the mystery."

CHAPTER FIVE

Captain Picot rose before dawn, walked to the grocery on the corner of Girod Street, and paced the banquette until the truck rattled to the curb and a worker tossed a stack of newspapers over the slats. He bent down, snapped the twine, and snatched the top copy.

He found the item on page four, carrying the headline "Police Correct Report on Woman's Death," and the byline of Reynard Vernel.

> Sources with the New Orleans Police Department have asked *The Times-Picayune* to correct certain details in a news item published in last evening's edition. According to these sources, there is no connection between the death of a woman whose body was discovered on Robertson Street yesterday morning and the deaths of any other women within the City limits.

The Captain did not leave a nickel for his copy. He folded it with a grunt of satisfaction and ambled back to his frame house to prepare for his workday.

Gregory found the morning paper on the brick walk that led from the gallery steps to the street and stood yawning in the morning sun. He didn't expect to read anything further about Robertson Street. There would be more ink soon enough. He turned around and mounted the steps, browsing as he passed back into the quiet house. From what he saw on the front page, New Orleans, America, and the world were in a sad state, the same today as yesterday and the day before. He had just started up the wide staircase to the second floor when he arrived at page four. He stopped, feeling his stomach twist and his cheeks flame. The paper crumpled in his hands. He climbed the stairs to the attic, where he stalked the boards, his brain seething.

That they thought it could be so simple! That some fat fool sitting behind a desk at police headquarters could simply pick up a telephone and inform an editor that no, the facts in the article were wrong, and that they expected to see this corrected in the next morning's newspaper. No woman had been found nude and sliced by a shaking hand on the banks of the river just east of the byway. Nor a second in an alleyway back-of-town, cut in the same way but by a steadier touch. This was *not* the case, even though both bodies had arrived at the city morgue, one in June and the other in August, savaged in the same manner. In fact, the woman in the crib on Robertson Street had suffered a random assault. Or an accident in which she managed to bind herself, suffocate, and then fall on a blade in a way that drew a precise design on her torso.

He rambled from wall to wall as his thoughts pitched in angry swells. He stopped at the round window, calming himself. *So this is the path you want to follow? To try and erase me with a few lines of newsprint?* He smiled grimly. *I think not.*

He left the window and rummaged through some boxes until he found a pen and a stack of stationery, then dragged an old table and chair from a dusty corner. With a final settling breath, he sat down to consider. It would have to be worded just right and in language too tantalizing to ignore.

He got it on the fourth try, including a detail so that there could be no question it was genuine and with the correct taunting tone.

After studying it over, he wrote out two more copies. Somewhere in the house was a packet of envelopes. He folded the three letters in careful thirds, rose from the table, and descended the stairs on his way to introducing Gregory to the city of New Orleans.

Justine heard the engine cough twice before rattling to life. She blinked from her half-doze and slid from under the covers, wondering if he was so eager to get back in the automobile again that he was about to drive off without breakfast. She slipped into a kimono and when she reached the front door, she saw him leaning into the carriage of the Ford with his shirtsleeves rolled up, twiddling some knob or another as the four cylinders settled into an even idle.

What was it about men and machines? Valentin was never one to care much about possessions and the roadster didn't belong to him. And yet he stood blissfully entranced by a contraption of sheet metal and bolts, as if it held the meaning of life. Presently, he glanced around to see her in the doorway. He reached back into the cab and shut off the engine. He wiped his palms on a handkerchief as he moved up the walk and climbed the steps onto the gallery. Before he reached the perron, he turned to inspect the roadster again.

"You want to bring it into the bedroom?" she said. The breeze fluttered her gown open.

He cocked his head. "Oh, you mean the car?" She laughed as he took her by the wrist and led her back inside.

A half-hour later, he was at the kitchen table, opening the morning paper as he sipped his coffee and waited for her to finish cooking their breakfast. He leaned forward to gaze through the front room and the screen door. As he eyed a red fender gleaming in the morning sun, he reminded himself that it was not his

49

property, but a rich man's convenient loan. If young Emelie came strolling in the front door of the mansion on Annunciation Street, he'd be back riding the streetcars.

He returned his attention to his newspaper, leafing with an absent mind. When his eye landed on page four and the correction, he knew what it meant. The byline was the same as the one on the original story: Reynard Vernel. He recalled the reporter as the eager young fellow who had dogged his steps when he was running down the murder of John Benedict. He had come to him with an idea about writing a book about a detective. Valentin found the notion ridiculous, but Vernel was so earnest that he was allowed to tag along while the case wound to its bloody conclusion.

Valentin had seen the name now and again over the years as Vernel moved from one paper to another. For this story, he had done his job, reported fairly, and for his trouble had been forced to eat his words. Too bad for him; but so it went with those who crossed the New Orleans Police Department. The detective had his own list of—

"Here you are," Justine murmured as she slid a plate onto the table. She glanced briefly at the open page. "Anything good?"

Valentin folded the paper and laid it aside, aware of her hawk eyes. "No, nothing much," he said and reached for his fork.

Reynard Vernel was in a foul mood as he walked into the building and climbed the steps to the third floor, avoiding the crowded elevator and the cheery morning faces of the bright sorts as well as the moaning and groaning from those who had arrived hung-over from nights spent in the saloons. It was his habit to snatch a fresh copy of the paper from the front desk, but this morning, he passed the stack and made directly for the stairwell.

So, Mr. Vernel, Captain Picot had said with a smile that was fish cold. *We got a problem with some information you put in the paper...*

It had gone downhill from there. Picot told him that there was no connection between the two dead harlots from over the summer and the woman in the Robertson Street crib. *Just one of them things,* he said, while his two detectives stood by like deaf and dumb twins. Salliers had fixed him with a hard eye, while McKinney regarded him with what he took as vague pity.

When he began to state his case, the captain cut him off and made a curt gesture to Detective Salliers, who snatched up the telephone handset, jiggled the cradle and murmured into the mouthpiece. A moment passed and he held out the candlestick in one hand and the earpiece in the other. Reynard put the cone to his ear and listened as his editor told him to stop being difficult. The reporter understood. With the matter settled, he handed the telephone back as Captain Picot resumed his seat behind the desk. Salliers shooed him out.

He made a lonely walk back to Gravier Street. When he got to the third floor, he sat down and raised his eyes over the commotion of the newsroom. What had happened to him? Growing up in Pass Christian, he had always displayed a way with words. As a student, he had devoured great writers and humbly wished to one day emulate them. His family could not afford college, but he had noticed how many of the authors he admired had cut their teeth at newspapers and had headed for New Orleans to talk his way into a job.

He opened the copy of the paper on his desk to page four and spied the piece retracting his prior evening's report. Folding the paper into a bat, he smacked it down on the desk, then threw it on the floor, leaving his blotter empty except for a cream-colored envelope. O'Neal, that drunken sonofabitch, had tacked his name on the item.

"You can always write a letter to the editor."

He looked up to see that same gentleman standing a few feet away, looking his usual rumpled self. Whythe O'Neal was composed of three globes – head, torso, and hips – atop two legs that were too thin for his bulk. This physique created a tendency to sway when he had to work to keep his balance, which given his drinking, was not a rare exercise. Button eyes were stuck into a red face that was splotchy from the effects of the bottle. At least he wasn't a mean drunkard and was in fact a quite decent fellow. Take away the whiskey, and he was a fine newspaper man. Reynard sometimes imagined himself in another twenty years as a taller, thinner, less inebriated version of the man.

O'Neal leaned a round shoulder against one of the columns that kept the plaster ceiling from collapsing into the newsroom in large chunks, wearing a look that suggested that he had read his reporter's mind.

"You forge checks, too?" Vernel inquired.

"We were in a pinch," O'Neal said. "We want help from the police, we have to do these things now and then. I'm sure Captain Picot explained that."

Reynard entertained an urge to opine that the help mostly went one way, but the editor was moving in with his whiskey breath and so instead he said, "You could have let me write it."

O'Neal waved a fleshy hand. "You weren't around." He stopped to cough for a red-faced moment. "But I'm here to make it up to you." He pointed to the envelope. "Go ahead, read it," he wheezed.

Reynard drew out the single sheet of paper and unfolded it. The words became clear on his second pass and he felt goosebumps rise on his arms. He sat up. "Good God!" he said. "Are you..."

"What? Going to run it?" O'Neal's eyes were as sharp as tacks. "Can't do that. We don't know if it's real. We could end up looking

52

like fools." He plucked the letter from Reynard's fingers. "But if it turns out there is a story there, it'll be yours," he said.

No matter how late he had been working the streets, Each was expected at the Café every morning at ten with a report for Mr. Anderson. He was one of a dozen or so citizens at the end of the King of Storyville's tentacles, each of them bringing information from various corners of the city. Anderson used what he needed for the moment and stored the rest of it away.

It so happened on this morning that Each was arriving as Anderson was clambering out of his touring car with the help of his driver, a Negro named Edward who always dressed in a near-perfect suit under a clean white duster, partially in appreciation that Anderson did not make him go about in livery.

Edward had his hand on Anderson's thick bicep, taking the weight as the old man climbed down. The King of Storyville appeared a bit pale as he stepped onto the banquette. He spotted Each and stopped. "How did the evening go?"

"Quiet again, Mr. Tom."

Anderson stood catching his breath, lingering with the other two men in the patchy September sun. Each exchanged a glance with Edward. Their employer did not look well.

"Did you see in the *Picayune* about that business on Robertson?" Anderson wheezed.

"No, sir," Each said. "What was that?"

"Seems the pattern is no pattern at all," the older man quipped. "That's what the morning paper says."

Each was about to ask what he meant when his eye was snared by a shiny red Ford roadster whizzing up Basin Street. The machine came to stop at the corner to allow a hack to cross over. Anderson pointed and said, "Well, well, will you look at that?"

The driver raised a gloved hand in an awkward greeting. The intersection cleared and the three men watched as the Ford lurched forward, rolled off, and rounded the corner at Canal Street.

Later, Valentin could not recall what had compelled him to take a route that placed him on Basin Street at that moment. It was the most direct line, though not the fastest, as automobiles and trucks and horse-drawn hacks crowded the cobblestones and passengers were risking their lives crossing to and from Union Station in random scurries along the four blocks. After he left the house, he turned north on Esplanade and drove along, the four cylinders humming in a steady rhythm that echoed off the white walls of St. Louis No. 2. He braked and turned at the next corner.

The view "down the line" was framed in the tall windshield, though after ten years, he could have made his way blindfolded. Between St. Louis and Conti, the mansions were sturdy if not stately, all narrow two-story red, yellow, and white brick. At this hour, only maids sweeping and drivers unloading food and drink from the beds of trucks were in motion, their rhythms unhurried in the morning sun.

He had just pulled his gaze off the familiar facade of Miss Antonia Gonzales' mansion when he noticed the three figures on the banquette in front of the Café. Two he would have recognized from a mile away. He fixed his stare on the street ahead and hoped they wouldn't notice the red roadster. But Tom Anderson missed nothing and he felt the stare as he passed by. At least Each hadn't shouted his name or come chasing after him on foot. He pushed the accelerator handle, rounded the corner at Canal Street and six blocks east, turned onto St. Charles.

~

54

Reynard Vernel telephoned Detective McKinney and asked if they might meet for a few minutes. He mentioned a saloon called the Crescent Café on Royal Street, midway between their offices.

The detective was quiet for a moment. "What time?"

"Eleven-thirty."

"All right, then." McKinney hung up.

Keeping one eye on the clock, the reporter typed in a machine-gun staccato as he dashed through a series of dull pieces about random bits of city business. The yellow paper chattered off the roll, and every few minutes, he'd rip free a length and yell "Copy!" It was eleven-fifteen when in one motion, he stabbed out the characters ###, threw the boy the sheets, and pulled on his jacket.

Lumbering along the aisle between the desks, O'Neal opened his mouth to pose a question, but the reporter rushed past and into the hallway before he could get a word out.

Ten minutes later, he was installed in a corner booth. The lunch trade was yet to arrive and the room was quiet. Two drummers leaned at the bar with samples cases at their feet, gazing dolefully into their beer mugs. For fellows who made their livings talking, they were a sad and silent pair.

Detective McKinney blocked the sunlight for the moment he was stepping over the threshold. He surveyed the room until he spotted the reporter, then crossed the floor and slid into the empty bench, eyeing the glass between Reynard's palms. "Is it some kind of rule that you people have to drink all the time?" he said.

"You'd think so, wouldn't you?" Reynard said. "And I'm one of the sober ones." He waved a hand. "Do you want something?"

"I'm fine." The detective turned his large hands upward. "So, what's this about?"

"Did you see the correction in the paper?"

55

"I heard about it."

Vernel sipped his whiskey. "We received a letter from a person claiming to be the murderer of all three women."

The detective's gaze fixed on the reporter. "Jesus Christ."

"And he says he's not finished."

McKinney lowered his voice. "Who else has seen it?"

"The editors. And me."

"What are you going to do with it?"

"Nothing has been decided."

"I'll be goddamned." The detective thought for a moment, then said, "So why are you telling me about this?"

"I felt like someone needed to know. Someone official, I mean."

The policeman almost smiled. "And you picked *me*?"

"Well, I wasn't going to tell Captain Picot," Reynard said. "I wanted to see what you thought about it, that's all."

"I've heard of killers sending notes to the police before. 'You can't catch me.' That sort of thing."

"Jack the Ripper," Vernel said. "He did that."

"Yeah, and it's been, what, twenty-five years now? And they never caught him."

The reporter drank off the half-inch of whiskey in his glass. "Maybe it's just a hoax."

"You saw the letter. What do you think?"

The reporter said, "I think it's real."

McKinney waited a few seconds, then slid out of the booth.

"What are you going to do?" Reynard said.

"I don't know. I guess wait to see if your paper runs it."

The room darkened again when the detective passed through the door. Reynard signaled for another whiskey.

CHAPTER SIX

Valentin pulled to the Annunciation Street curb. The racket of the engine died, leaving the street in silence as he sat studying the largest house on the block, a mansion of white stone. Behind the wrought iron fence was an expansive garden, still ablush in a rainbow of floral leaves and petals. The front gallery stretched thirty feet before curving around each side for another fifteen. The arched windows that shone out on the neighborhood from the upper floor and the garret were gabled.

The detective climbed down from the roadster and spent a minute surveying the block before moving to open the gate, make his way along the brick walk to the gallery, and push the button mounted next to double doors of solid oak and beveled glass. A mulatto maid with a compact body in a black and white uniform, a round pretty face, and dark worried eyes appeared at the door. "Mr. Valentin?" she said.

"It's Belle, is that right?"

"Yes, sir." She stood back. "Please come in."

The house was quiet save for the ticking of a wall clock. Belle led him through the foyer and down a hallway to a high-ceilinged room that was awash in buttery light from three south-facing windows. Reading chairs and lamps were arranged on a Persian carpet. The two side walls were lined with tall bookshelves and a long library table had been centered on the inside wall.

The maid gestured, inviting him to sit. "May I bring you a coffee, sir?"

He noticed how she had spoken the words and said, "Acadia Parish?"

She dipped her head. "Close, sir. Vermilion."

"Coffee will be fine."

She backed to the door. "And I'll fetch Mr. Alberton."

Valentin moved about the room, stopping at the table where a morning *Times-Picayune* was laying. He opened the paper to reread the page four correction and recognized Captain Picot's oily fingerprints on the piece. Did Picot truly believe that he could put a stop to a torrent of gossip about a string of killings so easily? He would have known better if he listened to anything beyond what stirred in his own dull brain. Now the Uptown tongues would be wagging over the possibility that a crazed murderer was on the loose.

Not so long ago, Valentin would have taken the little scrap of newsprint and ripped into the case until he had the perpetrator in his sights. But those days were in the past, as his wife would be too happy to remind him. As he folded the newspaper, he imagined Tom Anderson reading the piece and wondering what—

Footsteps padded in the hallway and George Alberton appeared. "Mr. St. Cyr." He spoke the name the French way, *sawn-sear*. He was wearing the trousers and vest from an expensive suit, a watch and chain, and a sober tie. He waved Valentin to the table and settled into a chair.

Valentin sat down. "When do you expect the call?"

The older man said, "So far, it's been eleven on the dot."

Valentin glanced at the wall clock. The call wouldn't come for another fifteen minutes. He was about to pose an initial question when Belle returned carrying a tray. She placed it on the middle of the table and gave each man a cup of coffee with sugar cubes in the saucers and a little pitcher of cream on the side. She said, "Anything else, sir?"

Alberton said, "No, Belle, this will be fine."

She moved to exit the room. The detective thought it odd that she was in the middle of the drama and yet still being treated as the help. Before she could reach the door, he held up a hand. "You should..." He glanced at George Alberton. "She should stay."

Alberton said, "Yes, of course," with the smallest hitch in his dry voice.

Belle laid the tray aside and lingered by the wall, her hands folded before her. Valentin sensed something odd in the room and perked an ear as he went to work on his coffee. Alberton had taken his black, lifting the cup to his lips for a small sip. Valentin felt the older man's stare as he stirred sugar and cream and then drew his notebook and pen from his coat pocket. He asked for a second account of the afternoon that Emelie disappeared.

Alberton frowned. "Why? What more can I tell you?"

"Today is not yesterday," Valentin explained. "We're in the house now. You might remember some things differently." He turned to Belle. "I'll want to hear anything you have to say as well."

Belle said, "Yes, sir."

Alberton said, "All right, then. She went to walk the dog, just like she does every afternoon. Ninety minutes after she left, the dog came back to the front gate. Belle went out to let him in. Emelie was nowhere to be found. We called the police right away. They searched the streets and the park. No trace of her. We heard nothing all through Sunday. Belle and my wife were frantic. We barely slept. Then on Monday morning, we got the first call."

"You took it?"

Alberton shook his head. "Belle did."

Valentin turned to the mother, who said, "She told me she was in a room in a house. She said she was safe. She said she couldn't tell me any more than that."

Alberton said, "She's called every day at the same time."

"You don't believe she just ran off?" Valentin said.

Alberton looked at the mother, who said, "She wouldn't. She's not that type of girl."

"We all get along very well," Alberton said. "My wife and I and my daughters adore her."

Valentin looked at his notes. "And what about the dog?"

Alberton gave Valentin a sharp look.

"Sorry," the detective said. "I mean, did the dog show signs of being injured? Anything like that?"

"The dog was fine," Alberton said in a cool voice.

"Who else is in the house?"

Belle spoke up. "Tante Dolores. She's the cook and she helps with the housekeeping. And her husband Thomas. He takes care of the grounds and all that."

"Are any of them suspect?"

"Not a chance," Alberton said. "They've been with us since..."

"Since Emelie was a baby," Belle said.

Valentin jotted a few more words. He closed his notebook and said, "I'd like to see a photograph of her, please." Alberton looked at Belle, who blinked. "What? Is that a problem?"

Alberton said, "We don't...she...it seems that her photographs... they're missing."

Valentin said, "Beg your pardon? Missing how?"

"Belle?" Alberton said.

The mother spoke up. "After she was gone. I went up to her room and saw that her pictures were gone. I mean down from where they was."

"How many?"

"Just two. Both was on the dresser."

A silence followed while Valentin waited for more. "It sounds like she was planning to leave."

Neither the maid nor Mr. Alberton offered any comment. Valentin kept his expression blank. "Could I see her room now?"

Alberton said, "Her— Oh, yes. Belle will show you to it."

Reynard Vernel walked into Fewclothes' Cabaret on Basin Street and found Each Carter with his elbow settled on the end of the bar, doing his best to assume the pose of a regular rounder. The reporter still saw the boy who had trailed along on the Benedict case five years ago. Both of them had dogged Valentin St. Cyr's heels until it was over.

Each straightened when Vernel stepped up. The two men shook hands. "Drink?" Each said.

The reporter remembered Detective McKinney's comment about newspapermen and liquor and demurred, though he could almost taste the smoking amber in the glass that Each held in his fingers. He said, "I want to tell you something. As a courtesy."

Each glanced to his left and right. "Go ahead."

Reynard told him about the letter from "Gregory."

Each was stunned. "It ain't no joke?"

"It's him, all right."

"Well, goddamn."

Reynard said, "You can pass the information on. Just don't mention my name."

He moved away from the bar and strolled out into the cloudy middle of the day. Each drained his whiskey in one quick swallow, then threw a dime on the bar and made a quick exit into the back alley.

~

Valentin followed Belle up the narrow wooden stairs, admiring the view. That he was a married man regarding her anatomy with such a frank eye gave him no pause. He had told Justine more than once that he would no longer touch, but if he ever stopped looking, she could bury him, because it would mean he was already dead.

When they reached the attic, he found that Emelie's bedroom took up one side of the gabled space. On the other, a wall had been built, blank painted wood with a door that was padlocked.

"What's in there?" Valentin asked.

"It's storage. Furniture and clothes they ain't using. Some other things."

The detective stepped to the door, rapped a knuckle, and called out, "Emelie?" Belle gave him a vexed look. "Just checking," he said.

"We ain't that kind of people," the maid said. Now she was upset.

"I know, I know," Valentin said. "It was a poor joke. Forgive me."

Hazy daylight filtered through sheer curtains, casting the room in soft curves. He stepped to the window and opened it. Fresh fall air wafted into the closed space. The room would be hellishly hot during the summer months; he assumed she slept somewhere on the lower floors or the back gallery.

He paused to survey a single bed with an iron rail frame, a vanity and a chest of drawers, and a small student desk. A few random pieces of art and pages from magazines were pinned to the walls and some entwined ribbons dangled from the rafters.

"Have you noticed anything else missing? Other than the photographs, I mean."

"No, nothing."

"She didn't take any of her clothes?"

"Not that I can see." Her expression was almost blank, but she was working at it.

He stood by the window in silence, until she raised her head and met his eyes. He was fixing her with the gimlet stare he had employed throughout his years as a detective in Storyville. Deep and flat, it was impossible to tell what was going on behind it.

He now could see Belle frowning, puzzled; and yet she didn't avoid the gaze, but held herself steady until he said, "Mr. Alberton said that Emelie took the dog for a walk and did not come back. Is that what happened?"

The maid caught herself. "What? Oh. Yes...Yes, sir. She, uh, she went out to the park like she always does on the weekends. Skipper – the dog – he came back maybe an hour after she left. I saw him out by the gate. I let him in and when Em–"

"Do you think she was taken, Belle? Or was it something else?"

Belle blinked. "Do I what?"

"Was your daughter taken? Or did she run off?"

"I...taken. I think." Her eyes fluttered a bit. He wasn't sure if it was a lie and shifted to another tack. "Tell me about her, please."

Belle took a moment's pause and then described a daughter in the only way a loving mother could, as the jewel of her life, pretty and polite, a student in the tenth grade at the St. Ann's School for Colored on Lasalle Street. She had spoken over dinner about going to college in Atlanta, but Mr. Alberton regarded this as folly.

Valentin stopped. "How did she take that?"

"She'd get quiet. Wouldn't say another word about it."

"But not angry?"

"No. Not angry."

With his back to her, he said, "Tell me about Emelie's friends."

"Her friends?" The maid's tone was absent. "There are some

girls at her school."

"A best friend?"

"Not that I could name."

Valentin now heard the way she had hedged and turned around. "Yes?"

"I suppose the person she talks to the most is Annette. The younger daughter. Because they're close in age."

"Then I'll need to sit down with her."

"Yes, of course."

The idea had distracted her. When he sensed her drifting away, he said, "Did she have a beau?"

Belle's mouth tilted. "Some boys have come around to sit on the back gallery. But there wasn't one courting her, no, sir."

"A pretty young girl, and she doesn't have a special beau?"

Now the smile widened and white teeth flashed. "Sometimes, I would be out there and some boy would be going on and on about something or other, putting on a show, you know, and she would catch my eye and make a face." She mimicked eye-rolling exasperation. "And I'd have to hurry out before I started to laugh."

In the next moment, tears sprang to her eyes. Valentin moved away from the window to stand before her, feeling the shadow of an old self paying a return visit, a fellow who didn't mind taking advantage of a woman in the throes of emotion. She dabbed her eyes, her expression now wary. He leaned away from her. *Good for you*, he thought. *Don't fall for any man's games.*

Moving around her he said, "Please, understand that I won't repeat a word of anything you say. Not to Mr. Alberton nor anyone else. But I want to know if Emelie would run off on her own?"

Before she could answer, George Alberton called up the stairwell. "Mr. St. Cyr? It's almost time."

Before they started down, Belle laid a hand on his arm. "Will you find her for me?"

"If she wants to be found," Valentin said. Belle looked startled at these words, but quickly turned away.

Each walked into the Café and found the King of Storyville looking so pallid that he wanted to ask the old man if he was ill. Instead, he offered a quick greeting and then got to the point with the news of the letter that had arrived at *The Times-Picayune*.

Anderson mulled the news. "And they're not going to print it?"

"No. Least, that's what Vernel says."

Now Anderson paused before saying, "We'll have to wait, then. Does Mr. Valentin know about this?"

The question had come from nowhere and Each was puzzled. "I ain't no idea about that, sir."

The King of Storyville considered for another few seconds before perching his glasses on his nose and picking up his pen. Each rose and made his quiet way out the door.

Valentin and Belle descended the staircase to the foyer where Alberton waited next to a telephone set of brass and ebony perched atop a waist-high marble column. The pale sun through the cut glass in the door gave the little room the appearance of a painting.

Presently, Alberton said, "How do you want to handle this?"

Valentin said, "Let Belle answer, just like every other day." He turned to the maid. "Hand me the earpiece so I can speak to her. I'll give it back to you before she hangs up."

The clock in the living room had struck a third time when the telephone chattered. Belle lifted the handset from the cradle. "Emelie?" she said, then listened. "Yes. Are you all right?" She held out the handset and the detective placed it to his ear.

"—fine. You don't have to worry." The voice was quiet, in the middle range, and Valentin listened intently. "I'm not going to go anywhere."

"I'm a detective," Valentin said. He heard Emelie catch a breath. "I'll be listening from now on."

Emelie said, "A detective?" Now she sounded almost amused.

"Is there anything you want to tell me?"

A pause followed, then: "No, nothing. I'll speak to my mother."

Valentin turned over the handset to the mother, who murmured a few words, listened some more, then dropped it into the cradle.

Alberton said, "So?"

"Her voice is calm," Valentin said. "Not like someone who fears for her safety." He looked between the maid and older man. "I'm not convinced that Emelie isn't a party to this."

Alberton crossed his arms and swung his head in a stubborn arc. "No, sir. I don't believe that's the case."

"We can't discount the possibility."

The older man's lips pinched. "I don't care why she's in this situation. Just do whatever you can to find her," he said. Valentin watched him march away. He felt Belle staring at him, but when he looked at her, she turned away so he couldn't see her eyes. It occurred to him that he had not seen Alberton's wife or any of the other staff, as if they were being hidden away. Another small puzzle.

"Well, then," he said. "I'll be back tomorrow."

Belle escorted him to the front door and wished him a fine day. She still wasn't meeting his eyes. He saw her standing in the doorway as he drove off. He was sure that she and her employer were playing with parts or all of Emelie's story. What he didn't know was why. If it wasn't for the presence of a distraught mother, he wondered how much he would care. There was that – and the money.

CHAPTER SEVEN

Terrebonne Parish Sheriff John Lasser had taken it upon himself to make weekly visits to Our Lady of Sorrows. This, though there had been only the one piece of real trouble in over six years, when a wife who had shot her cheating, beating husband to death, went on the run, and sought refuge inside those white walls. The Mother Superior had surrendered the poor woman on the promise that she would be offered every consideration, which the police in Mobile had been happy to do, given that the deceased had been no goddamn good and better off dead.

The sheriff was alert of the convent's needs. He believed that offering the special attention earned him prayers that his soul sorely needed and made up to some small degree for missing Mass.

Sister Jean was the liaison to the outside world and the hefty man and tiny nun strolled the quiet grounds, chatting about this and that and stopping at regular intervals to admire the varied foliage. They spoke of the odd weather of late, the way dark storms threatened, then didn't deliver. He gave her a report on charity baskets delivered to the poor in Houma. She told him about hunters from Chauvin who had been wandering too close to the property with their deer rifles. He promised to look into it.

There was nothing more to discuss and with their business concluded he offered a farewell, accepted a word of blessing, and started along the path to the front entrance, where his deputy was dozing in one of the department's Bakers. He had just reached the gate when he heard his name called. Sister Rosalie, a nun he knew well and looked upon with a particularly genial eye, was hurrying along the white gravel path to intercept him.

Lasser stopped and doffed his hat. "Sister?"

She bowed slightly. "Do you have a moment?"

They moved to one of the stone benches along the whitewashed wall and with a sigh the sheriff eased himself down. The sister followed, draping her skirt and folding her hands around her rosary. The branches of the live oaks between the grounds and the road hung overhead, still heavy with summer leaves, dappling the large man and the small, comely woman in patterns of light and haze. Once settled, the sheriff hiked a polite eyebrow.

"I'm hoping you can do us a small service," Sister Rosalie began. "A woman arrived at the front gate three weeks ago, on foot. She has no identity."

"No identity?"

"She has a condition of some sort." The sister touched fingers to her temple. "Her memories are mostly gone. She can't tell us where she came from. Her true name. Any of that. We've been calling her 'Evangeline.'"

The sheriff, a man of modest learning, noted the allusion. He didn't understand why the sister was bringing the matter to him. "So...do you want us to move her somewhere?"

"Oh, no." Sister Rosalie said. "She's welcome here. A kind and reverent soul. I'm asking if you could check for any reports of missing persons who fit her description. In case a family somewhere is looking for her."

Sheriff Lasser considered. "Where is she now?"

"Doing wash." The sister gestured to the dormitory. "So if you wouldn't mind..."

~

They stood in the doorway of the laundry room. Sheriff Lasser watched the woman sweating over the machine, her face, arms, and hands red from the steaming water as she cranked bed linens through the rollers. She was a Creole of color, her profile patrician, like an Egyptian queen or a Cherokee princess. He had been noticing such women since he was a boy because they often possessed a beauty that changed but did not fade. This woman's face was serene as she worked, as if she was adrift in a world somewhere far from a hidden corner of the Louisiana bayou.

The sheriff's eyes and memory were sharp and he recorded all he needed of her features and stature in a short minute. He stepped back from the doorway and addressed Sister Rosalie. "Do you want me to talk to her?"

"I don't think that will do any good," the sister said. "She doesn't remember. But if you wish."

Sheriff Lasser considered before shaking his head. "We'll leave it for now. If there are no reports, there'll be no point in going further. It will be up to you what to do with her."

The sister turned to watch Evangeline through the open doorway. "If that's the case, she'll stay," she said.

Gregory had no appetite for lunch and instead rambled the house from the top floor to the basement and through the garden and back again until it was time to leave for the market on Washington Avenue where the afternoon papers were dropped. He strolled along, sensing in his gut that his letter would not appear. He arrived and bought his copy, then stood on the banquette, away from the customers hurrying in and out of the store.

The editorial page featured a half-dozen tedious letters, one railing about the war, a second about the curse that God would visit on the nation should women get the vote, yet another on the opening of Xavier, the Negro college. Three others fools with nothing better to do prattled complaints about local issues. The last was a fond remembrance of a trainer at the Fairgrounds who had died after being kicked in the head.

Gregory gave the copy to a kid who was waiting for his mother to finish her shopping and began a slow walk back to Prytania Street. So the editors had considered his missive and had made the sober judgment not to indulge a villain, real or imagined.

Oh, but you can't dismiss me, sirs. I'll give you proof, if that's what you require.

He arrived back at the house and stepped into the kitchen, where he collected a heel of French bread and some slices of cheese and ham. The knife man had been around and he selected a freshly-honed blade from the drawer. He carried the utensil and his lunch to the attic to plan out his evening.

After Each left the Café, Tom Anderson sat for a long few minutes in a darkening mood. During all the years he'd held the reins of Storyville, he had considered Robertson and Claiborne the price he paid for Basin Street. He had never found a way to rehabilitate those foul warrens. The women were ugly and vicious and their customers the same sort who had been washing up in New Orleans since the days when the pirate Lafitte's ships sailed the river and red lights hung in the windows of hovels to mark a harlot's bed. Even as Storyville had come of age and earned a reputation for a certain luxury, thanks to Tom Anderson, the back end of the District never changed. The raw acts performed by the hundreds every night generated a stream of money that no one who mattered cared to halt.

Anderson thought about the woman in the crib, murdered in

such a strange fashion and wondered if they might have their own Ripper in the city. While it was a horrible prospect, as long as he plied his trade elsewhere, the District could carry on. But what if this creature, emboldened by his success, decided to stalk his prey on fancier streets? Who would be blamed then? Mr. Tom Anderson, of course. The thought made his breath come short and brought a flutter to his chest.

To calm himself, he sat sipping his brandy and casting his mind back to kinder times, when the sporting girls and the jass music and the champagne were all in full bloom. When Tom Anderson was in charge and everyone knew it. When Valentin St. Cyr was there to fix what went wrong.

The mist of memory evaporated at the sound of the bartenders moving about as they stocked the liquor for the night. He saw them sneaking curious glances his way; he was rarely at the Café so late in the day. They didn't know that he remained there, alone and silent, in vain hopes of forestalling a nightmare.

Driving through town, Valentin was in the mood for a good lunch and decided to take the chance and slip into the District and a particular address on Marais Street. He hadn't visited in weeks and it was a good a time as any to make a stop.

Each had understood Mister Tom's meaning without hearing the words, and as soon as he left the Café, went about tracking down the Creole detective. Time was, he would know that gentleman's location any time of the day or night. Now he didn't know where to begin, except for Mangetta's, the grocery and saloon on Marais where the detective often lit when he was in the city.

He had been standing on the corner of Conti Street for a half-hour, smoking one Regal after another and watching the sporting girls arrive for another day of work, when he saw the red roadster come rattling to a stop at the curb across from the storefront. The detective spied him as soon as he climbed down from the seat.

Each sidled over to inspect the Ford. "It looks like you're doing well."

"It's on loan," Valentin said as he pulled off his gloves. "You waiting for me?" Each noticed the edge in the question and shrugged. "Now what?"

"Have you been following the newspaper?" Each said. "About the three women that was murdered?"

"I saw that, yes."

Each explained about the letter that had arrived at the newspaper. "It said if they didn't print it, there would be another murder. But they're not going to."

He had spent years hanging on to Mr. Valentin's every word and gesture and now caught a tiny change in the detective's expression. The dark eyes narrowed and sharpened and the chin came up. He looked like nothing so much as a hawk, perched and watching the ground. But instead of grilling the younger man for more information, the detective gave a short shake of his head, brushing the news aside. In the next moment, he came up with a smile. "So you're getting inside information now?" Each blushed a bit. "Good for you," Valentin said. "Who was it?"

"You remember that reporter Vernel? It was him. He told me so that—"

"So that you could tell Mr. Tom. Who sent you to find me."

The game was familiar, a dance without music. Valentin's gaze wandered to the front window of the grocery and he raised a hand in greeting to the man who had stepped into the doorway of the saloon across the street. "I told him that I'm done with this place."

Each frowned. *Then what are you doing over here?* But he didn't

72

speak out of respect. It was the detective's business and none of his.

"He's just going to have to count on the New Orleans Police Department," Valentin went on.

Each said, "That would be Picot."

"I know. He has my sympathy. How is he, by the way?"

"He hasn't been looking so good lately right now. Kind of sickly. You should pay a visit."

"I will. Soon. But give him my regards." With a wave of his hand, he crossed the street.

Gregory knew the red mood was coming on by the way his image shifted in the cheval mirror. No one else could see it. To him, the change was as stark as when a sudden storm rose up with clouds the color of gunmetal and pushed away the crystal skies over the gulf.

The temper began with an electric tingle along his spine that brought a rise in the tide of his blood and the faintest stirring in his loins. His mouth went so dry that it made it hard to swallow and within a few seconds, small rags of saliva were forming at the corners. When he leaned to the glass, he saw in his eyes pinholes of light that glimmered like dirty diamonds.

Watching his features change, he imagined fairytale monsters, werewolves and vampires and whatnot, sprouting hair and claws and fangs, crude nightmares to terrify youngsters. He was something else. He had always been something else.

As a child, he had tried to hold back his dark urges as no way for a member of a proper old New Orleans family to behave, even an odd and sickly one. Or so he had believed when he was young and helpless before the cruelties he endured from others and the tortures by a malady he could not name.

His mother and father took notice of his odd behaviors and fretted.

They brought him to a specialist named Dr. Rochelle who looked into his eyes and asked him queer questions. Afterward, he spoke to the parents in another room.

He understood that there was something deeply flawed in his being. There were hints of a place far away for people like him. He understood the plan that was brewing and worked at a guise of a normal boy, enough to allow him to avoid the worst. The price for this was a weekly visit with a charlatan.

His adolescence arrived, and out of the vague horrors that had plagued him came a notion that was followed by a crude experiment. When he suffered no punishment, he added other wicked deeds. If he was meek in appearance and all but invisible to the world, the creature festering inside him could embark on a different life. He gave the dandy a name, a dark mantle: Gregory, the Watchman. That was his other self, the one only he knew.

A breeze passed through the trees, rippling the leaves beneath the September moon and causing a branch to scratch the round attic window. He turned back to the mirror to find other faces now swimming in the glass. The one who had terrorized him on the schoolyard. The matron who had chortled over the thought of him courting her daughter before sending him on his way. (The girl was *precious*, don't you know, and he was just a bit too *peculiar*.) Later, the fraternity brother who had dropped the black ball in the bowl when the lights were out, but made sure he heard about it later.

Oh, the fates that had befallen them! The bullying boy became a young man who ten years later hanged himself in a cellar. The poor woman had tumbled one dark night from a riverboat out near St. Rose. The brakes on the fraternity brother's motorcar failed and he crashed into a live oak along St. Charles, breaking his patrician neck. They, along with others, had gone to their final rest as payment for their sins against him.

The branch scratched the glass a second time and he left the mirror to peer out upon a Garden District that lay quiet under the blanket of night. A dozen blocks away, the noise of the city began in earnest, along with the glitter of lights that would not surrender until dawn. From where he stood, he could spy a scattered few of those artificial stars. Lost in his dark dream, he watched until he heard the bells of St. Ignatius toll twice for the half hour. It was time. He left the window and donned his jacket, dropping his supplies into the inside pockets. The final touch was the selection of a slouch hat of dark wool.

The house lay still, his parents and younger sister long asleep. The colored couple who took care of the place had left after the dinner dishes were put up. His other sister had taken the train to Mobile to spend the week with a friend who was planning her wedding. He descended the stairs to the first floor with the silence of a swooping bird and made a quiet creep through the kitchen and onto the back gallery. He closed the garden gate behind him and slid along the alley. The thought of his prey going about her foul business with no thought of a certain someone stalking through the shadows caused his breath to come so short and his brow to grow so fevered that he had to unbutton the collar of his coat.

Canal Street was as bright and loud as a carnival. Gregory crossed that boulevard and arrived at Iberville amid a throng of men dressed in good suits and derby hats, their cheeks shaved and hair oiled, drawn to the red light district by the promises of sultry flesh, painted lips, and powdered bosoms, the wet and lush destinations that hid between thighs tinted ivory, rose, and coffee.

He had once walked in their eager number. He, too, had found his giddy way to Basin Street, had been welcomed at a bordello door by a madam in a bejeweled gown, relieved of his coat, and invited into the parlor so he could inspect the girls as they twirled to the raggedy music a professor coaxed from an old piano. He had chosen one who captured his fancy and let her lead him upstairs. And then it had all gone wrong. For as it turned out, Gregory was no man at all, but a boy whose body would not come alive. He went back again and again to try different women, different colors, lily white to coffee brown. He remained lacking even when they worked him with their hands and took him in their mouths — *French*, they called it — to no effect.

The girls would murmur kindly or pat his head with shallow pity and reading the thoughts behind their eyes, he would feel a churning in his gut. They were all as false as the paint they wore, their honeyed whispers as hollow as the lies they traded for money. From the dawn of time, what woman could ever be true? And how many had ever had to account for their betrayals?

God, how he hated this place and all the warm flesh there for the taking — by others. It was true. A filthy sot creeping from the gutter or some lice-ridden tramp who hadn't seen bath water in years could summon enough life to poke into an old mattress whore. While Gregory, young and clean and of good breeding, could summon nothing but some color to his limp, pale hank. With no remedy, he remained furiously pure as he moved to majority.

From one end to the other, Storyville had insulted his dignity and in time he came to see what the fire-breathing preachers described: a modern Sodom, a pool of corruption that would bring down a terrible judgment on all those tainted by its filthy waters.

He approached Villere Street, the true boundary of the red-light district, the line beyond which Mr. Tom Anderson and the others claimed with some degree of pride. The few women walking the street were reasonably clean and generally sober. Each one would have a room to use for the few minutes the transaction of flesh and fluids would require. It was a far cry from the mansions of Basin Street, but it wasn't pigs rutting in mud, either.

The houses were narrow and tidy, the windows lit from parlors where the madams sat surrounded by three or four strumpets. A colored maid cleaned up after the girls and several places shared a roughneck to remove drunks and troublemakers.

Gregory strolled through the pedestrian traffic all the way to the white walls of St. Louis No. 2 and then crossed over and repeated the walk on the other side of the street, his eyes photographing an address with every step. By the time he arrived at the corner of Iberville, he had made his selection.

The house was halfway along the block between Bienville and Conti. He returned to study the simple brick structure with a vacant lot on one side and an alleyway on the other. Through the tall window, he noted that the lamps were turned down low as a favor to the customers, as few of the women were comely. He saw no light at all in the foyer.

Standing in a shadow, he took a moment to calm himself and think past the act as if it was already finished. By tomorrow at this time, the city would know the name Gregory. The heat was coming on. His palms had begun to sweat and his stomach quivered the way it had on his first fast ride in an automobile. It was time. He stole a final glance up and down the street before crossing over.

Captain Picot was settled on his couch, examining a collection of French postcards that had been confiscated from a local pimp. The detectives knew that the captain wanted lewd materials placed in his possession and every so often, an unmarked envelope would appear on his desk. Once he had examined the materials, he would lock them in his office safe until he could carry them home. He was studying a photograph of a woman bending over, giving French to one man while another mounted her from behind, cropped so the men's faces were outside the frame. The woman's expression was dull and bored, as if her mind was miles—

The telephone clattered and his hands jerked, sending the stack of cards fluttering like dirty leaves. He muttered an angry burst, got up, and stalked to the stand. Snatching up the handset, he barked a gruff: "Picot!" In the next moment, he came to attention as the New Orleans Chief of Police snapped a string of curt sentences. He was able to say, "Yes, sir," four times before the line went dead.

Across town, Detective McKinney had been roused from his bed by a knock on the door. He found a uniformed officer waiting with a police vehicle parked at the curb. The driver told him he had gone by Salliers' apartment on Girod Street, but the detective hadn't been home. McKinney didn't understand what Sallier's whereabouts had to do with him.

"I'm to carry you to Villere Street," the officer said. "There's another body."

Each was bending an elbow in Fewclothes' when some gadabout called Dirty Sam came rambling in the door, all aflutter over the police back on Villere Street because a whore had gotten cut up.

"Cut up as in dead?" one of the sports said.

"Dead as hell, is what I heard," Dirty Sam said, with a wise nod. "Dead as hell."

Each felt a sharp chill run up his back. He tossed a quarter on the bar, asked Dirty Sam for the number of the house, and made for the door.

~

78

Detective McKinney stepped down at the St. Louis end of Villere Street and walked through the gathering crowd until he reached the house that had been cordoned off by wooden barricades. He flashed his badge and was allowed to pass.

A copper he didn't know was lounging next to the front door, smoking a cigarette. He stepped over the threshold and glanced into the parlor to see a madam and three of her girls huddled there, their faces stricken. He climbed the steps to the second floor. The patrolmen standing a post at the top nodded down the hallway. McKinney stopped at the first doorway. Captain Picot, a detective named Conn, and a third patrol officer stood around the bed.

She had been stripped and bound and her flesh had been cut in a figure of a cross in the same manner as those before. Her eyes were open and raised toward the portrait of the Virgin Mary over the head of the bed. As McKinney moved around the bed, he heard one of the officers murmur in surprise and turned toward the door.

Captain Picot had been posing with his arms crossed, staring at nothing. Now he blinked and raised his head as he became aware of another body in the room. He produced a dumb stare, his lower lip dropping.

"Christ Almighty," he muttered. "What are you doing here?"

Valentin had left instructions that he was to be called with any news about the disappearance of Emelie Baptiste, no matter what the time. So when the phone rang, long after dark, he hurried to the foyer, wondering if the case was about to end before it began.

Justine heard him talking, his usual pattern of terse words. Then he was back in the bedroom and opening the closet door.

"Are you going somewhere?" she said.

"That was Each. Tom Anderson had a heart attack."

She sat up. "My God. Is he dead?"

"Still alive," Valentin said. "He's been taken to the hospital."

"And you're going to see him? Now?" The detective didn't answer as he pulled a shirt from a hanger. "Valentin?"

"I can't visit. Only the family."

"Then where are you going?"

"To Villere Street."

"What for?"

Turning to face her, he said, "Something happened over there."

"And?"

"And Mr. Tom wants—"

"Wants what?" Her voice went up a notch. "Wants you to go? Why would you do that? Whatever it is, it's none of your business."

"Do you know what it took for him to ask at a time like this?"

"What it took?" Her expression was one he had seen before, crimson spots rising to her latte cheeks and her black eyes smoldering. "He probably staged the whole thing to get you back."

"Why would he do something like—"

"Because he can, that's why. He calls from his sickbed. And you come running."

He said, "I owe him. You know that."

When she didn't snap back with anything, he crossed to the bed and kissed her forehead. Then he walked out. A half-minute passed before she heard the cough of an engine and he was gone.

CHAPTER EIGHT

Though most of the District didn't stir until after the noon hour, word of Tom Anderson's crisis and Valentin St. Cyr's arrival at the house on Villere Street was already swirling by the time the first rays of hazy sun topped the buildings.

The King of Storyville had survived his episode. After a few tense hours, he requested that the doctors and his sons leave him in his Mercy Hospital bed with only the nurse with the Chinee cast to her features to watch over him like a private angel. He dropped off to sleep not knowing if St. Cyr had heeded his request. Ordering Each to telephone the detective was a decision he made in the sudden moment when he realized that he might not greet another morning. He imagined Storyville in peril and beckoned the person who had stood as his right hand through a decade of battles both slight and treacherous.

He woke in the deep of night, relieved to find himself still alive. The pretty nurse dozed in her chair. A round moon had risen over the river, veiled in gauze and as lovely as a painting. He reclined in the quiet room, one hand splayed over the heart that had betrayed and almost finished him. Soft tears welled in his eyes and he used the edge of the sheet to brush them away.

He had been standing in his foyer, mulling over the call about the body found in the upstairs room of the house on Villere Street and feeling his blood beginning to boil over the murdering bastard taking another one, this time inside the true bounds of the

81

District. When he walked into the dining room, a hot spike drilled his chest, his left arm went numb, and his breath came short. His wife took one look at his deathly pale face and let out a wail. His oldest son caught him before he collapsed to the floor.

There was no time to rouse Edward or wait for an ambulance, so the boys carried him to the Maxwell and laid him across the tufted back seat. His younger son took the wheel and they raced across town. The streetlamps had whipped by one after another and he recalled with absent pride that his work in the state senate had brought those electric stars to uptown New Orleans. Now he wondered if the dazzling string of white orbs was the last vision his eyes would behold.

He lasted the trip and the doctors were standing by to treat him. Once they had him stabilized, they explained that even though it had been a small event, it was a serious one. He would have to take things easy, mind his health, and so on and so on. In the midst of the commotion, Each had arrived, and he was able to summon him close and whisper.

He was sitting up in bed, sipping a cup of weak tea, when Each walked through the doorway. He waved his wife and the two daughters who had arrived to fuss over him out of the room. Once again, he was touched by the worry on the boy's clownish face. While a new nurse checked his vital signs, Each delivered his report. Anderson thanked him, sent him on his way, and settled into his pillows with a sigh of relief, even as he understood that another kind of trouble would start. The Chief of Police would be livid and Captain Picot would pitch another of his tantrums over the meddling.

Neither man had ever quite grasped the simple fact that the District was nothing if not an extension of Tom Anderson's ailing but not yet deceased body and that he could feel its every twist and turn in his very bones. In this case, he sensed that the fellow preying on the women in such a ghastly way was no blood-hungry ogre, but a clever fox on a mission to wreak damage beyond the ravaged bodies. And he needed St. Cyr to stop him.

It was nothing new. Over twenty years, miscreants had sought to destroy Storyville and each time, the Creole detective had come to the rescue. He had made enemies in the police department and left some bodies in his wake, but the threats had been beaten back and the red light district had endured. Now a new villain had arrived, plotting to take down Storyville one corpse at a time.

Perhaps this was Tom Anderson's punishment for growing rich lording over an empire dedicated to sin. Or just an old man's fears getting the best of him. It was too late, in any case. St. Cyr had stepped forward. Another gruesome game had begun, and the King of Storyville knew that it wouldn't end until some other someone was in the ground.

Valentin had left the scene on Villere Street and driven home to find Justine awake and sitting up in bed. Any hope of making a quiet and cowardly entrance had evaporated in her steady stare as he began to undress.

"Do you have any blood on your shoes?" Her tone was cool.

"No," he said. "He was too precise."

She crossed her arms below what he had always thought the loveliest bosom in New Orleans. "All right," she said. "Tell me."

Valentin mouthed a silent prayer of thanks for this small salvation. From the start, Justine had been intrigued by his work and had revealed a country cunning as she picked apart the intricacies of the crimes and the dark motives of criminals, at times more sharply than he did. She never failed to be entranced by teasing details, so as he unbuttoned his shirt and trousers, he played up the scene in the house, with the ravaged body on the bed, the coppers milling about the cramped rooms, and Captain Picot glaring at him.

"What about the fellow who did it?" she asked.

"No one could make an identification," he said.

"The madam didn't talk to him?"

"She said he kept his face mostly turned away. And she was trying to save on the lights, so he picked one, paid his dollar, and they went up the stairs."

He didn't have to explain that many of the men did not want their faces examined too closely, lest they be embarrassed one fine day by a chance encounter. He saw Justine's brow stitch as she pictured the girl fixing a sugary smile in place, one that dimmed when he turned away. She would have climbed the steps to her room with him following behind, covering a yawn and entertaining no idea of the awful violence that was about to befall her.

"The hallway upstairs was even darker," he went on. "Once he got her in the room, she was finished."

He paused to bend and open a bottom drawer in order to tuck away his pistol, whalebone sap, and stiletto. It was an old habit. Then he remembered that he had stopped carrying weapons.

"Valentin?"

He closed the drawer and straightened. "I'm sorry. What?"

"Was it the same as the others?"

"It was, yes," he said and sketched a cross in the air. "And one hell of a mess." He lifted the sheet and slipped underneath.

She lay quiet for a moment before saying, "Is it your case now?"

"No one has said anything about that," he told her. "Mr. Tom asked me to visit the scene. He was in a bad state and needed my help. But if you don't want me to go any farther, say so."

"Oh?" Her tone mocked him. "Just like that? And you would

84

obey me?"

He turned to meet her gaze. "I would think about it."

They were quiet for another small moment while she curled against him, her head on his chest and arm stretched across his middle. His draped a hand so that his fingers touched the thin strap of her nightdress. He knew she was thinking about Villere Street and a poor girl who had wanted nothing but to make a few dollars the only way she knew how and got butchered for her trouble.

He had been a husband long enough to know when to hold his tongue and did so as the autumn leaves rustled in the wind outside the dark window. Presently, she said, "What about your lawyers? What will they think about you being back in Storyville?"

"I did a sick man a service," he said. "It doesn't mean I'm back."

"Oh, please." She let out a dark laugh. "You never left."

Once Gregory had finished his work, he exited into the alley and made his way to Prytania Street, where he settled into his bed for a good sleep. He woke before dawn and climbed the steps to the attic desk to inscribe a new letter.

> *Do you believe me now? When I did not warrant your attention, I had to go visit Villere Street. That is your fault, sirs. Will you kindly print this note? Or do you want more of the same?*
> *Signed, Gregory*

Satisfied that he had struck the correct note, he penned a second copy, then folded each page into a cream-colored envelope. It was barely first light when he passed through the kitchen, plucked an apple from the basket on the table, and began a fast walk to St. Charles to catch the streetcar.

~

He rode as far as Poydras Street, then stepped down and walked south to the corner of Gravier and Magazine. The lobby of the *Times-Picayune* building was busy with citizens crowding to the counter to place advertisements and employees rushing in harried knots to the elevators. Gregory stretched an arm to drop the envelope marked "To the Editor" in the basket on the counter and retreated to the door without being noticed.

He rode the St. Charles streetcar to the corner of Lafayette, dropped the envelope addressed "Attention: Chief of Police" through a mail slot, and slipped away. With the morning's tasks complete, his steps slowed and he surveyed the busy streets for a place where he might find a decent plate of eggs and ham.

Mayor Martin Behrman had finally managed to get to sleep after spending a fretful hour mulling what he would say in memory of Mr. Tom Anderson, the notorious King of Storyville, and another wondering if a murderer had begun a rampage in that gentleman's corner of the city, even as he breathed his last. He woke in the morning to find that Anderson saved him the trouble of the eulogy by surviving the blow to his heart.

From his upstairs bathroom, the mayor could peer through the hexagonal window and across the river at the familiar landmarks: City Hall, of course; the spires of St. Ignatius and those of a dozen other churches; the *Times-Picayune* building; a few more of the taller structures; Union Station and its web of tracks; and Anderson's Café and Annex, the anchor of the red light district.

As he stood at the mirror, running a small comb through his brush of a mustache, he pondered his own career, now into his thirteenth year and fourth term in office. Only Tom Anderson had lasted longer in the turmoil that was the City of New Orleans. How would history view them? He believed he had been a good mayor. The city had done as well as could be expected and he had not been touched by scandals of any weight. When he was gone his portrait would be mounted on the wall in the marble lobby and mostly ignored. He was a single mayor in a long line and New Orleans was one city among many. By contrast, there was nothing to compare to Storyville or its king. Though the time for that history had not yet begun.

As soon as Whythe O'Neal spotted Vernel, he whistled him into his office and dangled a sheet of stationery before his eyes. The reporter studied the delicately-scribed message. Before he could say a word, the editor refolded the sheet. "I'm going to vote for running it. I'll write copy to go along. Or you can."

Reynard didn't respond to this bit of baiting, replying instead, "What will the police say about that?"

"Well, I'm guessing they got one, too. But phone over there and see what you can find out. The mayor will want his say, too. So whoever you know at City Hall..."

Vernel said, "I've got something else. Word is going around that Anderson might have Valentin St. Cyr working on this case."

O'Neal leaned against the edge of his desk. "Is that a good thing?"

"Depends on who you ask," the reporter said. "He has his admirers. The coppers don't like him around, so they'll be unhappy. But so far, it's just a rumor. I haven't confirmed anything. Other than that he was on Villere Street last night."

"Then we'll run something on the rumor."

Reynard didn't care for the loose attitude. But he also understood that when trying to keep pace with the scandal rags, facts became pliable, even for a respected daily. So he would write a few terse words for the copyboy to carry away. It would fall into the hands of the mysterious character who assembled a column of gossip called "Talk of the Town" under the byline "Miss Arthur." No one knew if the writer was a man or a woman. Some said that O'Neal himself was the guilty party, others pointed to a grubby sot who drifted in and out of the newsroom at odd moments, then disappeared.

Vernel was studying the editor for any clues when the telephone on the desk rattled. O'Neal snatched it up with one hand and shooed Reynard out the door with the other. The reporter made his way to his desk, dialed the police department, and waited. As usual, the conversation with Detective McKinney was terse. Reynard told him they had a copy of a letter from "Gregory" and that the editor wanted to publish it in the afternoon edition. McKinney said he'd heard that a copy had arrived at the precinct that morning, addressed to the chief.

"Then I'll call his office," the reporter said.

"Do that," McKinney said. "Just don't mention my name." The connection went dead.

Valentin rolled out of bed, took a quick bath, and pulled on trousers, a cotton shirt, and his black vest. He had neglected to mention to Justine before she dropped off that he would be going back to the house on Villere Street for a full inspection. It would have been a waste of time searching for clues amid the commotion of the night before.

She didn't say another word about Storyville or inquire about his plans for the day as she placed a plate heaped with scrambled eggs with cheese and peppers under his nose, then kissed his forehead and disappeared down the hall. Outside, the weather was shifting, with a swirling breeze off the gulf and a sky all askitter with mottled clouds.

He gave the newspaper a blank scan and waited to hear the water running in the bathtub before leaving his plate for the telephone in the foyer. He first called the hospital and asked that Each Carter be summoned to the phone. When the kid came on the line, he learned that the King of Storyville was spending most of his time barking at the doctors about his release and sweet-talking the nurses. He told Each he needed Anderson to arrange permission for him to visit the house on Villere Street. Each uttered a quick few syllables and broke the connection.

Valentin next got Sam Ross on the line and asked if there was any new word on Emelie Baptiste. The attorney said there had been nothing since the call the day before. "Tell them I'll be there this afternoon," Valentin said.

"Not before?"

"I've got some business to attend to," the detective said. "Don't worry. I doubt the next call will be any different." He did not share his suspicion that Emelie's disappearance was some sort of a charade. That could wait.

He hung up and walked down the hall to find Justine standing before the mirror, naked except for the towel wrapped around her head like a *chignon*. He leaned in the doorway, stilled by the vision that took him back to the first time he had watched her shed a dress in the upstairs room in Antonia Gonzales' mansion on Basin Street.

It had been six...no, seven years ago that she had first caught his eye. After passing glances, they had circled each other for weeks. Finally, he made a small move and asked Miss Antonia about her. A country girl, the madam told him, from the bayou. A dancer in a medicine show who had decided to settle in the city for a while.

When one of the other girls whispered that she had been asking about him as well, the game went into a faster spin. Though they held out a while longer before coming together with a spark that flared into a crazy fire. That they could barely keep their hands off each other became a subject of gossip all down the line.

He couldn't afford her and she didn't want him that way. Still, she had to make a living and so she entertained some rich man or other for days or weeks before circling back to him.

That lasted until the one the papers called the "Black Rose Killer" began stalking the District and Valentin, fearing for her safety, took her out of the bordello and brought her to his Magazine Street apartment. She stayed and she left and she came back again. The heat between them flared and ebbed and returned a few degrees hotter. As much as he had loved his gypsy life, he found that he couldn't quite walk away from her. And so the months and years twisted and turned to arrive at the night that he almost lost her. When it was over, he decided his wandering was finished. A few months later, they were settled in their little house on Lesseps Street with silver bands on their fingers.

"Did I hear you talking on the phone?" she said.

He came out of his daze. "With Sam. I'll be heading out." She didn't question him further. The morning sun was pouring golden blades through the stippled glass of the small window, casting the curves of her latte body in an artist's light, and he felt his heart rising.

She was watching his face and smiling curiously. "Are you lost?"

He held out a hand to her and said, "No, I am not."

The mayor had been at his desk an hour when the Chief of Police called with the terse word that in the early morning hours one letter from a person claiming to be the slayer of the woman on Villere Street had been left at the precinct at Orleans Parish Prison and another at the offices of *The Times-Picayune*. The chief said he had called the editor O'Neal, who was ready to run it.

The mayor said, "And what's your opinion?"

"I say no. It only encourages these types. They're never satisfied."

"But he can run it if he wants, can't he?"

"Yes, sir," the chief said, keeping his voice steady.

Mayor Behrman was quiet for a moment. "I'd never hear the end of it if all this lunatic wanted was his little bit of attention."

The chief, hearing that the mayor talking mostly to himself, understood that it would be pointless to argue. "Maybe so," he said.

"I'll discuss it with my staff." The mayor switched directions. "Did you hear about Tom Anderson?"

"Is he still alive?" Chief Reynolds inquired.

"Oh, yes. Very much so. And he wants permission for that detective St. Cyr to visit the scene." Before the chief could protest, he said, "With the understanding that anything of value is turned over to your officers."

Reynolds stayed quiet long enough to signal his disapproval a second time. "I suppose it won't do any harm," he said.

The mayor ended the call before the chief changed his mind. After pondering for a moment, he called two trusted aides into the anteroom used for subjects to be kept from large ears, of which City Hall had dozens. The decision was affirmed to tell O'Neal to allow the letter-writer his moment.

While all this transpired in confidence, the news about the King of Storyville, the Villere Street murder, and the reappearance of Valentin St. Cyr had flown outward like a flock of startled birds until it seemed half the city knew all the grim details long before the first newspapers hit the street. After another call from City Hall to the hospital brought news that the patient was wide awake and giving orders, the mayor made arrangements for an afternoon visit.

He had returned to his office to stand at the tall window, pondering Tom Anderson and St. Cyr in vexation. The man was

91

dallying at death's door and who does he summon? His priest? One of his former wives? His old friend the mayor? No, he chooses a Creole of uncertain parentage, a one-time police officer who had lent a hard hand to maintaining order in his scarlet empire. The mayor paused to consider that he had no one he would trust that much and for that, he envied Mr. Tom Anderson.

CHAPTER NINE

Sheriff Lasser and his deputy finished their rounds and arrived back at the office in the parish building in Houma just before noon. After visiting a few minor matters and finding no business that required immediate attention, he asked for the file of missing persons reports. His clerk fetched it to his desk and he pored over the sheets as he enjoyed the lunch his wife had packed in a paper sack: a chunk of smoked boudin, a fat slice of cheese, and a small baguette. He perched his tin of chicory coffee on the window ledge behind him.

The files revealed some curiosities but nothing that matched the woman — Evangeline — now a ward of the sisters at Our Lady of Sorrows. Had it been any other circumstance, he would have laid it aside. Women were known to run off for all sorts of reasons and a citizen with a damaged mind could be a hopeless puzzle. Either way, most of them were best left alone. But he had understood Sister Rosalie's concern and so he dug through his desk drawers for the correct official form.

He wrote out Evangeline's description, guessing her age to be early sixties and adding *Creole de couleur*. He also noted the phrase *Victim of amnesia* and, as an afterthought, *not derelict* to reflect what he saw as her sound bearing. He noted her approximate height and weight. He left the rest of the boxes blank, brushed the crumbs off the sheet, and called for Corporal Marks. The clerk rustled some papers of his own and appeared in the doorway.

The sheriff instructed him to put the information on the wire and have a dozen copies printed for mailing to police departments in smaller towns. He presumed he would hear no more on the matter. Which might well be the best solution. A body could do worse than the peace of the convent on the bayou, a small corner of God's own earth.

Valentin parked the roadster on St. Louis, against the white walls that stood as a somber partition between the living and the dead. He crossed over to a Villere Street that was quiet at this midday hour and opened the front door of the house to find a policeman perched on a chair in the sitting room, flipping the pages of a copy of *The Mascot*.

"Anything good?" he asked.

The florid-faced copper eyed him over the top of the scandal sheet. "You St. Cyr? You can go on up." He returned to his reading.

The detective climbed the narrow stairwell and moved along a hallway that was redolent with the heavy perfumes the sporting girls applied, the disinfectants they used on their customers, and the rust from the old pipes. He reached the doorway of the victim's room, now draped in an eerie silence, and stopped, hedging. Once he crossed the threshold, it would be hard to turn away. A passel of grief would rain down on his head — from the police, the attorneys on St. Charles, and Justine. At the same time, standing there not yet inside the room and not quite out, was accomplishing nothing. After another few seconds' hesitation, he stepped back into an old habit.

Once inside the peeling floral walls, he waited to let the room come to him, bringing the imprints of motion and sound that the killer and his victim had left behind, his personal brand of *voudun*.

94

He pictured the girl turning with a false smile of promise of the delights to come, quick as they might be. All the while, she would be thinking about the end of the evening, after this one and the others were long gone and she could attend to her own pleasures. She would know of a music hall that stayed open and bouncing until dawn.

Valentin guessed that this thought had barely crossed her mind when the man snatched the pillow from the bed, threw her down, and was on her, his weight and the pillow muffling her cries. She would have thrashed for no more than a half-minute. Valentin could see how the corners of the sheets were pulled up where her feet had flailed. The rest of the work was quick, a few quick slices to split open the fabric of her dress and camisole and then two slower ones, the same as the other, from her lower lip, down her throat, over her sternum and stomach, to her *mons*. The second from the aureole of one breast to the other. They were delicate cuts with a minimum of blood loss.

He had likely paused for a moment to admire his handiwork before making a fast exit, moving down the hall to the window that opened onto the rickety back stairs. Valentin knew it took a certain kind of cold nerve to walk into a house, perform such a gruesome task, and then disappear clean. Just as it had required gall to snatch two whores off the street and take another in a dime-a-trick crib. In each case, there had been people close by. The murderer had counted on these citizens being too caught up in their own business to notice him.

The detective now began the same kind of slow circle he had walked in the missing girl's room on Annunciation Street, covering every square foot in a far different tableau. When he finished, he had nothing, not a slip of paper, nor a matchbook, nor an odd coin to guide him anywhere.

He had seen too many drab boxes where women who had done no wrong, but whose luck had run out, had died horrific deaths. He could not raise a single one of them from the dead and whatever punishment he had visited on their killers had been scant justice for their gruesome ends. The evildoers could suffer the same torture a hundred times over and it still wouldn't balance the scales.

He helped himself to the pack of Murads on the nightstand next to the bed and patted his pockets for a box of lucifers. Leaning against the jamb, he smoked and thought about a next move. The simplest would be a quick call to Each with a message to the ailing Tom Anderson that he had found nothing of value and with that, his work was finished. He had other matters to occupy him, including the puzzle of a young girl's disappearance.

The King of Storyville could find someone else. The police had decent detectives and the Pinkerton office on Carondolet was open for business. The murders couldn't go on forever. Sooner or later, the fellow would blunder and that would be the end of it. The question was how many innocent people would die on the way to that misstep.

No, sending a message wouldn't do. He would find time to visit Anderson at the hospital and explain in person, so he could feel at ease getting shed of it. Justine would forgive his truancy. The attorneys would never know that he had wandered off the path. With that settled, he stepped into the hall and closed the door behind him.

When he reached the first floor, the copper looked up from his paper and said, "The madam come by to collect some things. She's in back, if you want to talk to her."

Valentin hedged a second time while the officer regarded him in a blank way. *All right, speak to the woman and then be done with it.* That was it: address this bit of business, and leave it behind.

He made his way through a dim parlor and dimmer sitting room to the kitchen. A pot hissed gently atop the spindly iron stove. A small, thin woman he recognized vaguely was seated at a wooden table in the cloudy light of day with a cup in front of her. Her cheeks were pale and her eyes blank under graying hair that was parted in the middle and pulled back severely. She appeared composed as she looked up from her tea with eyes of pale brown.

"I know you," she said.

"Valentin St. Cyr."

"You work for Mr. Tom."

"I did before, yes."

"Not anymore? So what brings you here?"

"Having a look at the room," Valentin said. "What's your name, again?"

"Myra Kay," the madam said. She frowned over her tea. "Twelve years in the District. Five different houses. Nothing fancy, but they was all clean. My girls was clean. I never had as much as a bloody nose. And now this."

"What was her name?"

"It was Anna Rice." She sighed and shook her head. "Poor girl."

"You saw the fellow?" Valentin said, then spent a second wondering how the question got out. It was too late.

"Just barely," Myra Kay said. "He come in quick. You know, the way men do when they don't want to be seen. I said, 'Who can entertain you this evening?' The girls was on the couch. He pointed to her and said, 'That one.' But he didn't really look at her. She was just the closest to where he was standing. She got up and went to the stairs." She waved a hand. "He give me a gold dollar and followed after her, just like that. Kept his face turned away the whole time. That was the last I saw of him."

"And you heard nothing?"

"Not a sound," the madam muttered, her eyes grim. "When fifteen minutes went by and neither one come down, I went up. That's when I saw..." She clutched onto the cup. "Who does such things? Good lord."

"Someone with a sickness," was all the detective could think to say.

"And there's going to be more, ain't there?" Myra Kay said. "Ain't that so?"

Valentin climbed back to the second floor and exited the house by the path the murderer had taken. The wooden boards of the back landing and the steps down creaked under his feet, but if he stepped carefully, the sound was all but lost in the noise of the red light district coming to life. The streets would have been louder at night. He was on the ground in an easy ten seconds. The gravel alley was narrow and there were no light fixtures over any of the doors. He kept his eyes on the ground on the odd chance that he'd come upon a telling footprint or some other item, but saw nothing of value.

When he arrived back at St. Louis Street, he stopped to mull his choices. He could walk to the city morgue, where Anna Rice's body was being held. He could drive out St. Charles to the Alberton mansion and wait for a telephone to ring. He could point the roadster back to Lesseps Street for his lunch and a nap. Or he could choose another destination.

Frank Mangetta looked up from behind the counter when Valentin walked in on the grocery side, his heavy eyebrows arching.

"Twice in two days?" he said, stretching his arms in an operatic gesture. "Must be the end of the world."

"I was in the neighborhood," Valentin said.

The older man tilted his head and they passed through the doorway, out of the grocery with its thick aromas of imported meats and cheeses, and into the saloon on the other side. The room was its usual midday quiet. Two plates of prosciutto, salami, provolone, and hard rolls had been placed at the ends of the bar, but everyone knew that the proprietor was severe when it came to the free lunch. You didn't eat unless you drank and most of the daytime drinkers at Mangetta's Grocery and Saloon didn't display much in the way of appetites. They tended to be a sallow lot, mostly rounders, sharps, sots, and musicians in the wake of long nights on the town.

The place was recognized as common ground for those in legitimate business and in more suspect trades. This afternoon, the booths on the far wall where these characters usually gathered were empty, so that trade was slow, too.

The regulars barely looked up from their mugs and glasses as the detective made straight for the corner booth that was reserved for the owner. That gentleman spoke a few words in Italian to the cook in the kitchen behind the bar, then snatched a bottle of grappa and two glasses and joined Valentin. He poured, said "*Saluda*," and downed the liquor in one swallow.

Valentin said, "*Saluda*, Zi' Franco," and sipped.

The "uncle" was an honorific. Mangetta was a family friend going all the way back to Sicily. He and Valentin's father had crossed to New Orleans together. The saloonkeeper had watched over Valentin through his young years and did his duty as godfather after the family's tragedy. Mangetta's was a regular stop and Valentin had spent a few months living in one of the upstairs rooms after he and Justine had fallen out. Having some of the best Italian food in New Orleans never more than few steps away had helped ease his heartache.

A round plate of which now landed on the table between them. Frank waved an imperious hand. There was no point in arguing that Justine had fixed him a fine breakfast not two hours earlier. It was impossible to refuse the Sicilian or the meals he offered.

"Where's your friend?"

"Who? Each?"

"*Si. Each.*" Frank laughed. "*Viene qui ogni giorno.*"

Valentin said, "Comes every day for what?"

The saloonkeeper brought pinched fingers to his mouth in an unmistakable gesture. "*Mangiare.*" He poured another glass full and watched with a familiar narrowed eye as Valentin nibbled from the plate.

"You up here because of that business on Villere? What happened over there? A girl was murdered in her room?"

"She was cut up in a certain way," Valentin said. "Same as some others lately."

"What'd they have to pay to get you back?"

"Not a dime," Valentin said. "You hear about Mr. Tom?"

"Everybody heard. How is he?"

"Well enough to ask me this favor. I thought he might be on his death bed."

Mangetta shook his head. "No, that man will live forever."

"He just wanted me to have a look, Valentin said. "And I did."

"That's all?" The saloonkeeper poured again. "What's *Giustina* think about this?"

"*Lei dispiace.*" The detective downed his grappa. "Not one bit. Anyway, I've done what I said I would do."

"And now you're finished with it." The older man was treating him to a look he had seen before. "*E vero?*"

Valentin considered for a moments, then offered a quiet *grazie* and walked out, leaving the proprietor with his thoughts.

100

~

Captain Picot had begun fuming shortly after he arrived at his office and was presented with a scribbled copy of the letter that had shown up on the doorstep before the day shift arrived. That was on top of his foul humor over St. Cyr appearing like a snide ghost at the house on Villere Street. It was a mood that turned all the more sour when one of his detectives told him that Tom Anderson had survived his heart attack and was sitting up in his hospital bed, working his charm on the pretty nurses, and commanding Storyville with a long arm.

He wondered when in God's name Anderson would end his damned meddling. After Chief O'Connor had passed away, word had spread that the King of Storyville and the new chief had come to an agreement. The serious crime in and around the District would be left to the men with the badges. Anderson's people could handle petty offenses. Chief Reynolds had also made noise about cleaning out the street whores. Which brought quiet snickers from the working coppers; he'd have as much luck ridding the city of mosquitoes.

Picot stood at the window, staring out at nothing, a frown twisting his mouth. He was so fixed on his dark musings that he had forgotten the piece of paper in his hand. He now turned it to the gray light and read the terse paragraph. By language and tone, it was clearly the work of a person of schooling, but a devilish lunatic. The captain thrilled at the thought of his name attached to the arrest of such a monster. That wouldn't happen if St. Cyr got to him first.

He decided at that moment to put more men on the case and petition the chief to move the Creole detective out of the way. Meanwhile, he'd assign an officer to start tracking the meddling bastard's every move.

He returned to his desk. The letter was one piece among his morning mail and official documents and he shuffled through the stack, barely glancing at the half-dozen directives from the chief, the next week's duty roster, a few pages detailing regulations. He let a quick eye fall on a wire from the Terrebonne Parish sheriff requesting information on missing Creole-of-color females in their early sixties, then moved on to three wanted posters that were of little interest.

After jotting a few notes on a pad, he turned to the file of arrest and investigation reports. All hands would be expected later that afternoon for the weekly meeting and he needed to catch up on active cases. He was halfway finished with the fifth of these when something tugged at his mind. The wire from the parish sheriff was peeking from the pile of papers and he drew it out again.

Settling back, he read it more closely. The details sounded in an odd way familiar. He pushed his memory, hoping something hidden in a corner of his brain would be shaken loose. Nothing came. In any case, he had bigger problems. The first of which was Valentin St. Cyr, who could be at that moment stalking the city streets on the trail of Captain J. Picot's prey.

As Valentin crossed Canal Street, he tried to recall how long it had been since his last visit to the city morgue. Two years, at least. What he did remember were the attendants, two frowzy buffoons who ran a warehouse for the dead. As many times as they had been caught filching some late citizen's belongings, they'd still managed to hold their jobs. Though they were true fools, they had added a welcome note of comedy to what was a grim business.

Valentin walked the six blocks west, descended the steps to the basement of the Melpomene Street building, and passed along the dank hallway to find only half of the clownish team at work, along with a beanstalk of a youngster. The senior attendant, whose name was Randall, stepped out of one of the lockers, saw the detective, and came to an astonished halt.

"What the hell?" he yelped. "I ain't seen you in years." He turned to his assistant. "This here's Mister St. Cyr. Used to be a regular customer." Eyeing the detective, he snapped his fingers and said, "Villere Street."

When Valentin nodded, Randall waved a hand at his assistant. "Go on, pull that one for him." The beanpole grabbed a gurney and dragged it into a locker.

"Where's your partner?" Valentin said. "What was his name?"

"Walter." Randall snickered and produced a dirty smile. "He got caught selling bodies out the back door. Ain't like it never happened before, but he got greedy. Some of them was barely on a cooling board when they was gone again. Which was fine if it was some damn tramp. But then he sold off a city councilman's great-aunt."

Valentin coughed out a quick laugh and Randall grinned wider, revealing a mouth half-full of dark yellow teeth. "I ain't lyin'," he said. "You coulda heard the screaming over in Algiers."

"What'd they do to him?"

"He got four years hard time. Angola. It coulda been me out there with him. So I don't touch nothin' no more. Nothin' and no one." The wooden door banged open and the assistant pushed the gurney into the room, almost flipping the covered body onto the floor. As he righted it with a flurry of bony arms, Randall sighed and jerked a thumb. "And now what I got for help is *him*." He shook his head in woe. "She's all yours, Mr. Valentin."

Turning away, he muttered something to the assistant, who folded himself against the nearest wall. Valentin was pleased that his reputation was still worth something. They'd stay out of his way.

He pulled the sheet down to the shoulders. For all the times he had stood over a victim's body, the first small pang still came. Another poor and innocent soul taken. As paltry as the woman's life had been, it was all the sadder for ending up in such a place.

She was common enough, as Irish a face as he'd ever seen, with round pale cheeks, a pug nose, and a bow of a mouth. If he raised her lids, he'd likely find her dead eyes blue or green. Her hair was a greasy ginger straw.

He pulled the sheet lower to reveal her torso. Formaldehyde hit his nostrils and made his eyes tear as he bent to examine the bloody trail at a distance of inches. The cuts had settled and compressed, so that the figure of a cross was even more pronounced, precise and with not a quiver nor a jag. Even with only seconds to spare, the fellow had taken care to keep a steady hand. Maybe he'd been practicing.

Valentin examined her hands for any signs that she had struggled and found none. The reek of ether had been her last memory before she dropped into darkness. Valentin circled the body another time. As a street copper and later a detective, he had maintained no notions of vengeance or heroics. That was for storybooks. He was not bothered by the astounding stupidity of most of the miscreants he encountered. What he could not abide was the cruelty that a sick few displayed, the sort that had been visited upon the woman on the gurney. He sensed a familiar mood of pricking anger coming over him and grabbed the sheet to cover her again.

He glanced at the attendant and his assistant, said, "Thank you, gentlemen," and turned away.

"Mr. Valentin?" Randall said. "The police is finished. You want us to hold on to her?"

The detective said, "No, let her rest in peace." He stepped into the corridor and closed the door behind him.

CHAPTER TEN

The stacks of the afternoon edition were loaded on trucks and hacks for all the city stops and onto a narrow-gauge rail car for delivery to the outlying towns. O'Neal had held the line at giving front-page space to the letter from "Gregory," instead ordering mention of its publication in small type running the width of the paper just beneath the day's headlines and placing the text on page two below the fold. In any event, it escaped few readers' eyes and from Decatur Street to Metairie, the snapping of pages of newsprint was like thousands of tiny flags waving in the wind.

Though his appetite was coming back, Tom Anderson had no interest in the hospital lunch of pale chicken, wilted green beans, and dry white rice. He pushed the plate aside and sent his wife and two of his daughters downtown to find him some real food.

Each had lingered in the corner of the room and at his employer's beck and call all morning and into the afternoon. As soon as the women departed, Anderson directed him to go to the lobby and buy him a cigar. He was back in five minutes without the smoke but with Valentin St. Cyr. The Creole detective crossed to the bed and grasped the older man's hand. "I see you're not done yet," he said.

Anderson produced a bare whisper of a laugh. Valentin asked him how he was feeling, keeping the conversation light. They spoke of the way the weather had been shifting so oddly of late.

The King of Storyville grumbled about his women and his doctors, then lowered his voice to describe the nurse in the uniform that was a size too small for her ample figure. They steered clear of the subject of Villere Street.

Each interrupted the banter by clearing his throat in a pointed way. In the next moment, Chief of Police Reynolds, tall and natty in his dress blues, strode into the room. The two junior officers he had brought along waited in the hall. Anderson cocked his head in surprise. "Chief," he said. "What are you doing here?"

Reynolds stepped to the bed and laid a hand on the King of Storyville's shoulder. "Tom," he said. "Didn't I always tell you, only one girl at a time? How are you feeling?"

Anderson offered a sigh and a small smile. "Like I was run over in the street."

"But you're still with us and that's what counts." The voice was crisp with the timbre of a man who gave orders. Reynolds regarded the patient with concern for a moment before shifting his slow gaze to the Creole detective. "Mr. St. Cyr," he said.

"Chief," Valentin said.

"I heard you paid a visit to Storyville last night." The quiet words were followed by a moment of thick silence.

"It was at my request," Anderson said.

"So I understand." Chief Reynolds produced a smile that was next to invisible. "We appreciate any assistance we can get in dealing with this lunatic."

Valentin almost snickered; no matter what the chief said, help from him was the last thing the brass would appreciate.

"And now we have the matter of a letter?" Anderson said.

The chief drew a folded sheet of paper from an inside pocket and the three men around the bed waited for the patient to read through it twice. "I'll be goddamned," he said. "Insane."

Valentin spoke up. "Whose idea was it to run it?"

Chief Reynolds said, "O'Neal spoke to Mayor Behrman and they decided to go ahead with it." His eyes went blank. "The mayor asked my opinion. I was opposed. But it didn't make any difference."

"It was a mistake," Valentin said.

"They didn't print the first one and he went out and murdered a girl," Anderson said.

"He would have done that anyway," the detective said. "And he'll be back at it. I give him no more than three days."

Chief Reynolds nodded in somber agreement. The King of Storyville pondered for a few long moments before turning to the windows and the gray clouds forming in ragged patches over the city.

"Now what will we do?" he asked the New Orleans rooftops.

Once Valentin and the Chief had made their exits, Anderson decided he was done with lying around and demanded that the doctors release him. He created such a uproar that after an hour listening to gripes, his attending physician threw up his hands and signed the papers. The nurse wheeled him to the elevator and then across the lobby and out the door, where an ambulance was waiting. His charm had returned right along with his spirits and under his sweet cajoling and a promise of good pay, she and two of her sister nurses agreed to take shifts caring for him at the house on Marengo Street.

The nuns called her Evangeline and she accepted it as a mantle draped upon her. She had nothing else. Though it was true that at odd moments another name would flit by, too quickly to catch, resting on the tip of her tongue and then disappearing before she could say it. A chasm deep and wide existed between the woman who wandered the grounds of the convent and prayed in the chapel and another someone who had existed before. She was a jigsaw puzzle missing a dozen pieces.

The sisters were kind, flowing about her like angels, tending to her needs and asking after her with their kind eyes. In some of the faces, she read ancient grievings and smaller hurts; in others, the look of being lost without mooring; and in a few others, blades of wild light that told her that someone wasn't going to be inside those walls for long.

Faded photographs came and went: a handsome man with a heavy black mustache and warm dark eyes. Children swirling in busy circles, their chatter rising like music. A baby crying and a dead man laid out for burial. Roads and rooms and strangers, some wicked, more of them gentle, passing her along from one to the next, keeping her safe in a dangerous world. She was a blind woman with the gift of sight, a deaf soul who heard the world sing. She could always speak, but it was better to stay silent.

Of all the nuns, she knew Sister Rosalie best. She saw questions in the green eyes but had no answers. She didn't know her name or from where she had come. She didn't know who she had been, only that she was now Evangeline.

Valentin made a point of taking the long way around Storyville to arrive at the lot where the Ford was parked. The sky to the west was threatening rain and he raised the canvas top before cranking the engine and hopping up into the seat. With a flip of the wheel, he pulled onto the cobbled street. After the mostly cheerless morning, whipping the roadster through the downtown traffic buoyed his mood. He had never been much for things, but he was fast developing a hankering for a machine of his own.

~

When he arrived at the Annunciation Street mansion, Belle led him through the downstairs rooms to the study, where Sam Ross and George Alberton were waiting.

"No call," the attorney blurted as soon as Valentin crossed the threshold. "The first day that's happened."

Seeing Ross flustered and Alberton's face stitched with concern, Valentin took his time helping himself to a cup of coffee from the silver tray on the sideboard.

Alberton huffed with impatience. "So?" he said. "What does this mean? What can you do?" He was working hard to be stern, but Valentin could hear the weak note in his voice.

"I don't think it means anything grave," the detective said, stirring his coffee in a show of calm. "They might be worried about their pattern being detected. Or just trying to put a scare into you."

"Well, they're succeeding," Alberton said.

"They could also be ready to make a demand."

"And trying to up the ante," Sam Ross said.

The detective said, "Correct."

"But you're guessing," Alberton said.

Valentin said, "That's right. There's not been much to go on."

"Because you haven't found anything to go on." Alberton turned to stare at the attorney for a hard second. His gaze shifted back to Valentin. "Will you excuse us?"

The detective was leaning on the fender of the Ford, watching clouds that were building even higher over the gulf, when Ross appeared from inside the house. The attorney hurried along the brick walk and out the gate.

"I'm guessing he wants the car back," Valentin said.

"What he wants back is Emelie." Ross frowned as he dug into his jacket for a packet of Royals. He offered one to Valentin and struck a lucifer for both of them. "What is it?" he asked. "You don't like the people? You don't like the case? Or both?"

The detective studied the burning end of his cigarette. "I don't mind the people," he said. "This all seems..."

"Contrived?" The attorney smile in a lazy way. "I know what you mean. But doesn't that interest you? Why is anyone going to all this trouble? Why does Emelie sound so calm? Why no demands?"

Valentin smoked and thought about it. "I don't think she was taken at all, Sam. I think she ran off."

"We still need to find her," Ross said. "That man in there is worried for the girl."

"Why?" Valentin said."She's their servant's child. Why is he going to all this? Is he frightened for her or himself?"

"Maybe if you stay on the case, you can answer those questions," Ross said. "As long as you understand there are lines."

The detective blew another gray plume before dropping the butt. "All right," he said.

"All right?"

"Let's go back inside. Unless I'm fired."

Ross flicked his cigarette away. "You're not fired," he said. "You're the only hope he has."

They had just reached the gallery when they heard a telephone bell ringing.

George Alberton was standing over the ornate set as Belle waited inside the doorway, her hands clasped tightly. Valentin gave a quick nod and she picked up the hand piece. After listening for a few seconds, she offered it to the detective, who held it to his ear for a half-minute before replacing it in the cradle.

Alberton was tense. "What did she say?"

"It wasn't Emelie," Belle said. "It was a man."

The attorney's eyes widened. Alberton stared.

Valentin said, "He instructed me not to ask any questions. He told me Emelie wouldn't come to no harm. He said that he would be calling back. That was all."

"That wasn't all," Belle whispered.

"What?" George Alberton said.

"He spoke my name," Valentin said.

The attorney walked Valentin to the Ford. A hard breeze had come up and was shaking leaves from the branches of trees up and down the street. "What does it mean?" he said.

"Someone has been watching," Valentin said. "Or spying. That's how they knew when to call. They waited until I got here."

"What's the difference between watching and spying?"

"Spying would be from the inside." Valentin explained. "And don't turn around and look at the house."

The attorney caught himself doing just that. He laughed and shook his head as if Valentin had said something humorous. Keeping his voice low, he said, "Someone in the family?"

"It could be anyone in there."

Ross watched Valentin brush a leaf from the engine cowl, then reach over the door to turn the ignition switch and pull the choke. "How are you going to find out who it is?" he said.

The detective stepped around to the front of the machine, leaned down, and grabbed the crank. The engine started on the first twist. He straightened and winked at Ross. "Maybe we'll set a trap," he said and jumped up into the tufted seat, jerked the gearshift, and steered the runabout into the street, leaving the attorney in a cloud of white smoke.

Gregory had whiled away the morning and early afternoon hours in a state of agitation, pacing from room to room and climbing and descending the stairwells until his legs ached. His mother asked if he was ill. His father took no notice. The daughter of the couple who kept house was helping her mother and glanced up every time he passed, her brown eyes watchful. The way she studied him made him more nervous, though he guessed that she was one of those colored people who found much of what whites did peculiar.

He barely touched his lunch and when two o'clock rolled around, he took a fast walk to the store at the corner of Louisiana Avenue, where he paced some more.

The Ford truck emblazoned with the former *Picayune* masthead pulled up at last and the helper threw a stack at the feet of the paperboy, who sliced the twine with an expert flick of his pocketknife. Gregory snatched the top copy and flipped a nickel into the air. He made himself stroll down the block at an easy pace. When he reached Delachaise, he leaned against the trunk of a live oak to read.

He found the letter on the lower half of page two and studied it with eager eyes, wavering between annoyance at not getting front page billing and the thrill of seeing the words he had composed so carefully in public type. The editor had written a somber preface about the discussions that went on to reach the decision to publish the missive, *in hopes of saving lives...*

Gregory felt his heart pounding, as much with relief as excitement. If they had failed to print the letter, his hand would have been forced. Not that he was about to stop. Indeed; he was just getting started.

~

It was just after four when Justine heard the slap of the newspaper landing on the top step of the perron and crossed the gallery to collect it. She stood gazing up and down the quiet street. She had never in her life felt the kind of serenity she enjoyed at that address. After a raw childhood on the bayou, she had gone on the traveling show circuit before landing in Storyville, where she had made a good living serving men of means. And where she had met the man who introduced himself as Valentin St. Cyr. She found out later that his true name was Valentino Saracena.

They had orbited the red light district for five rocky years, breaking apart and then coming together until he at last surrendered his gypsy ways, made her his wife, and took her out of the District. Though she worried that they hadn't traveled nearly far enough. Now the magnetic pull of the scarlet streets had captured him once again.

Her thoughts shifted as she observed the patchwork of clouds mounting in piles of gray and white fluff that promised rain. Perhaps it was true he was only lending a hand in time of need to a man whom he owed more than a few favors and that once that gentleman recovered, he could make his way back to his wife and his work. She hoped that could be so.

She held fast to that wish for as long as it took to open the newspaper to page two and read the terse letter. The peace that she and Valentin had been enjoying since he had left Storyville behind was about to end.

Gregory perused the newspaper as he walked back to the house, smiling a private smile when he passed a street corner and saw some citizen gawking and muttering over the item on page two. At each turn, he stifled an urge to jab the fellow and then stab a proud thumb into his own chest. *That's me. I'm the one...*

He was strolling along, enjoying the secret thrill, when his eye passed over the "Talk of the Town" column. He stopped and stared at the print. A "certain well-known Creole detective" was on the case of the murdered women. For a moment, he was lost. What detective? What did *Creole* have to do with it? He felt his heart begin to race, as if he was already trapped by a ghost he had never seen. With a quick motion, he folded the paper and hurried to the house and up the stairs to the attic.

Standing by the round window, he read the item again, and again felt his pulse rise. With a mere minute of violence, he had thrown New Orleans into a proper fit. They had called upon some special person to track him down, like the hunters they sent for man-eaters in jungles. It was becoming a chess game. He moved, they moved. And now it was his turn.

He dropped the paper onto an old chair, bent to lift a loose section of floorboard, and plucked out a copy of *The Blue Book,* the handy little guide that listed every sporting house in the red light district, along with the names of the madams and the women who offered their talents. A paragraph on the first page welcomed gentlemen to take advantage of the guide and explained the code: *W for white; C for colored; J for Jew.* French houses were designated as such. Every few pages featured a small advertisement for a certain apothecary mixture or a badly rendered photograph of a particular house. Only Lulu White's Mahogany Hall claimed a page to itself.

Gregory turned the pages and ran his eyes over the addresses, rolling the names on his tongue: Ruth Templeton. Jane Corman. Miss Lily Dale. *Lily Dale.* That was a name he could savor. He could all but imagine her; indeed, he painted a miniature in the back of his mind. Yes; it would be her. And if by chance she did not live up to the picture, then he would pick another at number 334 Marais Street who did.

He crossed to the window to ponder. It wouldn't be as simple as before. Marais was a large step up from Villere and some sporting houses employed roughnecks to handle problems. The madams and the strumpets would be on alert for strangers, right along with the extra police who would be patrolling the streets. Finally, one person in particular would be stalking the Storyville shadows for the fellow who had already taken four women and was intent on the next one.

He stopped at the mirror. The image that stared back at him held the pose of a predator: cold eyes, sharp cheekbones, a grim line of a mouth, a spike of a chin. The hands that came up with palms out were more like talons. The thought of serious men huddling behind various closed doors plotting how to stop him sent a small thrill up his spine. They didn't know that before they were ready, he would strike again and the deed would be done.

CHAPTER ELEVEN

Whatever hopes the madams and saloonkeepers had been clutching, the afternoon newspaper erased. The madman's letter was right there in black ink for the city to see, along with the "Talk of the Town" column hinting about *a certain Creole detective* showing up in Storyville following Tom Anderson's sickbed request. Tongues went to wagging and ears perked.

Valentin arrived home to find Justine puttering barefoot about the back garden, wearing a thin shift and wide straw hat. She saw him and waved. He watched her from the shade of the gallery for a moment, thinking how completely at ease she looked working the earth. All the time she'd spent on Basin Street hadn't quite taken away her peasant instincts. He waited to be sure she was occupied, then slipped back inside and called the hospital. The nurse told him that Mr. Anderson had been released. He called the house.

Anderson came on the other end of the line sounding weak, though better than before. He wasted no time on small talk. "Are you going to be able to help me?" The King of Storyville was beginning to climb back into his old skin.

Valentin didn't reply, imagining Sam Ross's pique and Justine's wrath. Storyville was not his responsibility. Anderson didn't own him; he was free to go in whatever direction he chose.

"Valentin?"

The detective said, "Pass the word to get beat coppers on Marais and Franklin. They'll need undercover men on those streets, too."

He caught the faintest breath of relief coming through the little speaker. "I'll call the chief," Anderson said.

"And tell Each to get all his boys out there, too." He stopped, then started again. "Never mind, I'll tell him."

"Whatever you say."

"Do you think we can keep this in confidence?" Valentin said.

"I can't speak for the police," Anderson said.

"I know. As much as possible, is all."

"All right. Anything else?"

"Not at the moment."

"Then I should go lie down."

Valentin said, "Yes. Take care of yourself."

The King of Storyville coughed gently. "I have some help here."

Valentin allowed himself a small smile. He promised to call the older man later in the evening and broke the connection. When he stepped to the back door, he saw that Justine had moved closer to the gallery and was working her hands through the branches of the lemon tree, plucking dead leaves and singing a quiet melody that wove in and out of the twittering of the birds. He watched and listened until the idyll was broken by yet another squawking of the telephone.

A clerk called through the door. "It's the New Orleans police for you, sir. A Captain Picot."

The sheriff picked up the receiver. "John Lasser."

"Captain J. Picot, New Orleans Police Department."

The captain seemed to be waiting for some sign of recognition. The name didn't ring any bells and in any event, Lasser was in no way impressed by city police. From his experience, too many of them made a habit of looking down their dirty, graft-sniffing noses at country lawmen. He sat back and said, "What can I do for you, sir?" pushing his tone toward the brusque.

Papers rustled from the other end of the line. "This wire you sent out in regard to the woman in your parish with the amnesia."

Lasser perked an ear. "What about it?"

"Do you have anything in addition to what was printed here?"

"Such as?"

"Such as a photograph. Or any other information about her."

"What you have is all we know."

A pause followed and when the captain continued, his voice had shifted in the direction of genial. "Her description might match up with someone in our files. I'd like to send a detective out there. Let him have a look. Maybe talk to her."

The sheriff took his time as he puzzled over a high-ranking officer bothering with a minor missing-person report from a distant parish. "It's all right with me, Captain," he said at last. "But you'll need to speak to the Mother Superior."

Picot stopped, perplexed. "What, now?"

Sheriff Lasser explained about the convent and the sisters who were caring for the woman. "They're very protective of her," he finished.

"Well, then," Picot said, getting the drift. "Perhaps you or one of your people could go in there with the detective."

"I think that would be the best way to handle it," the sheriff said.

"What's his name and when should we expect him?"

"His name's Salliers and he'll be down there tomorrow," Picot said. "There's no chance she's going to disappear, is there?"

"No chance at all," Sheriff Lasser said. "She's not going anywhere, unless the sisters say so."

~

When the shower began, Justine put away her gardening tools and moved to the back gallery to sit with a book in her lap and watch the fat drops fall through the branches and make puddles in the soft earth. Occasional thunder roiled over the west end of the city.

She had become a busier reader when she moved in with Valentin and discovered his little library. It was not something he had announced. What did a private copper know of books? And though he didn't care much for the moving pictures, she dragged him out to see the little dramas and comedies now and then. A good tale was a good tale.

The rain was falling harder now and the light sky going gray. When Valentin stepped into the doorway, he was treated to a smile, which told him she either hadn't seen the newspaper, hadn't read the item that hinted at his presence, or was waiting until he relaxed to strike. He made a retreat into the kitchen to fetch a bottle and two glasses, intending to keep Storyville out of the conversation and turn it instead to Emelie Baptiste. He wanted to move his thoughts away from the night ahead and his worries over how cold his hand might have gone after being away for so long.

She closed her book and watched as he poured two glasses full and handed her one of them. Before she could inquire about where he had spent the earlier hours of his day, he told her about arriving at the mansion and the call with the voice muttering his name.

Her gaze went sly. "Someone's been watching."

"That's what I—"

"And talking."

He smiled. "You're quicker than I am these days."

"Most days," she said.

"So?" he said. "Who's telling tales?"

Justine curled into the chair. "There's Alberton and his wife and

119

daughter, Belle, and the housekeeper and her husband, correct?"

"Yes. The older daughter is in Baton Rouge."

"The one at home. What's her name?"

"Annette."

"How old?"

"Seventeen."

"Are she and Emelie close?"

"The father said they all love her."

"What's she like?"

Valentin cleared his throat. "I, uh, haven't met her yet."

"Oh. What about the mother?"

Valentin said, "I haven't seen her, either. I've been..." He gestured in an absent way.

Justine eyed him carefully. "Distracted?"

"I suppose."

She gazed into her glass. "I think that young lady needs to be next on your list."

Gregory ate dinner, amused as his father harrumphed and his mother sighed over the news of the murders in that awful Storyville. The newspaper had even printed a letter from the madman! Gregory shook his head in pronounced dismay before asking to be excused.

His father asked about his plans for the evening. When he announced that he would be visiting the library, the parents exchanged a glance of hope that their oldest child was taking a step in a constructive direction and might cease the endless creeping about the attic.

On the subject, his mother reminded him as he left the room that he had his appointment with Dr. Rochelle in the morning. He shook his head. Almost twenty years, all the money and time wasted, and for what? That was a man who might one day disappear.

Rain had begun falling at the end of the afternoon, first in a hard shower and then relenting into a light drizzle by twilight. He could not have asked for better weather. In the attic, he placed a few implements in an old oxblood briefcase, completing the deception of his library trip, and once outside, moved with what he thought a catlike gait. The notion of evading the police who would surely be lying in wait, along with a hunter so notorious that the newspaper had spent ink on him, had his nerves on a delicious edge. He imagined the looks on their stupid faces when he struck and walked away clean once more.

The streetcar appeared out of the rain with a ghostly headlight and pulled to a rumbling stop. Gregory stepped aboard and the car pulled away.

Justine prepared a plate of cold meats, cheeses, olives, and French bread. Valentin had little appetite and barely touched the food. When the sky went dark, she made a point of working in the kitchen while he retired to the bedroom to prepare for the night. After changing into his white shirt and gray trousers and jacket, he opened the bottom drawer and drew out the stiletto in the sheath and strapped it to his right ankle. The whalebone sap with the old leather grip went into a back pocket. Next was the Iver Johnson that he lifted from the linen where it had rested unused. He worked the revolver until it felt comfortable again. The weight in his jacket pocket took some settling before he got used to it. While he figured that on this night only the pistol might come in handy, the other pieces made a set, and he knew he'd feel lopsided without them. Last was the envelope filled with gold dollars that he had tucked into the back of the top drawer.

Perhaps his carriage was a bit uncertain, but as he stood before the mirror peering at the reflection of his eyes, he saw only the usual small flicker of nerves over what the night would bring. Once the game began, he would push that into a corner of his mind, as he'd done so many times before. After some quiet minutes, he stepped into the kitchen and, for the first time in almost three years, kissed Justine's cheek and left to track down a killer.

By the time he parked the Ford in the blue shadows along Rampart Street, the rain had ebbed into a soft mist that was tossed in swirls by small gusts of wind. The east end of the District was quiet as he made his way down Jackson Street, his riding cap pulled down over his brow and his shoulders hunched in his dark overcoat.

The uniformed coppers Tom Anderson had requested from the chief were using the rain as an excuse not to patrol. As he crossed over, he saw a pair dawdling beneath the canvas awning on the side of Julia Johnson's establishment. The sullen coppers looked his way, but offered no greeting. He assumed that the word had gone around that St. Cyr was there to make them look bad. Unlike a Pinkerton, who would know his place. He felt as if Picot's dirty green eyes were on him as he proceeded down the block.

Each was waiting on the corner of Liberty and Franklin. Valentin glanced along the street and saw two pairs of men on both the next corners. By their ragged attire, they belonged to Each's crew and they all would have colorful monikers: Two Dice, Gumball, Black Jimmy. They wouldn't have a Liberty half between them. The hope was that Gregory would ignore them as members of the small army of ragged layabouts who infested the District nightly.

Stepping onto the banquette, Valentin wondered if he was too smart for that ploy, too. "How many you have?" he asked.

122

"Eight in all," Each said. "I told them to keep moving, like you said. To take it easy and keep their eyes open."

Valentin reached into his pocket for the envelope and placed it in the waiting palm. Each tucked the coins away to be passed around at the end of the night. They both knew better than to pay such characters in advance.

"What's the signal?" the detective said.

"Three quick ones." Each had handed out the tin police whistles beforehand. "Where will you be?"

Valentin surveyed the streets in four directions, drawing in the panorama. After a moment, he raised his arm and pointed to the mouth of the alley that ran all the way through between Treme and Franklin. "There," he said. He turned back. "And I want you right here."

Each noticed a familiar set in those eyes, as if the detective had already spotted something. "What is it?"

Valentin clapped a hand on the younger man's shoulder and walked away. He wanted distance between them lest Each noticed that he was suffering a case of jitters. The notion that Gregory was already stalking Storyville had come over him as he drew closer to the meeting point. He couldn't tell if this was his rusty street sense coming back or his imagination running away. His gut had served him well in the past. If Tom Anderson understood Storyville as a machine of multiple moving parts, Valentin perceived it the same way a cat knew a the jungle. Though he was not such a fool as to believe that all his instincts would come back to him at the snap of two fingers.

Still, *something* was niggling in his brain and tingling up his spine. It was an old instinct that had never failed him; and so he let the dark alley and its shadows draw him close.

~

Gregory blended into the swirl of men moving along the Marais Street banquette. Eyes were darting at the doorways of the sporting houses where the painted ladies posed, through windows into rooms where sports sat cloaked in clouds of smoke, dealing their cards and rolling their dice, and at the sots and hopheads who staggered through and toppled into the gutters. Pickpockets loitered on the corners, flicking their gazes at this man and that in search of easy marks. The only police presence was the pair of coppers strolling unconcerned down the other side of the street. If anyone was on the lookout for a mad murderer, he gave no sign.

Did they still not understand what a threat he posed? That he had butchered four women right under their noses? That he had sent such fear through the red light district that they had printed his words in the newspaper? Or was all that already forgotten in the rush to the wet pleasures of the whores, the glasses pulled to the brim with Raleigh Rye, and the greasy cards?

He enjoyed a private smile as he passed along the block. *You will receive a reminder this night, dear citizens.*

He paced himself, at ease amid the foot traffic. Just before he reached the end of the block, he made a quick cut into the walkway that ran between a sporting house and the apothecary that dispensed everything from cures for gleet to paregoric to soothe an aching tooth or troubled mind. The passage was one he had selected on an earlier visit, and now, away from the glow of the streetlamps, he slowed his steps to glance over his shoulder. The foot parade continued on without pause. No one had noticed him.

Creeping in spite of the rats that scrabbled ahead of his feet, he traversed the passage gingerly. The alleyway behind the building was quiet and he leaned his head out. The back gallery of the house leaned on bowed timbers and a bare bulb offered a weak yellow light. Tossing from a fistful of gravel, he hit the bulb on the fifth throw. The glass popped and the gallery went dark.

With his soft-soled shoes, he mounted the sagging steps with barely a creak and stood at the back door. He surveyed the alley another time in both directions. When nothing moved, he pulled the thin-bladed knife from his pocket and inserted it into the keyhole. The innards of the old lock were loose and after a few seconds of jiggling, the bolt slid right.

He twisted the knob and opened the door a crack. Through the gap, he viewed the small laundry room with tubs and sinks. It was perfect for his purposes, unlit and close, a place where he could hide until the time was right. He was about to push the door wide when an odd sensation nudged him and he froze. Something had shifted on his periphery. A small motion? A shred of sound? A waft of strange odor? He turned his head in both directions a second time and still saw nothing.

He was leaning his shoulder into the flimsy wood when he heard a voice call his name.

Valentin had caught the movement and knew in that exact instant who it was. The world slowed and fell silent. He could no longer hear the traffic on the streets, the shouts from the banquettes, the music that trebled from the open windows. From the murk of the alley, he held his breath and watched, as first the head and then the body appeared from the passageway.

Head and body moved into the alley and his eyes narrowed as he registered the dark profile: round in the top and middle, set on spindly legs. The movements were cautious and yet steady as the figure mounted the steps to the gallery. At the quick flash of a blade, Valentin stalked a half-dozen soundless steps from his hidden spot to a closer one. Now the figure at the door stopped, held fast. The head turned in a slow arc, first to one end of the alley and then to the other. Valentin felt the probing eyes, but knew that unless they held magic powers, he was still invisible.

He stayed that way until the man on the gallery returned his attention to the lock, twisting the blade and then pushing the door open to reveal a gap of dim light from inside the house. Another pause, and the door opened a foot wider. At that, he moved to the center of the alley in two quick strides and called out, "Gregory!"

For a second night, Justine was awake and waiting when Valentin came in. An hour earlier, she had jumped when the telephone jangled and made herself get up to answer it. At the sound of his voice, she held back a sigh. In the next second, she bit down on the plume of anger in her chest over him putting her through this again. She had heard the edge in his voice and knew better than to ask for details. Once she caught a breath, she said, "When will you be home?"

"Soon," he said and broke the connection.

The minutes seeped by until she heard the Ford approach along the quiet street and come to a stop. The front door opened and in a few seconds, he was standing in the doorway. She saw the light in his eyes, like a boy after a fierce street game. He was broadcasting that same something that had first drawn her to him, the cool poise of a predator, whether the prey was a felon or a fine woman. She hadn't seen that look in a long time.

She kept her voice tight to let him know she was still perturbed. "So," she said. "Are you going to tell me what happened?"

Valentin stood in the center of the alley, his revolver draped against his thigh. As he figured it, Gregory had three choices. He could break through the door and try to flee through the house. He could run down the crossing alley and hope to escape onto Treme Street. Or he could stand where he was and let the detective take him down. Valentin guessed that he was making these same calculations. When a few tense seconds passed and he didn't budge in any direction, the detective shuffled a few steps closer.

"Why don't you just stay where you are?" he called in a steady voice, more a suggestion than a command. Gregory made a jerky wave with a one hand and produced a nervous laugh. Valentin couldn't get a clear fix on his features. Still in shadow and with the hat pulled low, the face seemed rubbery and indistinct. He needed to get closer.

Neither man was ready for what happened next. Valentin was pointing his pistol and stepping in to force him to his knees when the door was flung open. The madam of the house stood bathed in the light from the laundry room, her arms akimbo. "What the hell you doin' out here?" she snapped, her voice raw. "Why you breakin' my door?"

Gregory reacted by grabbing her hair and dragging her in front of him as he sidled down the gallery steps. Valentin extended the pistol with his finger on the trigger as Gregory wrestled the woman down to the alley, holding the blade to her throat. Her eyes flapped wide and she gasped as if she was drowning.

"You know I'll do it," Gregory announced in a voice so high it was almost girlish. "Back away." He crouched and ducked his head so that the detective could not take a decent shot. The woman wailed. There was commotion in the house and two sporting girls appeared in the doorway, shrieking and pointing.

"Get inside!" Valentin shouted. The girls gaped, then retreated in a gabble of cries.

The woman shuddered and moaned, her knees giving way. "Please...please..."

Valentin was now close enough to see the point of the knife jabbing her skin. He knew the madman might cut her open and take his chances. He shot a glance past the two bodies, hoping to catch sight of a copper or one of Each's boys. While he was looking, Gregory was moving, backing the woman farther down the alley. Another ten feet and Valentin would have no shot at all, but even then it was just as likely he'd hit the woman. So he stood helpless as his quarry shuffled deeper into the mist and shadows. Then, in a sudden second and a flutter of motion, he was gone.

The woman stood quivering, then collapsed to the ground. When Valentin reached her, she said, "Was that...was that the...?"

"It was," Valentin said.

"Oh, my dear God," she whimpered. "He was going to..."

The detective saw faces crowded at the back window and waved a sharp hand. Four sporting girls came tumbling outside and rushed to the madam's aid. He stood watching for a few seconds before turning around and making his way back to Iberville Street.

He found Each and told him to have his men on the lookout, even though Gregory, his bones shaking after the close call, would have fled the District. He walked a block to Mangetta's and used the telephone to call Tom Anderson. The King of Storyville cursed over the killer's escape.

"I wish I had finished it the second I saw him," Valentin said.

"At least he didn't get away with another one," Anderson said.

"I want to make go make sure he's gone for tonight."

"For tonight?"

"He's not going to stop."

"So you'll be waiting next time. And it will end differently."

Valentin murmured a good-night, dropped the handset in the cradle, and looked up to see the Sicilian standing in the office doorway holding a bottle in one hand and two glasses.

"You look like you could use something," the saloonkeeper said.

"I almost had him," Valentin told his wife. "It was that close."
"Nothing to identify him?" Justine said.
"Nothing I can use."

He drew the revolver from his pocket and placed it atop the chest of drawers. "It's been so long since I fired this."

"I know," she said. "I remember." Her pretty brow was stitching and he knew she was mulling the peril of his crossing paths with a murderer. She didn't understand that when he faced Gregory he had felt not the smallest tingle of fear, only a vague moment of hesitation that checked his once sure hand.

He didn't want to explain this and instead crossed to the window to watch the rain. "This weather," he murmured.

"Come to bed," Justine said.

CHAPTER TWELVE

Detective Salliers drove through the wet streets of Houma to the parish sheriff's office. He had caught only a few rushed words about what had happened in Storyville the night before, with the detective St. Cyr cornering the murdering bastard who called himself Gregory and then letting him slip away. He wanted to linger at the precinct to hear more details, but Captain Picot spotted him and asked why he wasn't on his way to Terrebonne.

He had his instructions, though in truth he didn't understand the captain's curiosity about one crazy woman. As if they didn't have enough of those in New Orleans. And with all the action with the madman Gregory. That's where he should have been, keeping his hand on the case or his eye on St. Cyr. Instead, he was on a foolish errand, steering around puddles in a backwoods bayou town.

He located the building, announced himself at the front desk, and stood snapping the rain from his hat. Sheriff Lasser, a solid, cool-eyed sort, appeared from the office in back. The two men didn't shake hands. "You're wanting to speak to the woman at the convent," the sheriff said.

Salliers said, "That's right."

"What's your department's interest in her?"

The detective gave a shrug. "My captain didn't give me much information. Just wanted me to talk to her and see if she might say something that ties back to our part of the world." He could tell at a glance that the sheriff wasn't buying it. "That's all he told me."

"The sisters have tried to get information out of her. No luck." Lasser paused before adding, "And she trusts them."

Lowering his voice, the detective said, "Look, I just need to be able to say I spoke to her, that's all. If she can't tell me anything, that'll be the end of it."

Sheriff Lasser eyed the city cop for another moment before reaching for the slicker that hung on the coat rack. "I'll drive you out there," he said.

Though Salliers had been told to expect this, he wasn't pleased at the notion of an escort. He bit down on his frown and produced a oily smile in its place. "I appreciate the courtesy," he said, then stood back to let the sheriff lead the way.

The Baker bearing the scars of five hard bayou years passed through a deep green tunnel of moss-draped branches hanging down like the hair of a weeping woman, the rain her tears dripping through heavy branches. Or so Sheriff Lasser imagined when he made the drive in a certain state of mind.

For his part, Detective Salliers, raised in Metairie and unused to the primeval backwoods, found that this place bordered on the menacing, all the more so because he could not see more than a hundred feet ahead. He relaxed only when they emerged from beneath the canopy and into a daylight drizzle. Ahead was the convent, enclosed in white walls. When they pulled to a stop at the front gate, he eyed the plastered arch over the gate and the angel of cast iron that stood guard at its apex.

"What's it like in there?" he asked the sheriff.

Lasser treated him to a sidelong glance. "Mostly quiet, is all. You haven't been around nuns before?"

"No," the detective said. "My people didn't care much for church."

"Well, it's pleasant," Lasser said. "Quiet. They're kind women. Devout. They do only good."

Salliers stared at the iron angel, wearing a dubious frown. "If you say so."

The sheriff was getting annoyed at the city cop's attitude. "You want to do this or not?"

"It's what I'm here for," Salliers said, and opened his door.

The Mother Superior had informed Sister Rosalie of the visit from the detective from New Orleans and the sister had in turn taken Evangeline aside to explain. They sat in the empty dining hall as rain whispered outside the tall windows. When the older woman heard mention of a police officer, her eyes clouded and she said, "Have I done something wrong?"

Sister Rosalie said, "Oh, no, nothing like that. They want to know if perhaps you have some connection to New Orleans, that's all." She smiled in a gentle way. "We all want to help you with your memories."

Evangeline was not reassured. "Will you be with me?" she asked.

"Yes, of course." Sister Rosalie patted her arm. "I'm not going anywhere."

They sat in silence, gazing out the window at the fat drops on the yellow and orange leaves, until a novitiate arrived to announce that Sheriff Lasser had arrived with the officer from New Orleans. The two women stood to wait for the policemen to enter and shed their rain-dappled coats. The sheriff in his uniform escorted the detective in his dull suit to the table.

"Sister," Sheriff Lasser said, turning a gentle eye on her. He offered the older woman a slight bow. "Miss Evangeline, is that it?"

Evangeline looked to Sister Rosalie, who said, "That's correct."

"This is Detective Salliers with the New Orleans Police. He's come to speak with you."

The women took seats on one side of the table, the men on the other. Salliers was regarding Evangeline with a probing gaze that made Sister Rosalie distrust him on sight. Sheriff Lasser had settled with his hands folded before him, quiet but watchful, which made her feel better. Evangeline kept her eyes cast downward and didn't raise them until the sheriff gave a nod and Salliers produced a notebook and pencil, at which point she caught and held the New Orleans policeman's stare. Sister Rosalie noticed this and smiled at another hint of the backbone that resided inside this puzzling woman.

Salliers said, "Thank you for your time, ladies." The sister noted that his voice was hoarse, probably from screeching at all the poor souls who had fallen into his clutches over the years. "I have a few questions, if you don't mind." Evangeline continued to hold his stare. "First, I want to ask—"

"I'm sorry. Who are you, again?"

She had caught him off-guard and he appeared piqued. "Detective Abner Salliers, ma'am. New Orleans Police." Evangeline nodded faintly. Salliers rearranged his notebook. "I want to ask what if any memories you have of the city."

"New Orleans."

"Yes, ma'am," Salliers said. "In particular, the First and Liberty street neighborhood."

Sheriff Lasser and Sister Rosalie exchanged a glance at the question. They had been expecting a general inquiry, a kind of fishing expedition. The sheriff knew the sound of an interrogation and came alert for any tick in the detective's queries or the older woman's replies.

Evangeline hesitated. "I know the words. The streets...I'm not sure."

"All right, then. What about Parish Prison? Do you recall anything about that place?"

"Prison?" Evangeline frowned and it dawned on Sheriff Lasser that though the questions were precise, Salliers had no idea where they might be leading. He was reciting from a list that someone else had prepared for him. That would be Captain Picot.

Salliers went on, inquiring about other places around the city. At the mention of Charity Hospital, Evangeline blinked hard but said nothing. Sister Rosalie cocked a curious eyebrow.

The detective moved to another of his notations. "Do you recognize any of these names?" He spoke each with a pause in between. "Bolden...Giovanni...Valentin...or Valentino." At this last mention, her eyes widened. Salliers said, "What? That one?"

"Maybe so," Evangeline said. "But I can't say for sure."

Salliers was watching her more closely. Her face went blank and she leaned away from him. Sheriff Lasser waited for a moment before saying, "Anything else, detective?"

The city cop looked over his notes, then closed the leather cover. "No, I guess that's it." He stood to don his coat.

"I'll be out in a minute," the sheriff said.

Salliers glanced between him and the two women, his eyes narrowed. Touching the brim of his hat, he said, "Ladies," and made his exit.

Once the door had closed, Lasser looked at Evangeline with concern. "Are you all right, ma'am?"

Evangeline's eyes shifted. "I remember."

Sister Rosalie turned and said, "Remember what?"

"Those words he said. The names and places." She laid fingers to the side of her head. "They're in here. I don't know how." Before the sister could question her again, she plunged on. "They're pieces of something." She summoned a smile that was half shy and half sly. "I didn't want to tell him," she whispered.

"I think you made the right decision," the sheriff said.

Evangeline turned to gaze out the tall window. After a long pause, she said, "Now I now there's a storm on the way."

"Well, it rained most of last night," Sister Rosalie said. "And off and on for a week. It's Louisiana."

"No, I mean a true storm," Evangeline said.

The sister was about to say something about bad weather blowing through all the time. Then she noticed Evangeline's grave face and how the serene light that infused it dimmed as the eyes turned a troubled gray. The older woman looked between Sister Rosalie and the sheriff. "It's coming. You wait and see."

In spite of the protests from his wife and the nurse, Tom Anderson summoned Edward and told him to fetch the car. With the help of the driver and his eldest son, he settled in the front seat and then rode into town, having sent word ahead for Each and Valentin to join him at the Café.

The landlady at Each's rooming house roused him. When the King of Storyville reached Valentin, the detective murmured that he'd do his best to be there as soon as he could. Anderson surmised that this was not a problem of transportation, but an unhappy wife.

The streets of the District had buzzed through the rest of the night and into the rainy dawn as the word passed from house to house to be wary of any customer who would not show his face or otherwise behaved strangely. And so not a few gentlemen who simply wished to enjoy the company of a strumpet while keeping their identities hidden went without. Though there were always the crib girls and mattress whores for the desperate. In any case, the hours went by without incident. While there was no new dead body, there was a quite evil one still alive and running loose.

Gregory had escaped the red light district with his heart lodged in his throat, his bowels churning, and his legs rubbery. This time, he had sensed his own life hanging on a terrible edge. With the day breaking, he recalled the frigid glare as the man with the pistol weighed killing both him and the madam.

But he couldn't do it and simply stood staring as his prey backed away and then fled into the maze of passages that ran among the buildings. Once he reached the Franklin Street banquette, he blended in with the eddies of menfolk until he could veer away and lurch across Basin Street and into the yard behind Union Station.

Once he was cloaked in the darkness, he had pulled off his coat and let the rain soak a shirt that was now clammy with sweat. As his racing heart calmed, he felt a rush of pride over his performance. He hadn't quailed at the hard face and the pointed pistol. He had not surrendered in a weeping, pissing lump. Something had taken over and in a sudden instant, he had grabbed the woman and used her to hold off his pursuer. Otherwise, he would surely be in chains — or dead.

He knew nothing of the man who had almost cornered him, but his gut told him that he was the one mentioned in the gossip column, a few lines of ink brought to life. Even in the murky alley, the eyes had glowed with such predatory light that all he wanted to do was escape them.

How long had he imagined himself a sick soul, a monster infected with diseased cells that drove him to horrid acts, a freak who would continue his cruel and miserable career until he was caught and exterminated? If he'd had any doubts, Dr. Rochelle was there to remind him of his malady and collect his fee.

But not anymore; now he was a dangerous character. And a

notorious one, having escaped such a skilled foe. *That's* what they would write about in all the afternoon newspapers. And what would the good doctor think of him now?

Replaying the scene in the alley behind the sporting house yet another time, he was assailed by a craving to know the one he had faced down, the one who had him in the sights but had let him escape in order to spare the life of a whore. What sort of man was this?

After Valentin finished the telephone call from Anderson, he made his way into the bedroom where Justine was tucking the sheets around the mattress. "That was Mr. Tom," he said. She continued working. "He's asked that I come to the Café to talk to him and Each about what happened last night. And what to do next."

"When?"

"Whenever I can get there," Valentin said, keeping a careful tone. She still gave no response, though she seemed distracted rather than perturbed. "I thought I'd go now. Get it over with."

Justine gave the top sheet a final tug and said, "Well, then. You can carry me to the French Market on your way."

He sat on the couch reading the morning paper while she dressed and fixed her hair. The presses for the edition he held had already been running at the time of the incident in the alley. So there would be a story in the afternoon paper. Until the drama ended, New Orleans would not be able to get enough of the mad killer whether on the printed page or hearing about him from some wagging tongue or other. That Gregory had been trapped and got away was too delicious. *The Times-Picayune* would be sober on the subject, but *The Mascot* and the other scandal sheets would be in full lather.

Hearing his wife moving about in the bedroom, Valentin felt his scalp prickle. His name was about to appear in print for the first time in years. He had never wanted it there in the past and less so now, but it was too late.

Justine entered the room, saw the look on his face, and said, "What's wrong?"

"I'd rather stay here," he said.

"Oh?" She perched her eyebrows. "Too bad for you."

He had no argument for that. She glanced at the paper that he had dropped on the side table and said, "What are your Garden District friends going to say if they find out?"

This thought had been squirming in the back of his mind, right along with his other guilts. If he had taken Gregory, the whole matter would be over. Now there would be no evading their wrath. "They're not going to be happy," he said.

"That's what I figured," she said. "Can we go now?"

Each was waiting outside when the Maxwell 25 pulled to the curb. He helped Edward maneuver Mr. Tom down to the banquette. The King of Storyville heaved a grunt and gestured impatiently with his cane. The day man was waiting and the front doors swung wide. The little entourage had just reached the threshold when a voice called, "Mr. Tom?"

Anderson turned and squinted. "You're..."

"Reynard Vernel, sir."

"From *The Picayune*."

"It's *Times-Picayune* now. But, yes, sir."

Anderson frowned. "What can I do for you?"

"I'm working a story. I'd like to observe your meeting, if you don't mind." Anderson turned to Each with a peeved look. "No one told me about it," Vernel said quickly. "I have my sources around town. People talk. I heard you were on your way."

The King of Storyville considered for a moment, then said, "Come along, then."

Vernel fell in behind. "Where's Mr. St. Cyr?" he asked.

Picot had just ended a call from one of his Storyville spies describing St. Cyr arriving for a meeting at Anderson's Café that included the reporter Vernel when Detective Salliers walked in. The captain said, "Well?"

"She didn't respond to any of the questions."

Picot folded his arms and waited.

"I do think she's hiding something. But I don't know what."

"All right, then, if you were to guess?"

"I'd say she knows something of New Orleans." The detective watched his superior officer. "What's this about, sir?"

Picot moved back to his chair and sat down. "This doesn't go any farther than this room. Understood?"

"Understood," Salliers said.

"St. Cyr."

"What about him?"

"Twenty years ago, his father got himself killed. It was in the middle of the Sicilian troubles. The Orange Wars."

Salliers frowned, puzzled. "I thought he was Creole."

"On his mother's side," Picot said. "The other half is dago. Why do you think he looks like that? After the father died, the mother disappeared. Lost her mind and wandered off, is what I heard. And no one saw her after that."

Salliers was a bit slow, but he wasn't stupid. After a moment, his eyes widened. "God damn," he said. "So you think...?"

"I've been wondering, that's all."

"Wouldn't it be a hell of a thing?"

"All right, Detective." The captain waved a dismissive hand.

"We'll leave it be for now. But remember what I said. Lips sealed."

Salliers left Picot gazing into space. As he closed the door, he saw a smile creeping onto the round face.

Anderson, Each, and Reynard Vernel were at one of the round tables sipping coffee laced with brandy when the door opened and the Creole detective entered. Valentin slowed his steps when he recognized the reporter. They hadn't seen each other in three years. Anderson noticed and said, "I invited our friend here."

"I'll leave, if you prefer," Vernel said. "But I'm filing a story for this afternoon. And I want to have the facts."

The detective understood that he would able to affect what was printed and nodded his assent. He took the empty chair, poured coffee from the brass-plated decanter, and topped it with brandy. Anderson waited for him to take his first sip to say, "So you saw this bastard's face?"

Valentin shook his head. "Not enough to make an identification. He's a clever one. He wore his hat pulled low and he ducked down behind the madam. Just enough that I couldn't get a clear view. He was daring me to take a shot." He gave a short laugh, breaking some of tension. "And I wanted to oblige him."

The King of Storyville smiled. "You didn't. That makes you a hero around here." His blue eyes did a cool shift and he tilted his head toward Vernel. "Our guest is going to make sure that the readers grasp that." Vernel began to respond and Anderson held up a hand. "You know those other rags will paint Mr. Valentin as faint-hearted because he wouldn't put a bullet through an innocent woman. You have only to say what happened."

The reporter sat back and drew out his pen and notebook. "That I can do."

The King of Storyville nodded to Valentin. "Go ahead."

Valentin recounted the scene in the alley, taking care to use words like "cringed" and "hid" to describe Gregory's actions. "These types are cowards of one kind or another," he said. "They only go after victims they know are weaker." He finished detailing how Gregory had run away – but only because he had allowed it. He tapped a hard finger on the table. "I wasn't going to be a party to another woman losing her life."

The reporter jotted, then looked up. "Anything else?"

Valentin produced a blank smile. "No, that's enough, I think."

Vernel closed his notepad and put away his pen. He took a last sip of coffee and rose to shake hands with the other men, murmuring thanks. He hurried from the table and out into the gray morning.

"You think he'll cooperate?" Anderson said.

Each said, "He wants the story, don't he?"

Valentin said, "He means Gregory. And the answer is yes. I think he will."

Gregory enjoyed a late breakfast, his appetite aroused by his Storyville adventure. After he finished, he sat at the kitchen table, pretending to read the morning paper, all the while watching the back garden until Henry the groundskeeper left to meet the trash wagon. He folded the paper, slipped from the kitchen, and hurried to the shed at the back of the property, where he helped himself to one of the jackets of blue de Nimes cotton hanging from one of the low rafters. Wrapping it around the pair of work boots he found in the corner, he carried the bundle back into the house without anyone noticing.

He dressed, relishing the prospect of walking back to the red light district when everyone would expect him to be cringing in fear. This time, he would not be on the prowl, but visiting as an everyday citizen. A working man, to be exact, with his foot up on a bar rail, elbow bent, and ears perked. By the end of the afternoon he would know the name of the fellow who had come at him in the alley.

He waited until he heard the noon bells toll to escape through a quiet house and walk to St. Charles, where he became one among the half-dozen ordinary riders on their way downtown.

Captain Picot spent the rest of his morning with one part of his brain fixed on the mundane tasks of running the Detectives section and another mulling Salliers' report from Terrebonne.

Once the Creole had retreated to his house in Marigny and his soft work for the law firms, the captain had tried to put him out of his thoughts. After what they'd been through, St. Cyr left Storyville holding a secret so deep and dark that it had given him what had seemed a perpetual upper hand. Picot thought that his chance to even the score had been lost, a bitter pill. But then the missive from a parish sheriff had landed on his desk, bringing a sudden glimmer of hope that the story could end in his favor. But only if he played his cards to perfection.

It was time to begin. He pushed his papers aside and called to Cassidy, the nervous clerk who sat at the desk just outside his office door. He heard the flutter of noisy motion as the young fellow disengaged from his work and jumped into view.

"Captain?"

"I have an assignment for you." Picot scratched on his pad, then ripped the page loose, folded it, and held it before him. Cassidy snatched it with nervous fingers.

"Go to headquarters," Picot said. "The records room is in the basement. I want you to take down the information off the cards on any murders or reported deaths on those dates. Do you

142

understand? You copy down the names and the locations of the incidents. Bring the information to me. In my hands only."

Cassidy's apple cheeks flushed at the gravity of the mission. "Yes, sir. In your hand."

"Well?" Picot snapped. "Move."

Cassidy backed out of the office, almost tripping on his own feet. Captain Picot returned to his papers.

Valentin parked the Ford on the corner of Decatur and St. Peter streets and sat waiting, the dutiful husband. Having a machine was a rare advantage and he guessed that Justine would take the opportunity to gather as much for the kitchen as she could manage.

The morning newspaper was folded on the seat and he opened it again. The news of the threatening weather from the west had moved from inside to the front page. Ships out on the gulf were reporting heavy storms. He lowered the paper to gaze over the river. In the distance, the mountains of gray clouds that had been a fixture for what seemed weeks were stacked high with shafts of sunlight cutting through them like blades.

He had seen bad storms, though none like the old timers related when it was late and the rain was pouring down and they were into their cups and casting about for new tales to foist on the younger men at the bar.

"This ain't *rain*," one of them would mutter. "Anybody here in the year of seventy-two? Didn't think so. We thought the goddamn world was about to end, like it says in the Bible. Skies opened up and just dumped an ocean on us. Up to the balconies in some places. The thunder was so loud you couldn't hear for the noise. People dropped dead of fright. Must have been a thousand drowned when the water come over the levees." The speaker would shake his grizzled head. "Ain't never going to see the likes of that again."

Valentin and the others would trade glances. No one had ever heard of a thousand people dying in a flood. But the old crank was entertainment on a dead afternoon, so they let him ramble on.

The detective stopped to cast an absent eye to the south and conjure the havoc the old gent had described. Forty years before, New Orleans was a far smaller city and still shaking off vestiges of the blockade. There were far fewer people to suffer such a tempest and far less property to destroy. After being battered by all sorts of wild weather over the decades, those who chose to live along the gulf were veterans not easily daunted. *Dropped dead of fright,* indeed.

He had no interest in continuing with the paper and settled deeper in the seat. It was the first gap of peace he had felt in eighteen hours and he now thought back on what had transpired in the alley. In that sudden second, Gregory appeared, a switch turned, and he went from reason to reaction. His three years away had not erased all his street skills. Though it was true that he hesitated. He could have fired for the madman's head and hoped for a hit; that, or a clean shot through the flesh of the woman's left shoulder. Or...

He stopped and sighed. *Enough.* He could roll it over a hundred times and never have it come out the right way. It was done; now the next step was at hand, one he had set into motion by way of the reporter Vernel. His taunts would be splashed in print where Gregory would see it, along with Sam Ross and George Alberton. Picot and Chief Reynolds and Mayor Behrman, and Justine, whom he feared the most.

He could hear her now. *What are you doing?* A second went by and her voice came back even sharper. "Valentin?" He blinked and turned his head to see her standing on the passenger side of the Ford, peering at him through the gap in the window flap. "Are you asleep? I called you twice."

He sat up. "I was...I'm—"

"Never mind. We have all these bags." She waved over her shoulder to the banquette, where a young Negro girl stood next to a crowd of sacks brimming with color. "Are you going to help?"

Valentin backed the roadster to the curb and climbed down. "Do you remember Mary?" Justine said. "The maid at Miss Antonia's? Can we carry her back?"

The girl smiled and Valentin offered a nod, though his memory of her was vague. He opened the boot and loaded the bags while the two women got settled in the machine. Rain was beginning to fall again as he slid onto the seat.

He let Mary operate the windshield wiper crank during the drive to the District, delighting her. He pulled to the curb in front of the familiar address, the very mansion where Justine had been working when they first met. She and Mary took a sack each and went ahead while he unloaded the rest of the groceries for the house and carried them to the gallery. He was in no mood to spend any extra time in the District, but then Miss Antonia pushed the door open and waved him to the foyer, an invitation he couldn't refuse.

The small, handsome madam looked him up and down. "Well, the married life hasn't done you any harm." Valentin saw her eyes shift and knew what was coming before it reached her lips. "I heard all about what happened last night. And that newspaper is going to carry the whole story this afternoon. Talking to a reporter? That doesn't sound like the Valentin St. Cyr I know."

He could feel Justine's icy stare on his face. Then it went away. She smiled at Miss Antonia. "It was so pleasant seeing you," she said. "We have to go now."

CHAPTER THIRTEEN

The afternoon edition of *The Times-Picayune* came off the trucks at two o'clock and into Storyville, Vieux Carre, and Uptown hands that were more eager than usual.

Gregory collected his copy from one of the ragged boys standing in front of the station terminal shouting, "Killer barely escapes capture! Read it here! Killer escapes capture!" He joined the file of men dropping nickels and snatching papers from the stack. The familiar thrill ran up his spine as he strolled from the station. *If only they knew who walked among them...* He crossed over Basin Street and perused the page as he weaved along the banquette. The story, carrying the byline of one Reynard Vernel, began on a factual note.

> Late last night, a private detective in the employ of Mr. Tom Anderson briefly cornered a suspect in the alley that runs from Bienville Street, a man authorities believe to be the repeat killer of women who has been calling himself "Gregory."

The reader of this narrative continued his stroll to the corner of Bienville Street, where he stopped to wait for traffic to pass.

> The detective, Valentin St. Cyr, told this reporter that he came upon the suspect trying to gain entry into the Marais Street sporting house of Miss Hannah Brown. When confronted, the suspect took refuge behind the

> landlady, who had opened the back
> door and stepped outside.

Gregory fixed on *St. Cyr,* an odd name that gave the face in the alley a whole new dimension. Engrossed, he did not move on, but lingered on the corner to continue reading. He did not care for the phrase "took refuge" one bit. The way it read made it sound like he was—

> "...a coward," the detective said. "He
> hid behind Miss Brown. I did not wish
> to risk her safety, so I allowed him to
> escape."

A *coward? Allowed him to escape?* He retreated to the shadow of the building on the corner, his blood stirring.

> The detective went on to explain
> that his years of experience have
> proven to him that such perpetrators
> are mentally defective in one way or
> another and the condition causes
> them to commit their heinous crimes,
> preying only on women.

Gregory crumpled the page as the burning rose through his chest and flashed in his brain and a red veil fell over him. He now remembered seeing in the detective's eyes not the recognition of a rival, but a piteous loathing for a weak and soulless creature that required extermination. He saw that the detective had not created a fiction. It was true that he had hidden behind that woman. And then he had run away, scurrying like a rodent. Yes, he *was* a coward...

The seizure lasted ten long seconds; then, as suddenly as it had come on, the heat resided and his cool returned. He glanced about to observe the day continuing as usual, except for the larger number of gentlemen loitering about the intersection with their noses buried in newspapers. Soon the talk would be going around, with the detective as the hero and Gregory the craven villain, like in the moving pictures.

He let out a girlish giggle. The news article was intended as a trap. St. Cyr was taunting him, hoping that he'd take offense, and rush headlong into view. As if he was too stupid or deranged to see through such a thin ploy.

He read the article again. The name Tom Anderson was known to all as the "King of Storyville," and for a decade, the state senator representing New Orleans. Gregory had listened to his father curse him as the devil who lorded over the lewd world behind the French Quarter. Who didn't know such a notorious character?

St. Cyr was another matter altogether, a riddle of a man, and Gregory was keen to learn what he was all about. The first step would be to locate a place along those scarlet streets where tongues were loose. Folding his paper and moving on, he smiled smugly. How hard could that be?

Since his earliest days on the force, Captain Picot had been paying copyboys to snatch the morning and evening editions of *The Picayune* the moment they came off the presses and rush them to the corner outside the building, where one of his clerks would be waiting to relay them to him. He wanted to read the news before the other officers in the department got a chance so he could appear in-the-know when it came to incidents around the city and have excuses prepared or blame to point elsewhere should something embarrassing turn up.

With this afternoon's paper, all he got was an early start on his bad temper. The story about St. Cyr and "Gregory" was on the front page and above the fold. He had offered information, flattery, and threats, and the reporter Vernel had just gone ahead and written the news as he chose.

This particular item featured a cool, stiff-spined St. Cyr recounting the standoff and offering snide opinions of the suspect. Picot shook his head over the detective holding his fire for fear of hitting the madam. He would have blasted away and too bad for her. What was she doing sticking her nose in anyway? It was just another episode of back-alley folly and Vernel had painted it as a moment of heroic drama.

He knew that the brass downtown would read about the confrontation and note that St. Cyr had drawn closer to the murderer in a matter of hours than any of his men had come in weeks. It did not reflect well on Captain J. Picot. He could only hope that the case wouldn't drag on as a litany of St. Cyr's exploits, to end in a capture that would be blasted in headlines for days after.

As to the detective's surly quotes, Picot understood that they were issued to bait Gregory into the Creole detective's clutches. He shook his head; the fellow might be mad, but he would be too clever to fall for such a ruse.

The captain tossed the newspaper aside. Let the Creole have his moment. It would only make it more delicious when the tables turned.

Justine's furious voice would have been a comfort to him, a sign of bearable ire. But she did not say a word during the drive home. She was seriously angry and Valentin guessed she was waiting until they were in the house to let loose. When they reached Lesseps Street and pulled to the perron, he hopped out and hurried around the front of the Ford, only to find she had already stepped down.

She marched past him and up the walk, leaving the market sacks. He lifted the trunk, gathered the bags into his arms, and began the slow hike to the front door, wondering if she would let him put them down before she lit into him.

She didn't get the chance. In a small stroke of fortune, the telephone began chattering just as he stepped over the threshold. A daily irritation became a gift and he hurried to drop the bags on the foyer floor and snatch up the handset.

"I'm holding the evening paper." Sam Ross was as livid as he could be while still keeping his voice to a fierce whisper. "What the hell is this? You're back in Storyville and you didn't tell me?"

"I was—"

"Mr. Alberton called. He saw it, too. He's furious. He thought we were providing him with a discreet private investigator. Private. Not some Storyville rounder."

When Justine stepped into the kitchen doorway to eye him, he wanted nothing so much as to pitch the telephone through a window and jump out right behind it. "I was asked to do this one service," he told the attorney. "For Tom Anderson. He was ill and...and I...agreed." He knew it sounded weak; it was all he had.

"Did that one service require getting your name splashed on the front page?" Ross hissed. "Do you have any idea how this embarrasses the firm? The partners will have my head."

Valentin said, "I'm sorry I didn't tell you. I thought it would be over quickly and that no one would know. Then there was this thing last night."

Neither man spoke for a few seconds. Justine bent to gather two of the sacks. She straightened, treated Valentin to a hard glance, and returned to the kitchen. He heard her unpacking groceries. Though not yet throwing any of them. "Now what?" he said into the telephone.

"Now, I don't know," Ross muttered. "Alberton is saying he wants you dismissed and for me to find a replacement." Valentin allowed a considerate pause. "But you're already so far into it," the attorney continued.

Valentin said, "I'm sorry, Sam."

"It's a damned mess, is what." After another pause, the attorney said, "Can you find someone to step in? Someone who has the skills?"

Valentin considered Each and a few of the Pinkertons he knew. None would do for this delicate business. He was distracted by the sound of Justine now humming a quiet melody, something she did to calm her nerves. A sliver of an idea crossed his mind, flew away, and came around again.

"Mr. Valentin?" Ross said.

"I might have someone."

The attorney said he hoped that was true. After another sigh of dismay, he said, "Oh, by the way. There hasn't been a call today. I think they're waiting for you."

"I'll call you back directly," Valentin said. He dropped the handset into the cradle and hurried into the kitchen to face his wife.

Gregory began by stopping a pair of sports passing on Basin Street to ask where a fellow might catch word of the action around the District, doing his best to play the wide-eyed hayseed, the sort any rounder would be pleased to pluck. The two exchanged a sly glance before directing him to Fewclothes' Cabaret, halfway down the next block.

The drizzle was keeping people indoors and he found the saloon busy, with the bar crowded and games going on at a half-dozen tables. Though there was a young mulatto rattling merrily on the keys of a rickety piano, *cabaret* was a laughable conceit.

The floor was laid with thick boards painted black and warped from decades of wet weather and spilled drinks. Some of the panes in the street windows were cracked with only the almost-daily rain to wash them clean. There were no women in sight, not even a house floozy.

The Raleigh Rye was flowing and Gregory crossed to the bar to order a shot, even though he couldn't stand the taste of liquor. He pretended to sip while letting it dribble to the floor. No one noticed him or the way his odd-fitting workman's clothes clashed with his faint, milky features. At the moment, all ears in the room were perked to the circle of men gabbing with animation about "Gregory" and the detective St. Cyr. He edged closer and listened, amused at how a few tense seconds behind a low-rent sporting house was already taking on epic proportions.

The speaker was a ratty sport who commanded the conversation with jerks of a glass, slopping whiskey to and fro as he posed as an expert on the confrontation of the previous night. Listening to his fierce recital, Gregory scanned the faces and noticed a thin young man in a worn gray suit who, unlike the others with their eager eyes, offered a mocking frown. The fellow peered with disgust at the faces and then around the rest of the room, his gaze landing on Gregory for a second before moving on. Finally, with a rude snort, he stepped forward to interrupt the speaker's tale.

"No, goddamn it," he said. "It wasn't like that at all. Jesus!"

The sport stopped in mid-sentence and glowered. "And you would know that how?"

"He works for St. Cyr," someone said. Now all heads turned. "Go on, tell him, Each," another voice called.

Gregory was confused. Then it dawned on him that the character's *name* was Each. He stretched for a better view.

Each said, "This fellow…"

"Gregory!" someone called out.

"Yeah, him. I can tell you there wasn't any *fight*. The yellow bastard hid behind that madam like a little girl. Mister Valentin had him cold, but he wasn't about to take a chance of hitting the woman, maybe killing her. So he let him run away. And that's what the chicken sonofabitch did."

Each stopped and sipped, eying the crew of louts over the rim of his glass. Licking his lips, he said, "You'll all have something to gnaw on when you see the paper. Mister Valentin told it his way. How it really happened."

A few of the men tried cajoling him for more details. In response he waved a sharp hand, quieting them. "Papers are out by now," he said and then snickered. "Read it for yourselfs." The joke being that a good share of the men in the room were lifelong street louts who couldn't read a newspaper or anything else. With that final word, he moved off to where the bar curved toward the wall.

Gregory spent a few seconds biting down on his ire at the way Each had described him, then sidled closer to the end of the bar. He beckoned to the barkeep and pointed to Each's glass. When the shot appeared and the bartender tilted his head, Each turned to look Gregory up and down. "Do I know you, fellow?"

"We met the one time," Gregory lied. "You and Mr. St. Cyr both. It was back at..." He jerked a vague thumb.

"Where, Mangetta's?" Each said.

"Right. That place."

"And this was when?"

"Been years," Gregory said. Recalling the gossip column, he added, "Back before he left."

Each considered, then lifted the glass. "Well, thanks."

Gregory toyed with his own drink, but did not sip. "I guess everybody's happy to have him back in business," he said.

Each blurted a quick laugh. "Everybody except his wife."

Gregory rolled his eyes, a fellow who knew about *wives*. "Oh yes."

Each's cool smile faded. "And that goddamn Captain Picot," he muttered, then caught himself and glanced sideways to see a face too hungry for Storyville gossip to carry back home. He drank off his whiskey in a quick swill, gave a quick nod, and crossed the room to make an exit onto Basin Street.

Gregory watched him go. He turned in time to catch the beginning of an spat over whose story about the incident of the night before was correct. In the next moment, a sot stepped close and eyed him in a friendly way. "You know Each, do you?" he said.

Gregory offered a vague flip of his palm. He noticed how the fellow was studying the coins he had left on the bar and said, "You friends with him?"

The sot slid his foul breath and reek of unwashed skin a step closer. "Oh, yeah, I been knowing him for years now."

Gregory nodded to the empty glass in the fellow's paw. "Looks like you could use a drink."

"I wouldn't say no." A smile that was mostly gums appeared. "They call me Panama." He extended a hand that Gregory pretended not to see as he waved to the bartender.

"What about Mr. Valentin?" he said when the drink arrived. "The detective. Do you know him, too?"

"Oh, yeah." Panama drank the whiskey in one gulp and wiped his mouth with a grimy hand. "I mean I know *about* him."

Gregory ordered up another round. As he offered Panama the fresh glass, he said, "Now he's some character, isn't he?"

Valentin was pleased that he had caught her by surprise and she had forgotten about berating him over the story in the newspaper that had yet to land on their doorstep.

"I'm sorry, what?" she said. "Are you talking about putting *me* in that house?"

154

"Alberton doesn't want me on the job anymore."

"Because..."

His face reddened. "He saw the newspaper."

"Oh," she said.

"But it's too late to quit. So I'll go away, but you'll take my place. And be my eyes and ears. By posing as a maid."

"A *maid?*" She appeared to find this humorous.

"I'll ask them to pretend to hire you on. And you'll see what you can learn." By her crossed arms and narrowed eyes, he could tell that she was wary of his motives. This was as he would have hoped; suspicion was a requirement for the job. "Anyway, nothing has changed since she went away," he continued. "Maybe if I'm gone, it will shake things up."

"What about Belle?"

"She can go someplace else for now."

She thought about it some more. "What if I say no?" she asked. "What's your next idea?"

"I don't have one," he said.

She peered closer to make sure this wasn't a story. Satisfied, she said, "So what now?"

Valentin got busy. "We'll put up the groceries. Then drive to the Garden District."

"I'm not saying I'm going to do this."

"But you'll take the ride?"

She paused for a moment before nodding.

Valentin called Sam Ross to explain his idea. The attorney listened, then snorted. He thought the plan was preposterous. "This is the best you can do?" he said. "Drag your wife into it?"

"I wouldn't suggest it if I didn't think it would work."

"It doesn't make sense. Mr. Alberton won't agree to it."

"Tell him she's been on cases with me before."

"Is that true?"

"Yes, it is." He hoped the attorney wouldn't ask for details.

Ross didn't. Instead, he said, "You're grasping at straws."

"Just talk to her, Sam," Valentin said. "Let Alberton talk to her. Then you can say no." When Ross didn't respond, he said. "I've never failed you. I'm asking that you give this a chance."

He could tell Ross was not convinced, but the attorney huffed and then said, "All right. Bring her. But expect nothing."

Gregory reached the third floor of the Public Library. He asked at the desk if there was a roster of New Orleans Police Department officers he could view and was directed to a thin booklet dated the previous January and listing all the officials on the city rolls.

He located the correct pages and found the name J. Picot under the First Precinct heading, located at Orleans Parish Prison. The map on the back page traced the actual lines of the precincts and the First covered Storyville, the French Quarter, and another half-dozen blocks to the east and west of their boundaries.

Gregory returned the book and mulled the information, adding it to what Panama and the loose-lipped drunkard named Jake who joined them had sketched out. In his ten minutes with the two, he had learned a good piece of the detective's story. That he had been born to a Sicilian father and Creole mother in an Uptown neighborhood. That one and perhaps both parents were long dead. That he had been a petty criminal before becoming a New Orleans police officer working the Storyville streets. Which was where Tom Anderson had spied him and later lured him into the position he had maintained for ten years before leaving.

"This bastard, what do they call him, Gregory?" Panama had groused in a loud voice. "Mr. Valentin, he only came back to deal

156

with him. And he will. You can be damn sure of that." Gregory held down an urge to chortle. He bought a final round then made his escape.

The plot had grown more tangled. St. Cyr had operated for years in Captain J. Picot's territory, had gone away, and was now back. The police had been finding bodies for weeks and had not even begun to pick up the trail of the guilty party. St. Cyr had come within a breath of stopping him the first night on the job. It amounted to an embarrassment. No wonder the captain despised him. And perhaps there was more.

Gregory pondered these facts with the detachment of an observer to events that did not involve him. As his thoughts meandered, he stopped to wonder if the detective's foe Picot could somehow be an ally.

Outside the library, the sky was mottled between gray and white. In another two hours it would be dark and he could make his return visit. In the meantime, he'd ride the streetcar back to the Garden District ahead of the end-of-the-day rush, retire to the attic to prepare for the night, and enjoy a leisurely dinner. Meanwhile, the madams and whores and rounders, their customers, and Valentin St. Cyr and Tom Anderson and Each, and Picot and his detectives, would all be waiting to see if and when he would strike again. Never dreaming that it would be that very night.

CHAPTER FOURTEEN

Evangeline sat with Sister Rosalie and four other nuns as they bowed their heads for the blessing and then shared a simple dinner. The sisters talked quietly, mostly about the weather and which ones were making trips to visit distant kin. There was also a bit of light gossip about petty intrigues around the convent. As usual, Evangeline did not speak, instead listening as if trying to hang onto every word, especially the talk of families.

One by one, the sisters finished, crossed themselves, and rose with their empty plates. Sister Rosalie, sensing that Evangeline had something on her mind, remained with the older woman until the hall was empty, save for the echoes of the two novitiates who were cleaning the tables.

"What is it?" the sister asked.

"That policeman."

"The one from New Orleans? What about him?"

"He made me think. I've started seeing pictures."

"Memories?" Sister Rosalie said.

"Yes, I think so."

"That's a good thing."

Evangeline pursed her lips and her brow stitched. "I'm not so sure." She turned to the tall rain-dappled window. The novitiates had finished their work, leaving only the sounds of the scratches of a branch on a windowpane. It was a peace beyond peaceful.

"This won't last," Evangeline said.

Sister Rosalie didn't understand at first. "The storm?"

Evangeline faced her companion. "You don't believe me. But it's coming. Remember that I told you." She crossed herself, rose from the table, and left the sister to her thoughts.

Valentin steered the Ford along St. Charles and then took a detour from his normal route, first turning north on Calliope, then southwest on LaSalle. A left turn on Third Street brought them into the Garden District. He steered down the alley that ran parallel to Annunciation and came to a stop at the Albertons' garden gate.

"I'll pull around the front and park," he said.

She treated him to a cool look as she gripped the handle. She was still angry. "It's not the first time I've gone in the back door of a rich man's house," she said.

She opened the door and stepped down. He watched her pass through the tall gate and when it closed behind her, drove two blocks down then cut over to the street. In another minute, he was standing on the front gallery.

Justine sat at the heavy oak table, a cup of coffee from the pot on the stove already steaming before her. Sam Ross gestured and Valentin shook his head. "Will Mr. Alberton be joining us?" he inquired.

"No," the attorney said. "He said he doesn't need to speak to you. But he's agreed to this arrangement." Valentin's eyes widened. "He knows that Miss..."

"Justine."

"Justine, yes, is part of the plan. He's the only one who knows about this. The family thinks you were referred by someone at our firm." He looked at Valentin. "I convinced him that it will be better if you are involved in a quiet way."

"All right," Valentin said.

"And...I didn't tell him that Justine is your wife." He paused to let this sink in, then said, "He's already unhappy about this situation. He called Mr. Mansell. So I don't know if you'll be getting any more work from the firm."

Valentin avoided Justine's eyes. "Is Belle still in the house?"

"She's been sent to Mr. Alberton's sister in Gentilly. She'll help take care of their mother."

"Is that a story?"

"Not so much," Ross said. "The woman is frail. And Mr. Alberton said it will be better for Belle to get away for a little while. Perhaps Emelie will contact her there."

A few seconds of silence ensued. Justine stood up. "Is what I'm wearing all right?" She had chosen a plain off-white shift.

"I'm sure it's fine," the attorney said. "They don't go in for uniforms and all that."

Valentin said, "I've explained everything else to her."

Ross nodded and the two men watched her straighten her spine and bring her hands together, weaving her fingers at the level of her waist. With her blank expression, she had slipped into the role of a docile servant. The attorney's expression eased, as if he was considering for the first time that the gambit might do some good. For his part, Valentin knew that the life she had been leading when he met her had required deft acting skills.

He was mulling that when Justine left the kitchen on her way to begin her spying mission. Valentin and Ross heard the voices from the dining room as Justine introduced herself to Mrs. Alberton. She used her maiden name, Mancarre. The lady of the house called to Tante Dolores and after some absent chatter, the voices drifted off as the matron led the new maid to the back rooms. Valentin went to the stove to help himself to coffee.

Ten minutes later, Justine reappeared. "Mr. Ross?" she said. "Mr. St. Cyr?" Her expression was placid. "Mr. Alberton says there's a telephone call in the library."

When Valentin heard the first words coming across the line, he thought he had been found out. "Very clever."

"Beg your pardon?"

"The newspaper. You made the front page."

The detective didn't want to discuss it. He said, "May I speak to Emelie?"

"Not today. Maybe tomorrow."

"I won't be here tomorrow." He caught the startled silence over the wire. "I've been asked to vacate."

"Because of Storyville?"

"That's correct."

"Do they think that you hold her and those sporting girls in the same regard?"

It was a rare instance when Valentin found himself confounded. "I can only speak for myself," he said.

"Well, I'm sorry. What will happen now?"

"I don't know. All this has gotten us nowhere. We have nothing from you. So I don't suppose it matters if I'm here or not." He paused for a second, then repeated his request. "I want to speak to Emelie."

"Why? You're leaving." Now the voice was petulant.

"We just want to know that she's still safe."

"She has not been harmed in any way."

"When will it be over?"

"When we get to the end," the man said. Valentin detected impatience. The next sound he heard was a click, followed by the static of a dead line.

George Alberton had been standing by the door, looking perturbed. After Valentin dropped the handset into the cradle, he said, "Did you have to get so brash?"

"I wanted to try it one more time." He shrugged. "Emelie's safe. I would ask that you allow Justine to answer the phone from now on."

"And what will you do?"

"I'm going to stay out of sight."

"That won't be so hard, will it?" Alberton gazed at him, his mouth tight with displeasure. He treated Sam Ross to a hard glance, then made his exit into the hallway.

Justine and Valentin stole a moment before he left for a few whispered words. "I'll come back for you," he said.

"No, I'll take the streetcar to keep up the appearance," she said. "Anyway, you'll be in Storyville. Isn't that right?" She didn't wait for an answer before hurrying off to find Tante Dolores.

The thought that no one would believe he'd have the gall to return so quickly to the scene of his crimes put Gregory into a giddy mood as he fidgeted away the hours. His strategy was simple: a house on Franklin Street, not a stone's throw from the back galleries of the Basin Street mansions. And what would they say about Mr. St. Cyr when this night ended? What would the King of Storyville think of his special minion then? Who would be the hero and who the goat in tomorrow's newspaper? The prospect made him quiver in every limb; though when he placed his fingers below his belt, he felt the same nothing. Perhaps even that might change once he had the girl cornered.

Valentin had told Each to meet him at the Café at five. He found the younger man waiting at the bar.

"Put anyone you can find on the streets," he said. "Make sure they go to all the houses and tell the madams no strangers. If they don't know the gentleman, he doesn't get in the door. And the maids and the girls don't decide. Only the landlady. Understand?"

"They're going to pitch fits," Each said.

"Let them."

"You think he's coming back?"

"He could be here right now. So we need to move."

Each got up to leave, then sat back down. Though much of the street kid still lingered, his face was finally taking on manly features.

Valentin noticed worried eyes and said, "What?"

"I might have done something wrong. I was in Fewclothes' this afternoon..." He shifted with discomfort. "And this here loudmouth was going on about what happened in that alley last night."

"Some loudmouth who was nowhere near."

"That's right. So I told the boys there that it wasn't a fight. You had him and he hid behind the madam and then he ran. Just like you said in the newspaper."

Valentin shrugged and said, "That's all right."

"That's not it, Mister Valentin. Just after that, this character I never seen before came along the bar and bought me a drink." He shifted again. "He was a stranger. But he said he had met you and me. At Mangetta's." He pushed away his glass. "I think it was him, Mister Valentin. Gregory."

Valentin stared. "I'll be goddamned."

"Or maybe not."

"No, if your gut says so, it was him."

Each was shaking his head in distress.

The detective said, "Did you tell him anything else?"

"Just what I said."

Valentin heard the faint ring of untruth. At the same time, he knew Each wouldn't hold back anything important. He had just gone to bragging. There was no harm in that. In truth, Valentin couldn't have plotted this part any better. As Gregory went about digging up information about the man pursuing him, Each had given him more bait. The kind he could gobble right up to a hook.

"Give me a description," the detective said. "Whatever you can remember."

Each's brow furrowed. "There wasn't nothing special about him. Don't know if I could pick him out on the street. His face was kind of..."

"Not there?"

"I'm sorry, I was only standing with him for a minute. And I never thought—"

"It's all right. I probably couldn't pick him out, either."

Each looked miserable. "He played me, didn't he?"

"I make mistakes, too." The detective thought about the mess with the Alberton case. "We can't worry about it now. Go get the word passed."

Each made a quick exit, his face still pale. Valentin knew the kid would take his shame and use it, making doubly sure that every house in the District was on alert. He now stepped to the bar, and asked for the telephone. When he got Tom Anderson on the line, he explained that he had men passing the word that on this night Storyville was closed to all but the regulars. In case Gregory came back sooner rather than later — as in that very evening.

The older man said, "Is he that brave?" He didn't comment on the detective making such a dramatic move on his own.

"He's not brave at all," Valentin said. "He's just sly. He'll think it's safer to make a strike while everyone's still getting over last night. And he'd be correct. But we're going to be waiting for him."

"What if he heads back to Robertson Street?"

"He won't," Valentin said. "He has ambitions. And that would count as failure."

"Well, you know we can't make this a habit," Anderson said. "I can't run the District with the doors shut. The madams won't stand for it. If they can't pay the rent, the landlords will start raising a ruckus. And you know what will come next?"

Valentin knew. Among the owners of Storyville sporting houses were some of the most wealthy and respected families in the city, as well as the major universities, and the New Orleans diocese of the Holy Roman Church. Though all stayed hidden behind walls of intermediaries, lest they soil the hems of their garments. That said, if they received reports of rent money drying up, those same agents would be in full howl at poor Tom Anderson's door.

"You need to get rid of him," the King of Storyville said. "I want him dead and buried or sunk to the bottom of the river."

"First I have to catch him," Valentin said.

"Then do that."

Captain Picot studied the city rooftops at the end of the day as he listened to Cassidy recite from his notebook.

"I found thirteen reports from the dates you gave me," the clerk said. "Thirteen male victims, I mean."

"Read the names."

"Bonneville, Andrew V. DeSalles, Charles Laine, Jacob..." Cassidy was on the ninth entry on the list when Picot stopped him and said, "That one. What are the details?"

The clerk directed a finger to his notations. "Male. Italian. Age thirty-three. Address, 2344 First Street." He moved to the next line. "Body was discovered off Levee Lake Road, April sixth, eighteen-ninety-one. Cause of death was asphyxiation."

A smiling captain turned from the window. "That'll be enough for now. You did good work. I won't forget it. Now I have something else. First thing in the morning, I want you to go to the *Picayune*. To the morgue." The clerk gave him a blank look. "Where they keep old copies of the papers. You know the building, don't you?"

"Yes, sir. On Gravier Street. "

"There's an alley around back. The morgue door is down from street level. I want you to go there and find funeral notices for any of those men on your list. Copy down the names of next-of-kin. Survivors and such. Understand?"

Cassidy gave an unsure nod, but said, "Yes, sir."

"Good. Bring those to me as soon as you get here. If anyone asks, we lost some arrest cards and we want to at least have notes on any important crimes back then." He waited to make sure the clerk understood, then waved a hand. "You're dismissed."

Cassidy evaporated and Picot went to his desk and settled in his chair, wearing a thick smile. He was fuming over why in all these years he had never thought to search the records when Detective Salliers came knocking on the door frame.

"I heard Storyville is going to be closed to all but regulars tonight."

Picot's smile and easy mood faded. "Was it Anderson's doing?"

"St. Cyr, is what I heard."

The captain gave a raw shake of his head. "You know they'd fight like hell before they'd do that for the chief of police. Or the mayor. But St. Cyr? *Of course. Whatever you say.*" He sat forward and placed his hands flat on the blotter. "All right, let him do what he wants. He'll only be in deeper when his good days come to an end."

Watching the glittering eyes, Salliers said, "Do you have something, Captain?"

Picot's smile returned, a harder line. "Oh, I do, indeed."

CHAPTER FIFTEEN

After an early meal in the kitchen, Justine set the dining room table and assisted Tante Dolores in serving the family. Mr. and Mrs. Alberton were reserved. Annette eyed the new girl curiously and asked her parents after Belle. Mr. Alberton explained that she was tending to their grandmother. "This is Justine," he said told her. "She'll be with us for a little while."

Justine offered a bow that hinted at a curtsy, then did her best to make herself invisible. Annette soon lost interest. By seven o'clock, dinner was finished and Justine carried the plates to the sink.

The father and mother were in the parlor listening to the Victrola and Annette had taken a book and a slice of lemon cake to her room. Justine took advantage of the quiet before it was time to go home to wander the second floor, carrying a stack of folded sheets as cover. She found a long hallway, four bedrooms, and two baths. She treaded softly as she visited first the parents' room and then the one that belonged to Beatrice, the sister in Baton Rouge.

Having grown up in raw deep bayou poverty, she was astounded by the luxury that young ladies of privilege enjoyed. The room was a page from a picture book, a place where a princess would enjoy her days and rest her pretty head at night. The bed looked so thick and soft that she was tempted to stretch out on it. Instead, she examined a bookcase crowded with dolls and other knick-knacks and another that was parked in a corner and lined with novels and young misses' guides to this and that.

The closet was something out of a fine store, with two dozen dresses on hangers, hat boxes on a high shelf, and a long rack of shoes on the floor. It was lovely, but somehow lifeless, as if intended for display, and she felt the sadness that came upon her whenever she happened upon the trappings of wealth. Who lived this way, far removed from the groaning hunger, the violent abuse, the shame that never quite went away? How could some be so lucky and fail to value it, while others were so cursed?

Justine pulled herself back from these dark musings. Look at how far she had traveled from nothing. She had a home and a husband who treated her kindly and understood her little mad places. She had survived three attempts on her life. Now she was safe and that was something, considering where she might have landed.

She carried the stack of bed sheets into the hall, reviving her blank servant's mask. As she pulled the brass handle, she sensed eyes watching her and peered along the hall to see that Annette's door was now open a few inches.

A soft voice called from the shadows. "What's your name again?"

"I'm Justine. Annette?"

The door opened wider. Annette stood in her nightdress, regarding her with a frank gaze. She and Justine were of the same height. Her hair, a deep brown, was tied back. A sweet-faced girl of French features that hinted at the elegant, her gaze gave the impression of a mind wandering elsewhere. Though at this moment the dark blue eyes were sharp. "I know why you're here," she said.

Justine covered her surprise. "I'm here to help your family."

Annette shook her head. "No. That's not why." She beckoned with a slow hand. "Please. Come in."

~

168

Gregory stepped off the St. Charles car at seven o'clock, crossed over Canal Street, and walked six blocks north with his ether bottle, cotton cloth, and knife tucked into his pockets. As he drew closer to Storyville, he played out the scenario in his head. This time, he would have a role to perform: a college boy visiting on a dare, about to taste a woman for the first time. He had dressed the part, in one of his finer suits. He pictured the girl hustling him up the stairs in hopes of claiming his regular business. Then he imagined her shock when she realized his true purpose. That was the best part, the moment when their eyes shifted from cold calculation to terror. He always wanted to draw it out, but couldn't risk something going wrong. Better to finish in a few quick seconds and be away, leaving behind another testament to his cunning.

So were his thoughts as he crossed over to Basin Street and then moved on to Franklin. Number 225 was a narrow three-story tucked between two larger mansions, modest but stately in their shadows. Stepping closer, he peeked through the lace curtains in the front window and saw two girls in evening dresses. There was neither a professor at the piano nor any sports lounging, the sort of place a discreet gentleman or a shy youngster would visit.

He mounted the steps to the gallery and lifted and dropped the knocker. After a few seconds, a woman's face stared at him from behind one of the panes of clear glass.

"Do we know you here?" she said, her voice muffled.

"No, ma'am," Gregory said. "It's my first—"

"We ain't open for new visits. Only our regulars."

Startled, Gregory cleared his throat. "I just— I wanted to—"

"Come back tomorrow."

She retreated before he could plead his case. He stood for a few baffled seconds, then descended the steps and crossed to the gallery of another of the smaller houses, where he found a hand-lettered sign on the door: CLOSED FOR THIS EVENING. Scanning the street in both directions, he saw parlor lights turned down low or windows gone dark, and a few gentlemen ambling off as if it was the end of the night rather than the beginning.

In the next moment, he muttered, "St. Cyr." In one swoop, the detective had accomplished what those who railed against Storyville day and night had failed to do: closed down the District, except for clientele known on sight at this or that address.

Gregory knew he could wander the foul back lanes of the District and take a crib whore with ease, but what would that prove? The sudden setback dogged him as he spent a quarter-hour roaming, his hands in his pockets and his eyes down, another frustrated caller. He wandered to Basin Street and past Fewclothes' Cabaret and heard chatter and laughter and the rattled of an old piano. The shuttering of the sporting houses was a boon to the saloons.

He wasn't about to go home and give St. Cyr a victory, so he ambled on to Iberville and crossed over to lurk on the corner. One of the heavy double doors of Anderson's Café had been propped open to clear the close air and cigar smoke and the light from inside was dazzling, a golden glow cast by rows of electric chandeliers.

He could view the bar that ran the length of one wall with its long mirror and a small mountain range of bottles. It was no less crowded at the twenty-odd tables around which gentlemen sat dining, drinking, and playing cards. A six-piece orchestra tootled happy jazz music from the low stage at the far end of the room. Here and there, a dusky quadroon passed by, attached to the arm of some well-heeled gent.

Gregory stood still. The knowledge that he could never be part of that world brought a sour taste to his tongue. He had lived all of his life cast outside, so far beyond the pale that he was like a drifting planet in another universe.

So it was; and he had managed to turn his shame into a private pride that had carried him through his lonely years, had kept him from downing arsenic or slashing his veins, and later had driven him to punish the world that had tormented him so. If he did not belong anywhere, he would occupy a place of his own making, where no one could touch him and where he dictated who lived and died. That was his grand construction, and it had barely begun when the bastard St. Cyr came along.

A burst of laughter broke into his thoughts and he watched as two men in suits lurched out the door of the Café to stand swaying beneath the streetlamp. One was tall and thin and the other as short and plump as a barrel. The taller man held up an umbrella. Neither noticed Gregory watching from the opposite corner. They chuckled over something, shook hands, and then bid each other loud farewells. The taller man lurched east on Basin Street. The round one tugged at the brim of his hat and headed up Iberville Street at a slow rolling pace, as if climbing a hill. Gregory could hear the lines of the song he sang between wheezes.

Watching the fat fellow's grudging progress, he entertained a sudden blade of an idea, such a wild notion that it made the hair on his arms rise. He tapped his pockets to check his equipment before starting up his side of the street, slowly drawing abreast of the heavy man in the three-piece suit.

Valentin had taken a covered pot from the icebox and placed it over a low flame. The stew that Justine had prepared from the roasted chicken came to a low simmer, filling the kitchen with the warm scents of garlic, peppers, and sweet basil. Once it was set, he went to the closet for a jacket and an umbrella and walked along the banquette to the corner to wait for the streetcar.

~

171

The headlamp came ghostly through the evening mist and the car rumbled to a stop. Justine was down from the step before the door had opened all the way and ducking under the umbrella. He saw the shine in her eyes and said, "What is it?"

She smiled and took his arm and they began the trek back to their house. As they walked along, she told him what had transpired on the second floor of the house on Annunciation Street.

"She said she thinks she knows where Emelie is."

"Where?"

"That's what I asked her. She just changed the subject. To why she had disappeared."

Valentin steered her around a puddle. "Well?"

They had reached their door and she climbed the steps to the gallery while he folded the umbrella. He knew she was drawing out her story, as he himself had done so many times. By the time he had locked the door, she was in the kitchen standing over the simmering pot. He pulled a bottle of Madeira from the cabinet over the sideboard, poured two glasses, handed her one, and waited for her to take a first sip before saying, "So?"

"To begin, this is not the first time. Emelie has run away before. But only for a few hours."

"Why didn't Alberton tell me this?"

"They didn't want you to know that she's been ruined. That's what Annette says. And that she probably went with the boy. Well, not such a boy. He's twenty."

Valentin said. "What's his name?"

"She said Paul. She wouldn't give me his last name." She took a sip of her wine. "I didn't want to push her. I think she's playing a game of her own."

"No, you got enough for one night." He mused for a few seconds. "Why didn't she come and tell me any of this?"

"I would guess that she doesn't think she can trust you. Why should she? You're the man spying for her father. She knows I'm not just a maid. But she wanted to talk to me."

Valentin sat back, quietly astonished. Over the years, he had told her about his cases, but hadn't realized how closely she had listened.

She cocked her head, trying to read his expression. "What?"

"Nothing, go ahead," he said.

"Anyway, she asked me if I would be back tomorrow. She goes to that finishing school and comes home at three. So maybe I'll find out some more." She yawned and sagged back. "I'm not used to this kind of labor. That reminds me. How much am I getting paid?"

Each was standing on the corner, explaining to Black Jimmy that he wanted to make one more round before calling it a night when two coppers came running across the intersection of Liberty and Bienville. He and Jimmy hurried to the corner in time to see one of the Model T touring cars used by the police slide to curb at Sally Mason's sporting house. A pair of detectives hopped down and the four officers climbed the steps.

Two of the sporting girls appeared on the gallery, wrapping shawls around their shoulders against the evening chill. Each left Jimmy to draw closer and beckon them to the railing. "You know who I am?" he said.

The auburn-haired girl said, "Your name's Each. You work for Mister Tom."

"That's right," Each said. "What happened in there?"

The girl leaned at the banister, providing him a generous view of her anatomy. "Man came to the door. He was all bloody. Been stabbed. Miss Sally let him in and called the police."

"Do you know him?" Each said.

"Don't know him at all," the girl said. Her companion, a pudgy blonde, shook her head.

He was about to ask if one of them could let him in the back way when the door opened and two of the coppers stepped onto the gallery. The taller one went into a pocket for his packet of Omars. He offered one to his fellow officer, and when he struck a lucifer, Each could make out his face in the light from the flame.

"Detective McKinney?"

McKinney snapped the lucifer away and looked down at him. "What are you doing here?"

Each said, "Mr. Valentin had me and some others out on the streets telling the madams to keep out anyone they don't know."

McKinney said, "I heard he had a hand in all that."

"Yes, sir, he did." Each glanced at the other copper, who was chatting with one of the girls, then nodded toward the door. "Girl says a fellow was stabbed?"

"That's right," McKinney said.

"Who is he?"

"Said his name's Gillette."

"What happened?

"He says he left the Café and was walking up Iberville when someone jumped him. Stuck him with a knife." McKinney tapped his chest. "Got him right there. Good thing he's so heavy, or he might be dead. Lost a lot of blood, though."

"Was it a robbery?" Each said.

"Far as we can tell, he's got his valuables still on him. So if—" The detective stopped as a siren whined from the direction of St. Louis Street. An ambulance from Charity covered the two blocks in a matter of seconds and slid to a stop. The driver and an attendant, both in white coats, hopped down and ran around to pull a stretcher from the back.

"He's on the floor of the foyer," McKinney said as they climbed the steps. He let them pass, then turned to the girls. "You two come back in before you freeze." He gave Each a wink and the two shivering floozies disappeared inside.

Each thought about staying to check on the victim's condition, but he needed to report to Mr. Tom. He left Jimmy to keep an eye on things. Walking back to the Café at a fast clip, he thought about making a second call to Mr. Valentin, then decided against it. The detective's only concern was Gregory and this one was not his doing. His steps slowed as he turned onto Basin Street.

Unless it was.

Gregory had trailed the thick-bodied man along the street and watched as he took a look around and then slipped into the alley to relieve himself. The traffic was light on Iberville, but enough cars and trucks were passing that he could cross over without attracting notice. The fat man had just zipped his trousers and closed his coat when Gregory made a sudden rush and plunged the wicked blade through the wool lapel.

The man's eyes went wide in shock and he slapped both gloved hands over the spreading red stain. With a loud groan, he tottered and then collapsed onto the cobblestones, his hat rolling away. Gregory turned on his heel, trotted to the street, and dodged the traffic to the west side and down Liberty. When he looked back, the body was an inert mound in the alleyway.

On the next corner, he turned south and strode directly to the St. Charles streetcar stop and so did not see the gentleman struggle to his feet to stagger along the banquette and up the steps of the house on the corner, where he summoned the strength to pound on the door.

~

175

Justine guessed that Valentin was being careful with her because he knew he was still in trouble over ruining his arrangement with the lawyers. So she didn't lift a finger as he went about setting the table, then serving the stew with a baguette and bottle of red wine. By silent agreement, they did not talk about Storyville or any more about the house on Annunciation Street. After the bottle was empty and the dishes were cleared, he took her by the hand and led her into the bedroom.

Justine was not surprised that time and stability had tempered the heat between them; and yet when they did frolic, it seemed fresh, as if they were always finding a bit of new ground. Or finding new places in the ground they had covered hundreds of times.

On this evening, with the rain pattering the windowpanes and the lamp turned down low, he drew her close and worked the buttons on her dress, one by one. He often started this gentle way with her, and the thought of what was about to come caused her to sway as if her knees were going weak. All the more so because it was no longer a near-nightly habit but a random surprise. She chose to let her anger ebb for this little while. The Valentin who had crossed her by letting himself be lured back to Storyville could go stand in the corner while the one who brought sinuous bones and hard muscle to her pliant flesh took over.

Her dress dropped from her shoulders on its own, and then her brassiere and her slip and when she felt his fingers and his mouth sweeping her like a breeze, the heat rose from just below her navel and spread outward by inches. Her heart began to drum and her breath came deeper and faster.

Now he lowered her to the mattress and moved back. She watched his shadow shed his vest and shirt and trousers with the silent twist of a half-dozen buttons. She was aching to draw him down and into her, to absorb him into her very pores as he spread

176

over her, but he made her wait in a sweet fever. No matter how many times he did this, the effect was the same. Of all the men – and the number hadn't been few – no one had come close to moving her the way he had and still did.

That she could go so woozy after so many years vexed her, but beneath the bedcovers, she surrendered, falling onto her back as if she was made of a liquid poured thick and slow. The feeling lasted only until the sudden moment when he drilled into her with a spike that was charged with electricity. She let out a gasp and then a loud moan and he snickered like a devil who was too pleased with himself. She closed her eyes and dissolved in a wash of pleasure.

An hour later, they were both asleep. When the telephone chattered and Valentin began to get up, she laid a hand on his arm and said, "No, no. Enough for one day." He saw her eyes glowing in the darkness and drew her close.

The King of Storyville was appalled at what Each reported. "What?" he said. "What the hell is going on over there? How does someone get away with an attack right out on the street?"

"No one saw. Not many people out tonight because of the−"

"And it wasn't a robbery?"

"The copper said nothing was taken off the man."

"Nothing taken?" Anderson paused. "Do you have his name?"

Each searched his memory. "Gillette. That's it. Nobody I know."

"Where did they take him?"

"To Charity."

"I'll be damned."

"Do you want me to call Mr. Valentin?" Each said.

"Why?" the King of Storyville said. "This is not his concern." He heard the silence from the other end. "It's not, is it?"

"I'm not sure," Each said.

"Christ in heaven," Anderson muttered. "Call him."

Officer McKinney followed the ambulance and sat in the waiting room for the hour it took the doctors to tend to the victim. He had been through the man's wallet a second time and found a card identifying him as Laurence P. Gillette and another with his occupation as an insurance broker at the Southern States offices on Tulane Avenue. His home address was on St. Philip Street near Bayou St. John. He was no rounder, but a man of modest means who lived in a good neighborhood.

The detective used the book at the nurse's station to locate the gentleman's home number. When Mrs. Gillette answered, he explained that her husband had been the victim of a crime. Stunned, she began to sob. He told her that the wounds were not fatal and she calmed down and asked where the attack had taken place. He told her it had been Iberville Street with no inflection in his voice. Mrs. Gillette paused before saying she would have a neighbor who owned a machine drive her to the hospital.

After the detective finished the call, he paced the halls until the doctor appeared to tell him he could speak to the victim. As they walked to the Emergency Room, the doctor explained that Gillette's girth had spared him worse damage. The single thrust was accurate but the blade hadn't plunged far enough.

The policeman and the physician stood by the bedside. The patient had been given medicine for the pain and could tell them little. What he did have to say came out in dry gasps. He had been making his merry way from Anderson's Café to his automobile in a Canal Street garage when a man leaped at him. Then he was on the ground, bleeding from a hole in his chest. He managed to reach the bordello before he collapsed again.

"You didn't see who attacked you?" McKinney said.

Gillette shook his heavy head. "Happened too fast."

"And he didn't try to rob you?"

The patient said, "No...he just cut me...and then ran away."

"Is there anyone who would want to harm you like this?"

"No one." Gillette grimaced. "I sell *insurance*."

From the baffled, anxious eyes, McKinney believed him. He told the man that his wife had been notified, then thanked the doctor. Walking along the echoing corridor, he mulled the crime. Who attacked a citizen for no reason? Perhaps robbery had been the intent after all, but who knew? As if things weren't bad enough with that madman Gregory wreaking havoc, now some maniac had committed an assault on a nobody. He wondered if Storyville was coming apart in pieces and if that was the case, if there was anything Valentin St. Cyr could do about it.

CHAPTER SIXTEEN

Gregory had awakened from a nightmare of being pursued into a dead end alley, cornered by a mob without faces, set upon, and torn to shreds. He tried to scream as his hands and feet were ripped from their limbs, and then the rest of him, a few blood-soaked inches at a time, until clawed fingers reached into his torso and began pulling out his red, green, and brown entrails. Other sharp nails were coming for his eyes when a rumble of thunder as loud and sudden as a bass horn snapped him awake and he lay with his heart pounding and a helmet of sweat populating his scalp.

Even as the images dissolved, a red rush came over him, and he again saw himself in sudden relief as an ogre who could not turn away from his terrible impulses any more than he could crawl out of his skin. It was his horrible fate to have been infected with urges that drove him to wreak such gruesome havoc on his way to an appointment in hell.

The suffocating heat passed and he reminded himself that it wasn't the same anymore. He was no longer simply driven by a murderous sickness and his delight at getting away with his crimes. The detective St. Cyr, Mr. Tom Anderson, and the twenty blocks they stood for had given his work – no, his *life* – a grander meaning. When it was all over, they would understand that the lives of a few slatterns was a cheap price to pay for eradicating the polluted swamp. It was a thread he could clutch fast to keep from leaping through the attic window or into the Mississippi.

180

In small motions, he rose from the damp sheets, then lurched into the quiet hallway and climbed the steps to the attic. The sky outside the round window was angry, suiting his mood. That wouldn't do at all. He forced past the stirrings in his head with thoughts of how important he had become, how feared. And his stature would now grow larger. After spending another minute pondering the new day, his calm recovered and he sat at the old desk with fountain pen poised over a sheet of paper.

You see you have nothing to place against me, he wrote. *I will not stop until I'm ready. Will I take another? You won't find out until it's too late. Pay heed to me and it will end. My price is Storyville. Signed, Gregory.*

Writing the words helped; a purging of bile. Not to mention another stroke of genius. People would read the letter and wonder if the red light district was worth the terrible cost.

Drawing a new sheet of paper, he copied the message in a more precise hand and folded both pages. When he wrote the words *To The Chief of Police* on the first envelope, the captain named Picot crossed his mind. Whether or not the officer realized yet, they were cohorts, with the Creole detective as their common enemy. In any case, it was time to inform him. He selected a third sheet of paper and scripted a different letter. He kept it brief, just enough to tantalize, and let it go at that.

The last ragged shreds of his nightmare vanished as he sealed the final envelope and carried all three downstairs. His appetite had returned and he hurried to dress and make his way to the kitchen, where the cook had breakfast waiting.

Officer Cassidy arrived at the *Times-Picayune* building at eight o'clock. He found the back alley that Captain Picot had described, descended a set of stone steps to the oak door, and stepped into a deep, narrow, and dusty cavern. A long table, chest-high for reading while standing, had been placed in the middle of the room. Beneath it was a wide shelf stacked with newspapers. The floor-to-ceiling shelves that lined both walls held thousands more copies. The air hung heavy and the new electric lights overhead offered light that was still too poor for the room's purpose.

In the far back were two desks and at one sat a stooped man with skin the approximate color of the newsprint that filled the room. Wire-rimmed spectacles perched at the end of his spike of a nose. Behind them rested two pale blue bird eyes. A bronze nameplate identified him as GILBERT ROYCE.

Gilbert Royce lifted his head and called out, "Help you?"

Cassidy made his way along the stacks to the desk and produced his identification. "My captain sent me to locate some old copies. From March and April of eighteen-ninety-one."

Royce stood to study the clerk's badge. "Ninety-one?"

"Yes, sir," Cassidy said. "Do you have them?"

"You haven't been here before," the custodian said. "We have copies back to eighteen-thirty-seven. The first year they printed."

Cassidy made sure to nod as if deeply impressed and Royce's frown uncurled a bit. "And every day in between, including during the blockade." He began a crabbed walk down the left side of the morgue, stopping about halfway to slap a hand on a stack. "March of ninety-one." He eyed the visitor. "So this a police matter?"

"Yes, sir."

"And who was it sent you?"

"Captain Picot, sir."

"Uh-huh. Well, then. You take the copies you want up there by my desk. When you finish one, you place it the basket. No place else. You don't leave it lying out. You don't put it back where you found it. In the basket. Understand? Or you won't be permitted to use the facility again."

The clerk said, "Yes, sir. In the basket."

"All right." Royce pulled the stack from the shelf and dropped it into Cassidy's arms. "You looking for something in particular?"

Cassidy repeated it the way the captain had instructed him.

"Sounds like a waste of time." The curator started off, then stopped and turned back. "That was when Chief Hennessey was shot down." The clerk responded with a blank look. "You probably weren't even born yet."

Cassidy smiled. "Not for another two years."

Royce waved a hand at the stack. "Well, that's one crime you'll find in there for sure." He moved to his desk and sat down. Officer Cassidy drew pen and notebook from the pocket of his coat and went to work.

The telephone rang a few minutes after eight and this time Valentin rolled out to pull on his trousers and shuffle to the foyer to answer it. In a few tense sentences, Each told him about the stabbing on Iberville Street and the details that had come from Detective McKinney. Valentin listened without saying a word. When the explanation was finished, he muttered a thank you and dropped the handset into the cradle.

He stood gazing out the window as a selection of their neighbors moved along the Lesseps Street banquettes to the streetcar stop. The moment Each had begun describing the assault, he knew it was Gregory's handiwork. Bloody fights were uncommon in Storyville; attacks on regular citizens even more rare. Tom Anderson had kept it that way by putting a hefty price on the head of any reprobate who targeted innocents.

Valentin had blocked Gregory from his quarry, never guessing that he would simply shift his sights to different prey — likely the first warm body he could reach and still make a clean escape.

183

The stabbing was as clever as it was wicked. With one bloody move, Gregory had changed the game. No longer was he a sick beast ravaging helpless harlots; he was a nimble force who was apt to take down any man or woman on any street in the city, and right under the Creole detective's nose, if he so chose. Or that's the way it would play in the scandal rags and on busy lips.

Valentin slumped on the couch with the weight of the calamity settling on his shoulders. Against his wife's wishes, he had let himself be tempted back into the maw, where his vanity had taken over. Thoughts of another rescue, another villain erased, and another opportunity to humiliate Picot had all teased him. But this time he had misjudged and had fallen into a trap of his own making.

It got worse. The victim had just left the Café when the assault occurred. Tom Anderson would be furious and he'd want answers. When the phone shrilled a second time, Valentin knew it was him calling. But when he lifted the handset, he heard no blustering shout of rage. The King of Storyville kept his voice under control. Valentin understood; he couldn't let himself become agitated for fear of landing back in the hospital — or dead on the floor.

"It was him, wasn't it?" Anderson began.

"I believe so," Valentin said. "He couldn't get at a woman, so he went after this fellow. I never expected it."

"No one did," the King of Storyville said. "Now what?"

"I'm going to talk to a police detective who was at the house and the hospital. I'll see if he can tell me anything more."

"And if he can't?"

"Then I'll think of something else."

"This man has to be stopped, Valentin. Or the next thing we know, they'll be trying to close us down again. We'll be finished for sure." He grunted in frustration. "Can you believe it? After all we've been through?"

Valentin heard the older man's overwrought tone and kept his own steady. "I'm not done with this, sir. Not nearly."

"I hope not. I don't want it to end this way. For either of us." After another long sigh, he asked Valentin to keep him informed and then broke the connection.

A few minutes later, when Justine called his name, he was still holding the telephone and staring at nothing. He now replaced the handset and returned to the bedroom to deliver the news that the madman who called himself Gregory had outdone him again.

She sat up as he related what happened in a few terse sentences. When he finished, she said, "And you're sure it was him?"

"Who else?"

"My lord." She leaned back against the headboard and watched his face. She had never seen such a look in his eyes, with the light so dull. His shoulders stooped as if he had taken a beating and the words from his mouth were listless. The thought *He's in some kind of shock* crossed her mind.

Silently, she cursed Storyville. If only he had refused Mr. Tom. If only he had listened to her instead of granting that old man's plea. If only they had left the District farther behind and moved to some place where he couldn't reach them.

But Valentin wouldn't do that, because of unfinished business that, for as long as they'd been together, she could still only guess at. She knew only that it was a jumble of tragedy from his childhood mixed up with the sad saga of his friend, the crazy King Bolden. He had never admitted anything; she had drawn her conclusions from a pattern of clues over the years. She had allowed him into the deepest, darkest corners of her history while he kept his hidden from her. She understood that this was a product of fear and not mistrust, and so she allowed him to protect his last secrets.

This was not the time to try and unlock that door. Nothing she could say would change anything at this moment. And she had a job waiting. She slipped from under the blanket.

Captain Picot had been alerted of the assault in Storyville when he arrived for the day shift and as he hurried to his office, he had to work to mask his glee. He closed the door behind him and paced the floor in a state of wonder. Could it be true? Had an innocent citizen been nearly killed in the red light district the very first night that St. Cyr tried to put those streets under his protection? It was almost too perfect.

He was rolling this marvelous news around his brain when Detective McKinney appeared with a copy of the incident report. Picot ordered him to wait while he read it through. Looking up from the sheet, he said, "You're sure that this..." He peered at the name. "...this Gillette fellow isn't involved in anything?"

"He has no record," McKinney said. "I found the man he was with at the Café. James Dubose. His name's on the sheet. He said that Gillette is just an ordinary family man. He likes to have some drinks and play faro. He mostly loses, but it's small change. He's not a drunkard and doesn't make a habit of visiting the houses. I also spoke to his employer. He's been with them for over ten years. No problems."

The captain said, "So it was random."

"As far as I can tell, yes, sir."

Picot nodded crisply. "That's all, then."

Officer Cassidy arrived as McKinney was stepping out. "Report from the morgue, sir," the clerk called out.

Picot didn't notice McKinney's glance as the door closed. "Well?" he said. "Did you find them?"

Cassidy opened his notepad. "All but two."

"Which two?"

Cassidy read the names. "Jones and Racine."

Picot was studious in his disinterest. "All right, then, leave the list with me." The clerk tore three pages from his pad and placed them on the captain's desk. "You can return to your duties," Picot said. Cassidy made a nervous bow before exiting. The captain picked up the three sheets of paper, dropped two, and read the third with a lazy smile. Once he had finished, he sat back and gazed out the window, imagining that the dark clouds in the distance were meant for Valentin St. Cyr.

Evangeline was waiting at one of the dining hall tables when Sister Rosalie arrived from morning prayers. The sister stepped through the arched doorway and stopped in her tracks at the sight of something illuminating the older woman's features. She hurried to join her. "Evangeline?" she said. "What is it?"

"I woke up with the pictures in my head," Evangeline whispered. "I remembered more. There was a house on a sunny street. We had a little garden in back." She stopped as her eyes fixed on something. "Where the children played. I had a husband. But..." The light dimmed. "But I lost them."

Sister Rosalie waited to see if there was more before saying, "And your house was in New Orleans?"

Evangeline nodded slowly. "Yes. In New Orleans." She turned to the window and gestured in a vague way. "I grew up someplace green. But then I went to the city." She dropped the hand.

"Anything else?"

"Other pictures come and go. Faces I don't quite know. I still hear voices. And music sometimes."

The sister held Evangeline's wrists in a fervent grasp. "This is good," she said. "God is offering a helping hand."

"Is He? That's a pleasant thought." Evangeline's smile returned. "I'm hungry," she said.

Sister Rosalie released her grasp and stood up. "I am, too," she said.

Justine spent her morning in domestic chores under the direction of Tante Dolores. The older woman was a kind but no-nonsense sort and the suspicion in her black eyes did not go unnoticed. But she wasn't about to pry and Justine knew to keep her mouth closed and her mind on her work. Even so, she couldn't shake the feeling that there was something playing out just out of sight and earshot, and so she kept watching and listening.

Each rode a half-block past Orleans Street before he realized who he had just seen. It took that span of time for him to recognize the figure walking away from the parish precinct in a gray coat that was too heavy for the fall weather and connect one dot to the next. It was the fellow who had approached him at Fewclothes'. It was Gregory.

He jerked the rope for the bell and jumped up from the seat with such a sudden motion that the woman dozing next to him was startled awake. He all but tore the closed doors open and the conductor, fearing that he was about to be sick all over some well-Garden District dressed passenger, pulled the air brake to bring the car to a grinding halt and hit the lever for the door, all in one swift motion.

He hit the ground in a leap, then forced himself to a fast walk. Mr. Valentin had taught him that, too: run or behave in some other odd way on an everyday street and you might as well shout your intentions to the world. He said that guilty people could feel hostile emanations in the air and evaporate just like that.

Which was exactly what Gregory had done. Each's eyes darted this way and that until he was seeing the murderer in every man on the street. He asked the air what the Creole detective would do. The answer was to stand still, take a breath, and allow the panorama to come to him. That's what he did, and a curious movement caught his eye.

The strolling fellow had almost reached Bourbon Street. Each hadn't made a sound and the street was noisy, but somehow the man sensed danger, because he looked over this shoulder. Though the distance was too great to pick out features, the recognition was so immediate that they could have been standing a few paces apart.

Gregory had felt something poking at the edge of his vision as he walked away from the building. Maybe it was the sudden, screeching way the streetcar had come to a stop. He slowed his progress, as if his attention had been snared by the nearest store window. After moving a few steps from the window, he cast a glance back and saw the young fellow from the Basin Street saloon a half block away, edging into the street and staring his way. What was his name? Each?

Their gazes met and Gregory drew a sharp breath. Fighting an instinct to bolt, he held the wide-eyed stare for a few seconds before turning to the next store window, then sauntering off. He kept an even pace until he slipped around the next corner, leaving the spot where he had been standing vacant.

From fifty paces back, Each saw him leave his place at the window at an even pace and felt a rush of doubt; wouldn't a guilty man have bolted? What if he was seeing things and was about to embarrass himself by disturbing a harmless citizen? He reached the corner, expecting to peer down the street and see only an innocent gentleman going about this day.

The man in the gray coat was nowhere in sight, telling him that his first notion was spot on. With his brain whirling at the thought that he had let the killer escape a second time, he trotted along the banquette, stopping at every door and at the walkways between the buildings. He saw nothing but blank stares.

He picked up the trail at the Bienville Street entrance of Fong Le. Though it was too early for the restaurant to be open, the door was cracked. He stepped inside to find a cook in an apron standing over a case of bottles with a notepad in one hand and gaping in puzzlement toward the kitchen. Each entered, raised a finger to his lips, pointed and hiked his brows. The cook, a small, round Chinaman of middle age, shrugged his shoulders. A door creaked.

Each ran through the dining room and into the kitchen to find the door that opened onto the cobblestone alley that cut through to Bienville Street flung back. He came to a sliding stop on the stones and grabbed fast glances one way and then the other and saw a gray coattail flapping on the west side. By the time he reached the street, he found only a sot who was just then lurching to his unsteady feet.

Each rushed up, scaring the drunkard out of his wits. "Did you see a man out here?"

The sot's red-veined eyes rolled crazily. "Didn't see nothin'," he croaked.

Each walked back down the alley to the restaurant. As soon as the cook saw him, he jabbed a finger to the front door. Each loped to the banquette and scanned the street. Gregory was nowhere in sight and he stepped inside again. The Chinaman must have taken him for a copper, because when he pointed at the telephone, the response was a quick nod of invitation. He called the St. Cyr house and got no answer.

~

190

Gregory had hidden behind the door of the cold locker and waited until the footsteps slapped past and out into the alley. After peeking around to find the kitchen empty, he walked through the restaurant, admiring the rack of cutlery on the wall, and exiting with a smile that left the cook in a dither of confusion. He moved quickly to slip into the alley on the other side of the street.

The envelopes intended for the editor at the newspaper were still stuffed in his pocket. The delivery would have to wait; he couldn't chance another close call. The banquettes would be busy in another hour and he could take care of it then. He felt a flush of anger at St. Cyr and his meddling ruining his plans, by intention or chance. The Creole was far too wily a foe to be eliminated by some act of violence. It would take a different strategy. As he went casting about for ideas, a certain New Orleans police captain came to mind.

Captain Picot had been so enthralled with the delicious debacle unfolding in Storyville that he forgot the important detail of ordering Officer Cassidy to keep the particulars of his errands to himself. So later that morning, when the clerk and Detective McKinney happened to be climbing the main stairwell at the same time, the detective struck up a conversation that was at first idle. The younger man was so abashed at McKinney's civility, asking about his family and how he was enjoying his work, that he didn't realize that he was sharing a confidence.

McKinney had never trusted Picot, a feeling that was frankly mutual, and always kept a corner of his eye peeled for odd happenings around the office. Over the past week, as the captain fretted over the fellow who called himself Gregory and then fumed when St. Cyr took on the case, he had noticed Salliers and Cassidy scurrying here and there.

191

Now the captain's clerk was explaining how he had spent part of the previous afternoon at the Records Room downtown and his early morning at the newspaper morgue.

McKinney raised an approving eyebrow. "Both of those are good experience for anyone who wants to move up in the ranks," he said.

"And I do, yes, sir," Cassidy said.

"Were you able to find what you were after?" the detective inquired in a casual way.

"Yes, sir." The clerk concentrated as if his memory was being tested. "Reports of murders in the files and death notices from the old newspapers," he said. "From March and April of ninety-one"

They had reached the fourth-floor lobby and McKinney patted his shoulder. "Well, you keep up the good work," he said.

Cassidy's cheeks blushed a happy pink and he said, "Yes, sir, I sure will."

The detective watched him stride back to the section, mulling the reasons that crimes twenty-three years in the past would be of such interest to Captain Picot. He walked to the window at the end of the corridor to smoke a cigarette, recalling Salliers whining as he went out into the Wednesday morning rain about having "to drive all that goddamn way."

Instead of returning to his desk, he descended the four flights and walked to the police garage on the next block. After a few jovial minutes with the supervisor who stayed half-drunk while he managed the facility, he learned that when Detective Salliers checked out a vehicle, he had scrawled *Houma* as the destination on the dispatch sheet. As in deep-in-the-bayou Houma, too far to drive except on business that couldn't be handled by telephone. He thanked the dispatcher and took a slow stroll back to the precinct, wondering what was happening in Terrebonne Parish that had not appeared on any reports or bulletins.

As he was crossing the lobby, the desk sergeant called him over to hand him a note. The message was in the code that he shared with Valentin St. Cyr.

Valentin had called Parish Precinct twice in an attempt to reach Detective McKinney and was told both times that the officer was out on cases. In between, he telephoned the hospital and located a nurse who had graduated from Storyville a few years before, married, and studied for a new profession. Her name was Mariette and Valentin had once protected her from a bad character who wished to claim her by force. When warnings didn't work, the detective threw him down a staircase, then placed the muzzle of his Iver Johnson between the furious eyes and asked his opinion of what might happen next. The angry suitor got the message and was never seen again. Mariette believed Valentin had saved her life. He and Justine had danced at her wedding. Now she was happy to serve as a reliable source of doings within the walls of Charity.

"Mister Valentin." She sounded breathless. Before he could ask, she said, "The man who was stabbed. I wondered if you'd be calling, so I checked on him."

Valentin murmured his gratitude. "What's his condition?"

"He's stable," the nurse said. "He won't be up and about anytime soon. It was a deep wound, but he's a large man. Lucky for him."

Valentin said, "I'm going to ask you to keep an eye out for a police detective. His name is McKinney." He described the officer. "If you see him, tell him to call me. He has the number."

Mariette promised to keep an eye out for the detective. She asked after Justine and he after her husband, a former rounder who had straightened his path. After they hung up, Valentin mused on what she must be thinking. She, her husband, and his wife had all managed to escape the red light district. Only he had gone back.

With nothing to do and nowhere to go, he fetched the newspaper from the front gallery and settled down with a cup of coffee laced with brandy. On this morning, he needed the lift. It didn't help much; he found he couldn't sit still and tried tidying the house while he decided on his next step.

An hour into this domestic torment, Detective McKinney rescued him with a telephone call. "I just got your message."

"I'm hoping you have some information you can share," Valentin said. "In regard to the incident last night."

"I might."

"Are you able to meet me in town?"

"When?"

"This morning."

"Which location?"

"The one with the sweets."

"I can be there at eleven-thirty," McKinney said.

He clicked off without a further word and Valentin smiled. They had met over a dead body on Rampart Street some six years before, when McKinney was as green as they came; now he displayed all the jadings of a New Orleans veteran. Valentin had recognized something of himself in the younger man and now and then offered advice. Over time, they had formed a wary alliance. Of course, this caused Picot to distrust McKinney all the more. Which meant Valentin appreciated the officer all the more.

He was relieved to be finishing his dressing in advance of hurrying out to the roadster that was parked at the curb. From Lesseps Street to downtown was no more than a twenty-minute drive. But leaving early was better than roaming an empty house.

CHAPTER SEVENTEEN

A jolly Mr. Louis Martín looked up, winked, and fetched a cup of chicory coffee as the customer made his way to the corner table. Along with the beverage, he brought a small plate of *beurres* laced with almond liqueur, his wife's specialty. "Is anyone joining you?" he said as he arranged the cup and saucer.

The detective offered a faint nod. Martín and the proprietors of another half-dozen other venues around the city were acquainted with his cautious habits. He had stopped using Mangetta's for regular meetings when one of Picot's spies started hanging around. Now, for the few times he needed secrecy, he moved from place to place in a random fashion. He hadn't seen Mr. Martín in months; though by the welcome, it could have been two hours. The Frenchman was delighted to see him.

He sat sipping his coffee and nibbling a *beurre* as he watched the foot traffic along Magazine Street. He knew this part of New Orleans better than any except Storyville, having lived in a flat over the tobacconist just a few doors down from Martín's for seven years, the one where he had brought Justine when the Black Rose Killer was stalking prostitutes.

Later, in that same place, he had shot down the man who had caught her in his bloody web. That episode had pushed him to marry her and take her away to another part of the city. Had it been far enough? From what was transpiring now, it appeared that was not the case.

He was fretting on this when McKinney arrived and crossed to the table without casting an eye about the room. If there had been anyone suspect in the cafe, Valentin would have intercepted him outside. He doffed his hat and settled in a chair. They hadn't seen each other in almost a year and Valentin noticed that the ginger hair and beard now held a few flecks of gray. Time was passing for all of them.

The policeman regarded Valentin in turn while he waited for his coffee. Once Mr. Martín had served him and moved away, he said, "Are sorry you went back over there?"

"I don't know what else I could have done," Valentin said.

McKinney said, "You could have told Anderson no."

"Well, I didn't," Valentin said. "And it's getting worse all around. That stabbing last night..."

The detective said, "I went to the house on Franklin Street. And then at the hospital. He is one lucky gentleman."

"He didn't see who cut him?"

McKinney gave a shrug and said, "He stepped into the alley to piss. He had just finished and turned around when whoever it was stabbed him. And then ran off." He sipped his coffee. "You think it was our friend?"

"It was," Valentin pondered for a moment. "You know your captain is going to help as little as possible unless he can figure a way to get the credit for putting an end to it."

"I know that would be his choice."

"I want it to be your arrest. Or whatever else stops him."

"Not you?"

"I don't care about that."

McKinney put down his cup. "But you don't have him in your sights."

"I will."

"Are you even close?"

"He's not going to get away with it."

The policeman looked thoughtful. He wasn't about to challenge the detective's conviction. And he knew it wasn't bluster; not from Valentin St. Cyr. "All right," he said. "*When* it happens." He sat back. "And what do you want in return?"

"There's nothing you have that I can use." He noticed the expression on McKinney's face. "Is there?"

"Do you know anything about Houma?"

Valentin didn't follow the change of subject and cocked his head. "Small city. Terrebonne Parish. Not much more."

McKinney said, "Picot sent Salliers out there on Wednesday morning. Two hours each way. I read the reports and make all the briefings. And I haven't heard Houma mentioned once. I'm wondering what he was doing down there." He paused. "It might be worthwhile finding out."

Valentin thought about it. "Any copper making a visit would check in with the city police or the parish sheriff." McKinney sipped his coffee and waited. "And you can't be asking questions. The captain might catch wind of it." The policeman shrugged his reply. "So happens that I know a fellow down that way," Valentin continued. "A while back, I got him out of New Orleans when he crossed the wrong people. He's a Pinkerton now. I can ask him to poke around a bit."

"If it's no trouble."

"I've been meaning to see how he's faring anyway."

The policeman gave a nod and rose to leave. Valentin caught the hesitation in his eyes and said, "Something else?"

McKinney said, "Captain sent one of the clerks to the records room and then to the newspaper morgue. And he had him looking up deaths by violence on certain dates."

"What dates?"

"Spring of eighteen-ninety-one. March and April."

Forcing his hand steady, Valentin placed his cup in the saucer. He regarded the detective for a few seconds, then shifted his gaze to the window. "Do you know why?"

"No. Do you?"Valentin shook his head. McKinney said, "With this business with Picot and Salliers and Houma, I can't get rid of the notion that the captain is up to something. And that it concerns you."

"Why? Because he despises me?"

McKinney produced a short laugh. "Well, there's that. But, no, this is just a feeling I have." He waited to see if Valentin had any response before rising to his feet, offering a quick wave and walking out.

Once the door closed, Valentin released the breath he had been holding at hearing those months in that year spoken, a soft call from the shadows of a long lost past. In the next moments, questions began to swirl. Why would Picot care about that particular time? And what of the business of sending a detective to Houma on a secret errand? He considered that it might all be a coincidence. On the other hand, he knew better than to dismiss a good copper's gut feeling – or his own.

McKinney was right; the captain was plotting something. Wasn't he always? So he would call his friend in Terrebonne sooner rather than later. And perhaps pay a visit to the newspaper morgue for himself and have a chat with his friend He wasn't about to give Picot an edge.

After another few minutes, he carried his cup and plate into the tiny kitchen and stopped to shake Mr. Martín's hand before making his exit into the back alley.

~

198

He left the Ford parked on the lot and walked to Storyville. He wondered when George Alberton would want the machine returned. What if he did Justine's bidding and simply drive them away to some place where they could make a new start? How hard could it be? The police would be looking for a Ford roadster, when Fords accounted for four of every five cars on the road. He could hire someone to return it once they found a likely destination.

It was an idle but impossible notion that he enjoyed all the way to Canal Street. Crossing the tracks, his thoughts shifted back to McKinney's suspicions about Salliers' errand away from the city. He ran Houma through his memory another time and still came up with nothing. He couldn't recall even passing through the place.

At the Café, he drew a cup from the urn that was kept steaming. The day man told him that Each had called twice. He had left messages for Valentin to meet him at "the dago's" at one o'clock.

Valentin asked for the telephone. He gave the operator the exchange and number and waited almost a half-minute before he heard an intermittent buzz. The voice that came on the line belonged to Ray Lee Townes, like him, a former New Orleans policeman.

One night some twelve years before, Townes had reached his fill of rich men buying their way out of crimes and instead of taking the money to ignore the beating of the young sporting girl, made an arrest. That mistake could have been rectified. The one that couldn't be was alerting a newspaper reporter, who showed up at the precinct with a photographer in tow. Within twenty-four hours, he was dismissed from the force and instructed to get out of New Orleans for his own good. Valentin helped him find a position with the Pinkertons, working the western half of Louisiana. He lived in

Morgan City and ranged north as far as Baton Rouge and south all the way to the Gulf, a territory that included Houma.

Valentin got to the point. Townes listened, then said that he knew the Terrebonne Parish sheriff and could speak to him about the matter.

"You'll be helping me and sticking a police captain here," Valentin said. There was no need to speak a name. Townes snickered and said in that case, he'd get on it immediately. Valentin recited his telephone number.

"So how's the married life?" the Pinkerton inquired.

"It suits me," Valentin said. Adding, "I never would have guessed."

"Maybe I'll try it someday," Townes said before breaking the connection.

It was a quiet day at the mansion and with Mr. Alberton at his office and the lady of the house off shopping the downtown stores, what little work there was got done quickly. Justine didn't want to be sent home before Annette arrived back from school and miss a chance to learn more about Emelie. So she went looking for something to keep herself busy.

She was in Mr. Alberton's office, replacing books to the shelves and tidying the newspapers that were strewn about when she heard the creak of a floorboard overhead. Tante Dolores was working in the kitchen and Thomas was raking in the back garden. Another board creaked.

Placing the pages back on the table, she slipped out the door and along the hallway to the bottom of the staircase and called "Hello? Annette?" She began to climb. Halfway up, she stopped, hearing what might have been the whisper of feet along the hardwood floor. When she reached the top, she looked up and down the hallway. Nothing was moving. The door to Annette's room was open a few inches.

She made her quiet way along the corridor and paused in the doorway, listening. When she heard no sound, she slipped inside, and saw that the closet door was also open. She crossed the room and pulled the cord for the overhead light. The clothes on the hangers had been disturbed and at least two no longer held dresses. As she mulled what this meant, she heard a hinge squeak and then a flurry of rapid steps from out in the hall.

By the time she reached the corridor, footfalls were tapping on the back stairwell. She gave chase, rushing to the top and then descending the stairs in small leaps. The stairwell opened into the kitchen, meaning Tante Dolores would see whoever appeared. But when she reached the bottom floor, the older woman was nowhere in sight. She looked out the window to see her standing behind Thomas with her hands on her hips, giving orders as he raked and ignored her.

She made a fast circuit of the downstairs, peering out every window in hopes of seeing someone making an escape. The streets and banquettes were empty and there was no one on the south side of the house, either. She thought about questioning Tante Dolores and Thomas about an intruder, but that would only raise more suspicion. She spent a few moments pondering before returning to the second floor. The door to the attic was shut tight, but when she turned the knob, it opened. She climbed the steps to the dark and quiet space beneath the eaves. Here, nothing appeared out of place.

She moved to the window, putting together the pieces. The intruder had gone into Annette's room, then have moved down the hall and just unlocked the attic door when Justine called out. That person hid until the new maid was inside the closet and then made a rushed exit to escape being cornered. So Justine had come within a few seconds of a confrontation and perhaps the solution to the puzzle.

She paced in the hall for a few minutes, calming herself before returning downstairs and making herself look busy. Even if every speck of the housework was finished, she would linger long enough to intercept Annette.

Valentin entered Mangetta's on the grocery side and the proprietor took a second away from a customer to wave him into the saloon. He walked through the archway and made a line for the booth in the corner, sliding in so that he was hidden from the rest of the room.

Frank followed after a few moments, hiking a dark brow as he ran a towel over the table "You eating today?"

"Whatever you have," Valentin said. "Each will be here in a few minutes."

"*Each*." He shook his head. "The way he eats, you think he wouldn't be so *magro*. Too skinny, that one. *Un bastone*. A stick."

Valentin saw the party in question crossing the floor and tilted his head. The Sicilian turned to give Each's cheek a savage pinch. Valentin smiled. With his own children long gone, Mangetta needed a *nipote* and Each could do with a *zio*. Valentin was happy to relinquish both roles.

Each sat down with his flesh bursting red from the fingers and the embarrassment. Frank left them alone and went to fetch their lunches. Valentin saw that he was even more jittery than usual and said, "What is it?"

Each leaned forward and described in a low voice how he had spotted Gregory and then the chase that ended with him losing his quarry. Valentin felt his stomach sink at Gregory's ongoing gall even as his pulse quickened. "He was by Parish Precinct when you first spotted him?" he said.

"Just down the street."

"Then he probably dropped another letter for Chief Reynolds," Valentin said. "And he carried one to the newspaper, too. He's going to crow about the man on Iberville now."

Each said, "I'm sorry about this, Mister Valentin. I didn't—"

"It's all right," Valentin said. "It's a damn wonder you happened to spot him. He's stupid to be out, after you and I both saw his face. He thinks he's clever. So far he's just been lucky."

"So what do we do?"

"We keep going until we catch him," Valentin said. "And we will."

Mangetta appeared with two sandwiches, a bottle of wine, and three glasses. He settled the plates, poured the glasses full, and sat down. The chatter began in English and Italian. Each watched Valentin, hearing something in his voice and thinking, *He's starting to sound scared, too.*

Whythe O'Neal caught Reynard's attention as the reporter crossed the newsroom and waved him into his office. "Another cordial message from our murdering friend." He held up a sheet of paper. "A fellow was stabbed in Storyville last night. Gregory says he was the one wielding the knife." He handed over the letter.

"Is the man dead?" Reynard said as he began to read.

"The bastard failed this time." The editor thumped his thick torso with an open palm. "Something to be said for a little extra meat on the bone."

Vernel returned the sheet. "Are you going to run it?"

O'Neal settled his chair and laid the letter aside. "I don't know. What's the point of doing his bidding? It's not helping the police get any closer. Or Mr. St. Cyr." He leaned back. "You know it happened on his watch. When he had his own men on the streets."

"I heard," the reporter said, keeping his tone bland.

The editor drummed fingers on his blotter. "Can you reach him?"

"St. Cyr? I can try."

"Do that. Tell him about this. As long as he's around, I'd like to hear what he thinks we should do." He looked at his watch. "I'll need to make a decision one way or the other in the next fifteen minutes."

"And if I can't find him?"

"Then I'll flip a coin."

Frank appeared just as Valentin and Each were readying to leave. He waved at the empty plates and said, "*Sta bene?*" It was a meaningless question; nothing but fine dishes came from the kitchen at that address. "I got someone on the telephone in the office," he said. "That newspaper fellow. Vernel."

Valentin and Each exchanged a glance and rose to follow the proprietor out of the saloon. When the detective picked up the handset, Reynard Vernel told him what he already knew about the morning's letters from Gregory. "My editor would like to to know your opinion on running it in the evening edition," he said. "He's going to find out if the police received a letter and if–"

"They did," Valentin said.

"Then what do you suggest?"

"I suggest not doing it," Valentin said. "It won't matter one way or the other. He's just toying with you and the police." The words *and with me* crossed his mind, but he kept them to himself.

"I'll tell Mr. O'Neal what you said." The reporter told him to watch for the evening edition and clicked off.

Frank and Each had been able to overhear most of the exchange by way of the squawky speaker in the handset. Now they both watched Valentin's face for a reaction. He produced a smile that was more of a grimace. "That sonofabitch."

"*Que cosa farai?*" Frank asked. *What will you do?*

Valentin said, "I'll take him down, that's what. Sooner or later."

He looked from the saloonkeeper to Each, who was staring at the floor, and realized that the words had come out hollow, as if he didn't believe them, either.

CHAPTER EIGHTEEN

Captain Picot heard about another letter dropped through the precinct mail slot that morning. By midday, when the chief was huddling with the officers who advised him, he was not among them. So be it. Since he wasn't important enough for their precious inner circle, he decided to take an extra long lunch.

When he returned, he found the envelope that Officer Cassidy had placed in the middle of his blotter. He sat very still for long seconds, studying the handwriting before picking it up. Random bits of information landed on his desk on a regular basis. A network of spies meant a steady stream of gossip and hard fact, delivered by way of ragged slips of paper and whispers in corridors and over the telephone. The envelope before him was of a quality paper and the handwriting florid. He knew without opening it that it had come from Gregory.

The realization caused his breath to come short and his heart to flutter. Could it be true? Had the murderer who had been holding the city on edge somehow learned his identity? And sent one of his mad screeds to Captain J. Picot's direct attention? As if he was important, no matter what the brass thought. His hand went to shaking.

A moment later, he stopped to wonder if it could instead be someone's idea of a prank. He had enemies in the department who took pleasure in embarrassing him. The memory of arriving at a full-dress police event at the Opera House only to learn that the invitation had been a fake still galled him. As did the tip that had him rushing to corner a fugitive wanted in five states, only to find a local lunatic screeching like a lewd parrot. A fake letter from Gregory would fit the pattern. And yet something told him it was genuine. So he sat down and spent some time calming himself before cutting the seal, turning back the flap, and extracting the single sheet of cream-colored paper.

Captain Picot, it began, *I believe that you and I have interests in common. I do not wish to cause any more harm, only to achieve my goals. If you are willing to hear more, please place something of a red color in a street-facing window on your floor. I will take the next step. Signed, Gregory.*

The captain sat perfectly still, hearing nothing but his own breathing as his thoughts pitched forward. Department procedure dictated that he rush the letter to his major, who would carry it directly to the Chief. They would devise a trap, with Captain Picot offering the bait. His only involvement would be the signal in his window. The action, the arrest, and the glory would belong to others.

That construction was now overturned. As long as he held the sheet of parchment, the power was in his hands. He closed his eyes, opened them, read the words over again, and then spent the next hour fuming over his choice, knowing that with every minute he held onto the letter he was risking deeper trouble. He got up and paced.

Just before three o'clock, he made a decision. After hiding the letter deep in a desk drawer, he descended three floors to the storage locker, where he found hanging from a hook a burgundy scarf some officer had left behind. He carried it back to his office and draped it over the latch so that it would be visible from the street.

The figures of pedestrians on the banquettes below were pieces on a board. Standing there, he imagined that one was Gregory, a second St. Cyr, a third the mysterious woman in the Terrebonne Parish convent who went by the name Evangeline. Also represented were Tom Anderson, the street weasel Each, the reporter Vernel, Detective McKinney, and his man Salliers. Then came the sports and madams and hussies who populated the District and the army of customers that flooded the streets night after night. And now he imagined his hand directing the game, moving the pieces in a pattern that led to an inevitable end, a collision that would see them breaking on each other, leaving nothing but shards and dust. And when it was over, J. Picot would claim credit for a victory that had been a long time coming.

At four o'clock, the jitney from St. Boniface School pulled to a stop and Annette stepped down. Tante Dolores cut her a slice of coconut cake and poured her a glass of milk. Annette finished her snack and went on her way.

Justine was waiting when she reached the second floor. "Someone was here today. I think in the attic. And in your bedroom." She described hearing footsteps and the intruder escaping down the back stairwell and out of the house.

Annette's eyes gave a cool flick as she walked away. "It must have been her. Emelie."

Justine followed behind. "Why do you think so?"

"Who else would it be? Who would want to be up there? And know about the back stairs? It was her."

"She could have told someone. Maybe Paul."

"I don't think so." Annette was making it clear she wasn't interested in another opinion. They had reached her bedroom. "You don't know her," she said.

Justine changed tack. "Did you leave your closet door open?"

Annette produced a sharp frown and said, "No, why?"

"Because that's how I found it."

She made no attempt to examine the closet. Instead, she stood waiting in a pointed way until Justine retreated to the hallway. "Are you going to tell my father?" she said.

Justine paused, sensing a drift. "No."

Annette studied her for a few seconds. "You'd be surprised to learn the truth," she said.

"Why don't you just tell me?" Justine said.

Annette smiled as she closed the door.

Justine walked off mulling what had just transpired. Maybe *Annette* had been the visitor, slipping away from her fine school, making her way to the house, and then stealing back before she was detected. Justine couldn't fathom any reason for this subterfuge, unless it was just to render the puzzle even deeper.

Sheriff Lasser had worked with Pinkertons, though not often by choice. He could manage his parish without any outside assistance. Also, he had found the freelance detectives even quicker to corrupt than sworn officers. A fair share were no better in character than the reprobates they were tracking. As a last straw, there was the annoyance over their slapdash investigations.

Ray Lee Townes was an exception, a professional who had impressed the sheriff since the day twelve years before when he visited on a case he was working. At that first meeting, he told Lasser that he had been on the job in New Orleans and explained why he had left. He guaranteed to keep his nose out of parish business and had been true to the promise. He had in fact been an asset. So when the clerk told him that Townes was on the line, he was pleased to take the call.

They traded some small talk and the Pinkerton got to the point. Had by chance a New Orleans detective visited the parish during the past week? The sheriff paused, then answered to the affirmative. Townes asked for whatever information about the visit that the sheriff could share. Lasser hesitated for a longer beat. Had it been any other person asking, he would have turned him down flat. But Townes had never betrayed a confidence; and the sheriff was curious about the inquiry.

"He was investigating a woman who's staying at the convent," he said. "She came here out of nowhere about a month ago. She had lost her memory. The sisters took her in. This detective wanted to interview her."

"Do you know why?" Townes said.

"I don't. And I don't think he did, either. He was on an errand for his captain."

"Picot," the Pinkerton muttered.

Lasser said, "How did you know that?"

Townes explained that word had come to his New Orleans friend that there was something suspicious about the matter. "I don't know what that is. But he has an interest."

"I see."

"He suggested that you be careful about any further contact from that officer."

The sheriff understood. "The woman won't be bothered here," he said. "The sisters are taking care of her. And I take care of them."

"I'll pass that along," Townes said with a quiet laugh.

After he had hung up, the sheriff sat reflecting on the chain of events. It was all questions and no answers, and he decided to pay another visit to Our Lady of Sorrows, just to make sure that Evangeline was safe. And to spend some more pleasant time in the company of Sister Rosalie.

~

Gregory arrived at the corner at two o'clock, just as the afternoon editions were hitting the banquettes. This time, he strolled into the store and made the casual purchase of a packet of Wings that he would not smoke. Cigarettes made him ill. He stepped outside, dropped a nickel in the boy's palm, and accepted his copy of the paper. He tucked it under his arm and meandered along Prytania Street, stopping in the middle of the block to lean against a spreading oak.

The story about the stabbing had not made the front page. Nor the second or third. His nerves began to pinch as he flipped to the editorials, only to find the usual array of inane crowings about the war, the new Negro college, and other matters of interest only to dullards and lunatics. He straightened as a spike of heat rose through his throat to his face. It had not occurred to him that they wouldn't run the letter.

A woman approached, pushing a baby stroller, humming a little melody as the infant gurgled, and he felt a wild urge to attack mother and child right there on that quiet street, throw them under a passing truck, and see if New Orleans would pay attention then. In a few seconds, the moment of red rage passed, leaving him shaking.

He stood staring at the newspaper without seeing a word and imagining the detective St. Cyr offering his opinion that there was no point in placating the madman a third time. Of course, the editor of the paper and the police followed right along. He completed his walk to the house thinking that they, too, would be sorry.

Valentin and Each strolled the two blocks to the Café and stood on the banquette watching a train creeping into Union Station. If they lingered there, they would be greeted by a throng of men

211

arriving from this hamlet or that and looking for a night of revelry, another wave in the tide that had been rolling in for the better part of forty years, long before the ordinance that made the District legal. Though the flow they observed was a trickle compared to the mobs that had once rushed from the terminal and into the red light district.

"What about tonight?" Each asked. "What shall I tell Mr. Tom and the madams?"

Valentin considered. "Tell them it's business as usual. But they should all be careful about who walks in the door."

"Will Gregory think we're giving up?"

"I don't care if he does," Valentin said in a sharp voice. "We're not going to let him run Storyville." He softened his tone. "Get your fellows back on the streets. Tell Mr. Tom to ask Chief Reynolds for any officers he can spare. That will make the coppers happy. They'll think we can't handle things." He laid a hand on Each's shoulder. "And you be careful, too. You've seen him up close."

Before Each could announce that he wasn't worried, the Creole detective gave a short wave and walk off in the direction of Canal Street.

Gregory returned to the District at the end of the afternoon, wearing a slicker with the collar turned up and his hat pulled low. With the bad weather rolling in, the apparel would raise no suspicion. The storm clouds were already high and dark over the rooftops as he walked on with the bearing of a man on important business.

He crossed Commerce Street, walked halfway down the block, and stopped. He entertained a brief few seconds of alarm when he couldn't locate the window. Then he saw it; on the fourth floor near the middle, solid red, just as he had requested.

So now the final act could begin. It was time to erase the Creole detective St. Cyr, Mr. Tom Anderson, and the blight that was Storyville, all in the same clever stroke. No one except a solitary police captain would catch the twist in the plot. Who would suspect that he could have gained a partner of such a high rank? The one person with a cause of his own and a hunger to play that role? It was yet another brilliant move that no one could have predicted. *Surprise, ladies and gentlemen.*

He stood relishing the thought of what was to come for a few moments before moving on. The Western Union office was four blocks away on Poydras Street. Among their services was a bank of telephones in booths that offered the privacy that a confidential call would require.

Valentin arrived home feeling the day weighing on his spine and went to the kitchen to help himself to a short brandy. He drank it off and was about to pour a second, then decided on something with more heat. He took down a fifth of Raleigh Rye he hadn't opened in months and carried bottle and glass to the back gallery.

The garden was quiet, the twittering birds absent from foliage that was still a lush green. It was too early for the racket of late day traffic. Far off, he heard the mournful horn of a freighter plying the Mississippi. He took a small sip of the whiskey, sighed, and settled into the chair.

As he watched the raindrops on the leaves, McKinney's words came to the edge of his musings, carrying memories of the terrible weeks of a spring some twenty-three years in the past. Now, by the thinnest of threads, they had come back to him and he felt something stirring that had been long dormant, as if a net had closed around a dark liquid shape and was dragging it from the bottom of the river.

In his weary state, it was too much. He laid his head back and fell into a half doze. As his mind began to unwind, he pictured a woman standing on the other bank of that same river, waving a hand and calling through the mist. Calling to who? Someone she had lost? Was it him? He could not discern her face or hear her voice clearly, but there was no denying the plea. What was she saying? Was it—

The telephone chattered and the image swirled away. He blinked, sat up, and made his way to the foyer. He recognized Ray Lee Townes' voice through the tiny speaker. Behind it, he heard rumbles of thunder. The last shreds of his dream scattered.

"Is it storming down there?" he said.

Townes said, "Yes. It's looking nasty."

"Here, too," Valentin said.

Townes repeated his conversation with the parish sheriff. Valentin listened, working to keep his thoughts from running down any wild paths.

"Did he tell you anything more about the woman?" he asked when the Pinkerton finished.

"That's all of it," Townes said. "I don't believe he was holding back anything important." He waited for a few seconds, then said, "Do you want me to go to the convent?"

Valentin said, "Not now. I might drive out there. And we can go together."

"It will be good to see you again," Townes said. "I'll buy you a drink."

Valentin thanked the detective and broke the connection. He returned to stand on the back gallery and watch the rain until he heard Justine coming through the door.

~

214

Gregory stepped into the booth, dialed the four digits, and was connected to the switchboard at Orleans Parish Precinct. He asked for Captain Picot. After a few seconds of static, a young voice came on the line. "Detectives' Section. Cassidy speaking."

Gregory said, "Captain Picot, please. He's expecting my call."

As he had guessed, this was not an unusual ploy, and Cassidy asked him to hold for the captain.

"Captain Picot." The name came out in a quick and guttural spurt, the sound of an angry man.

"I saw the window," Gregory said.

After a weighted silence, the captain said, "I'm listening."

"I know I'm sick," Gregory began. "And I want to stop. But first, I want to be rid of that party who's been meddling. The man who runs that awful place and his kingdom, once and for all."

For a wild moment, Picot wondered if the madman was announcing a plan to murder St. Cyr and Anderson in cold blood. Was he that insane? These thoughts were interrupted when the caller said, "I have reason to believe you share these hopes." He sounded quite composed and Picot relaxed, thinking *Maybe he's not so crazy after all.*

From the booth in the Western Union office, Gregory paused to gaze out at the shapes moving along the Poydras Street banquette. "You don't have to say anything unless you disagree." He waited to see if the fish would take the bait. Captain Picot kept his silence. Gregory's lips curled in a childish smirk, but he kept his voice steady.

"My hope is that you have some information that I can use to end this matter." This time, he didn't wait for a response. "If this is the case, please remove the cloth from your window. If it's still there at the end of the day, I will assume that you have nothing to offer and will find another solution. I thank you for your time."

He dropped the handset into the cradle and walked outside to retrace his steps to Parish Precinct. By the time he arrived, the red cloth was gone.

Justine spent the first part of the streetcar ride thinking about Annette. Surely, the girl was hiding something; maybe that she was involved in Emelie's disappearance right up to her deep blue eyes.

Mr. Alberton had arrived home as the new maid was gathering her things to leave. He beckoned her into the study. "No telephone call today?" It was the first time he had spoken to her about anything other than domestic chores since she had taken the job.

She said, "No, sir."

Alberton sat down in one of the chairs, a weary slump that made him look older. "Do you think Emelie has come to any harm?"

Justine said, "No, sir. I don't."

Alberton stared at her, trying to decide if her opinion mattered. "And why is that?" he said, still in a grudging way.

"Because no one has asked for anything," she said. She was thinking, *Like there's no need for her to ask.*

Alberton appeared about to continue the conversation, but instead waved a tired hand and said, "I guess that's all for the day."

As the car crossed over Canal Street, she paused to consider the possibility that everyone in the house was in on it and that she and Valentin were being played for fools for a reason neither of them could yet fathom. She wondered if with all the moving shadows and whispers, her husband the detective would be doing any better.

The streetcar came to a stop at the corner of Basin Street and she surveyed the lights of that broad boulevard without seeing them. She was back in the Alberton mansion, feeling the first tingle when she heard the footsteps, the electric charge of the chase, the thumping of her heart, and the quivering of her nerves.

216

She guessed that another woman would have run to fetch Thomas at the first errant sound. That had never occurred to her. The seconds that followed had been tense, but not in the dark and bleak and helpless way she knew from when she was young. Being the hunter rather than the prey was a strange sensation. Was this why Valentin still hankered for Storyville? Because he craved one more chance to play a dangerous game? She smiled a private smile, thinking he had better hope that *she* didn't develop a taste for it.

The car passed down North Rampart Street. As she rolled toward home, she couldn't decide whether Valentin would be pleased or angry over her trying to run down the suspicious someone. As the car came to the stop, she decided she didn't care.

Sheriff Lasser drove the flooded roads and parked at the gate and tugged the brim of his hat down low before climbing out. When he stopped to pull the rope for the bell, he glanced up to see the iron angel peering back down at him, her face dappled in raindrops that might have been tears. *Our Lady of Sorrows, indeed.*

One of the novitiates opened the gate. He took the umbrella she was holding and together they hurried along the stone path to the dining hall. The young woman, a girl really, left him there while she went to fetch Sister Rosalie. He crossed the hall to stand by one of the tall windows and watch the rain until he saw her figure moving through the drizzle. She looked up and saw him. Even at that distance, her smile was bright with life, and he considered what a good wife she would have made for some man. In the next moment, he felt ashamed that he had entertained such a thought about a woman who had given herself to God, doubly so because the man he had in mind was John Lasser. Had she known these thoughts, she would of course forgive him. He doubted his wife would do the same.

He returned to the door and opened it for her. She ducked inside, folding and leaving the umbrella against the wall. She peered at him. "Sheriff? Is there trouble?"

Lasser gestured to the nearest table and said, "Sit with me, please."

They sat. In a few brief sentences, he told her about the call from the Pinkerton and the interest in Evangeline that was stirring in New Orleans.

"What does it mean?" Sister Rosalie said.

"That someone has an idea about her identity. Or thinks he does." The sister's eyes widened and the sheriff said, "I know you want to protect her. So, for now, if anyone comes looking for her, find me."

"Do you think she's in danger?"

The sheriff shook his head. "Not here. She has a right to her privacy, that's all." He reached into his shirt pocket and handed her a card. "I know Mother Superior has my telephone number at home. I want you to have it, too." He stood and picked up his hat.

Sister Rosalie said, "You know you didn't have to drive all the way out here. The roads are terrible."

Sheriff Lasser gestured, his arms wide to encompass the room and grounds beyond. "It does me good." He noticed that the sister's expression had turned pensive. "Something wrong?" he asked her.

"Evangeline. I do worry."

"God will abide with her. And with you. Isn't that how it goes?"

"That is how it goes, Sheriff." She did not appear comforted.

Lasser touched the brim of his hat and left her there. When he reached the gate and looked back, he could make out her figure standing in the open doorway.

~

Justine found Valentin on the back gallery, half curled into one of the willow chairs. He looked up with a vacant smile. He had fetched the dusty bottle of rye from the cabinet and she saw a glass that was mostly full on the table between the chairs. She stepped back into the house, took off her hat and shoes, and poured herself a short brandy from the flask on the sideboard.

After she had settled into the second chair, he made a small gesture, as if brushing something aside, then said, "So?"

"I had quite the afternoon." She related her adventure with the intruder and then her conversation with Annette. Valentin listened without saying a word. The tale finished with her walking out the door to catch the streetcar home.

He sat back. She sipped her brandy. He hadn't touched the whiskey and made no move to pick it up now. "So she's probably in on it, too."

"I think they're all in on it, one way or another.' She swirled the liquid in her glass. "But in on what?"

"Tell me about the mother," Valentin said. "I never saw her out there. Not once."

"She's a society lady," Justine said, "She's younger than her husband. By maybe twenty years. She kind of drifts in and out of the rooms. I get no feeling of anything from her. Like she's made out of wood. I think that's because of her medicines."

"What medicine?"

"Patent medicines. Elixirs. Dr. Bartell's. That kind. She has bottles all over the house."

"Is she ill?"

Justine gave a slight shake of her head. "You know some women take potions to make themselves happy? I think she's taking them to not feel sad." She shrugged. "But I'm just guessing."

"It sounds right to me," Valentin said.

"Maybe. You know I've never been around rich folks." He hiked an eyebrow and she said, "I mean a rich family. Are they all like this?"

"Just the ones that have too much money. They get into trouble worrying about it. Fighting over it. Little things get blown up." Now he did lift his glass, though only for a small sip. "Watch the girl. She's the only opening you have right now." He looked at her face and smiled. "All right, you know that." Now he turned to survey the garden, a tangle of autumn greens, golds, and browns.

"What about your day?" Justine asked.

"My day?" he said. "I'm still trailing behind."

"Are you going to Storyville tonight?"

Valentin said, "No, that's what he wants. Each's men are out. And the police." After a moment, he said, "But I might have to go to Houma. It's in Terrebonne Parish."

"I know where it is. Go there why?"

"Because of a woman in a convent. She wandered in about a month ago. She lost her memory and doesn't know her true name or where she came from. Now some people are trying to find out who she is."

"What people?"

"Captain Picot, for one."

That stopped her for a moment. "What's it got to do with you?"

When he didn't answer her, Justine noticed a shadow on his face and began to sense something strange and terrible arising along the horizon. He held her gaze, sending a message that he could not form with words, until her eyes widened and she whispered, "Good God, Valentin. Could that be? Your..."

He held himself still, as if balancing some delicate something that any motion could shatter. "Probably not," he said. "But I won't know anything until I go down there."

"It's been almost thirty years," she said. "Do you think you'd remember?"

He didn't answer as he watched the night draw close.

Captain Picot left his office at six o'clock, earlier than was his habit. He had spent the last hour of the afternoon planning his next move in the game that would soon end with him as a hero and a certain Creole detective in disgrace. The thought made his heart trip as he made his way along the evening banquette.

The day was fading and the captain retreated to the doorway of a closed store to watch the passing citizens, many of them fairly glowing over leaving work after a long day or embarking on a night on the town. He had never been in their number. After so many years, he was still a stranger in the city he called home.

From the moment he had first donned a uniform, he had been devoted to his police work, caring for little else. His family was gone and he had lost interest in friends years ago. Women whom he helped with criminal problems satisfied his physical needs. His career was his life and the thought of ever having to leave the department haunted him, his worst fear.

This didn't mean that he played it safe, like some officers he could name. His arrest numbers were always outstanding, partly because a share of them were inflated with poor innocents. He had spent those same years gathering information that he had then used to carve a path inside the department.

He believed without question that a law officer of his superior skills and complete devotion could have been — no, *should* have been — promoted to chief by now. Instead, he had yet to reach even the rank of major, and at the age of fifty-four, his future was dim. All because of those who over the years had thrown obstacles his way.

Primary among those tormentors was Valentin St. Cyr with the secret that had been held to Picot's throat like a sharp knife. But now, at long last, the tables had turned. *He* was the one with the dark knowledge. He would use it to trap and then destroy St. Cyr and achieve the glory he had long deserved. It was too late for chief; commander would do. That this would require making a pact with a devil didn't signify; he'd done that more times than he could count. He had always found a way to rid himself of an evil partner and would again. In time, Gregory could be lured into a trap and eliminated, while Captain J. Picot would be left to bask in the glory.

With that notion to lift his spirits, he stepped back into the flow of citizenry and, for a lingering moment, drifted in the swirl of sound and motion that was New Orleans at night.

CHAPTER NINETEEN

Morning arrived with no reports of trouble. The madams had been vigilant, the police visible, and word had gone out that there were private coppers about, just in case the information reached the killer's ears. It was also true that the weather put a damper on business. That was the other story. Overnight, the storm that had been hovering in East Texas came awake and turned toward Louisiana.

Thunder was rumbling and lightning crackling when Sister Rosalie woke. Her next thought after her silent prayer to God was Evangeline. She dressed and hurried to the foyer, where she found a slicker to drape over her habit. When she reached the second floor, she found Evangeline's bed empty, but made so perfectly that she imagined the older woman tidying up before wandering off into the same invisibility from which she had come.

She crossed the grounds at a slippery half-trot without seeing any sign of her. She was about to turn for the Mother Superior's office to call Sheriff Lasser when she noticed the door of the dining hall standing open a few inches. She climbed the wet steps and pushed inside. The hall was empty, except for Evangeline, who stood by one of the windows, gazing at the fuming sky, her eyes pensive.

Sister Rosalie caught her breath. "How did— What are you doing in here?"

Evangeline didn't turn at the sound of the voice. "It's a good place to watch," she said.

A jagged branch of lightning flashed in the distance. "Please don't stand by the window," the sister said. "Sit with me. I'll start coffee."

A few silent seconds passed before Evangeline moved away from the glass. Sister Rosalie removed the slicker, laid it on a table, and pulled out a chair. "Sit. Please."

Evangeline did as she'd been asked. As the sister started for the kitchen, she said, "Chicory."

Sister Rosalie stopped. "Ma'am?"

"I always made it with chicory. He liked it that way."

"Who did?"

"My husband," Evangeline said. Her eyes took a distant set. "I had a husband. I was married. His name was..."

Sister Rosalie felt her heart thump. "Was what?"

The gray eyes closed. "I don't remember. It's in my head, but I can't find it."

"It's all right. Don't fret." The sister moved off in a gradual way, in case there was more. By the time she reached the kitchen, Evangeline had bowed her head and begun murmuring under her breath.

Captain Picot rose that morning in a mood that continued to be bright in spite of the clouds looming to the south. He had spent the hours after he arrived back at his house on Mallard Street fretting over the scheme to use Gregory to rid himself of St. Cyr, so that Tom Anderson and Storyville would fall like dominoes in a row. After attacking it from a half-dozen directions, he decided that not even the Creole detective would be able to trace it back to him. Gregory had no proof that they had ever talked and anything he said could be dismissed as ravings. The letters to the newspaper would be all the proof he would need.

As to that deranged citizen, he would eventually find himself trapped. And this time, he wouldn't be able to count on a soft heart to ease his escape. This time he'd die, his end having been wrought by the fearless hand of J. Picot. The captain would have succeeded where St. Cyr had failed. The fancy St. Charles Avenue lawyers would have already sent the Creole detective packing. His reputation shattered, he'd slink off in shame. Without him, Tom Anderson's failing grip on the District would weaken even more. Storyville would begin its decline into ashes.

Standing still in the center of his living room, the captain closed his eyes to savor that last sweet detail. The end of Valentin St. Cyr's career as a New Orleans detective would not be the last word. That would come when it dawned on the Creole that his old enemy had engineered his downfall. It might take years, until it would be too late for St. Cyr to exact revenge. But the day would arrive.

He took these joyful thoughts with him as he dressed, ate his breakfast, and telephoned the department. Cassidy was on duty and the captain told him he would not be available for most of the day due to police business in another part of town.

Cassidy was saying, "Yes, sir. Shall I—" when the line went dead.

The captain sat down to wait. As the minutes crawled, the glow dimmed, and the thought that he had misread Gregory began to stir. Someone who committed such gruesome acts was not right in the head. Who knew what he might do, no matter how composed he sounded on the telephone? What if he decided to go off on a tear?

These notions were still gnawing at him when the telephone bell chattered. He stared at it without moving. After the fifth ring, he sat forward, lifted the handset, and placed it to his ear. "Picot."

"Good morning, Captain." A pause. "Sir."

Picot took a breath to calm himself. He needed to put this fellow in his place and so didn't return the greeting.

225

Gregory said, "Nothing happened last night. Though it would have been easy enough. Those women care more for money than they do for their lives." Another pause. "So, do you have something for me?"

Picot hesitated, experiencing another flash of doubt. For all his careful scheming, things could go very wrong. And yet, if he was ever to prevail, this was his chance. Not acting would mean St. Cyr would continue until he caught or killed Gregory, and his star would be back shining brighter than ever. Tom Anderson's handle on the District would be restored. And J. Picot would remain J. Picot.

"Captain?"

Picot steadied himself. Once the words were spoken, there would be no taking them back. "I have information about that individual you met."

"Oh? What would that be?" The words were cool, almost disinterested.

Picot said, "He lost his father over twenty years ago. And his mother about a year after. The father was killed. What happened to the mother was never determined."

Gregory said, "Yes, and?"

The captain shifted the handset from one ear to the other. "A month ago, a woman appeared at a convent in Terrebonne Parish. She showed up at their door. Seems she had lost her memory. The nuns are taking care of her. They don't know her true name, so they gave her one." The captain halted again, feeling his flesh prickling as he approached the largest leap. "It's possible that she's St. Cyr's mother."

He could all but hear the gears grinding over the line. "Does he know about her?" Gregory said at last.

"He does not," Picot said.

"I see."

"I'm going to send two of my men down there to bring her back to the city," the captain said. "The reason being to find out if she matches a missing person in our files." Gregory stayed silent. The captain sensed a shadow creeping and turned away from it. "Once we've determined that this is not the case, she'll be released."

"Released."

"Onto the streets of New Orleans. And I'll make sure that information gets to him." He held back from choking on his next words. "And to you." At this Gregory let out a small humming sound. "But I want to be clear on something," he continued. "The woman is not to be harmed."

"I suppose there would be no point."

Gregory sounded a bit too vague, giving Picot pause. "Do we agree that we want him gone from the city for good?"

"Yes," Gregory said. "Gone. I can see that happening." His voice held a gloating note.

"Just as long as no harm comes—"

"I heard you." Gregory was sounding snappish and Picot backed off, not wanting to upset him now. This was a man with an insane pride. The captain was counting on it. "At some point, we'll arrange for her to be carried back to that convent."

"And then what? What will happen once it's finished?"

"Well, you'll write one of your letters to the newspaper."

"And mention a certain New Orleans police captain?"

Picot wanted to laugh out loud at pulling the maniac so easily into his web. "That would be part of the arrangement," he said, sounding earnest." I'll see to it you're not pursued. The crimes will become one of the great unsolved mysteries. With St. Cyr gone, Anderson loses his right hand. Storyville won't last."

If Gregory was at all troubled by Picot's trust in him or his shaky logic, he voiced no doubts. "So," he said. "What do they call her?"

227

"Evangeline."

"Poetic."

Picot did not understand the comment. But who knew what was circling that mad brain?

"Is she his mother?" Gregory said.

"I have no idea," Picot said. "The facts fit in a loose way. It doesn't matter. He just has to believe she could be."

Gregory paused for a few moments. "All right, then. I'll call you again this afternoon at four and then every morning and afternoon until it's finished."

"I hope that will be a few days at most," Picot said.

"It will be, Captain." Gregory clicked off.

Now that the scheme was in motion, the captain felt some of the pressure he had been carrying relent. It was an odd feeling. Murky fears that he would one day be made to pay for his misdeeds had lurked in the back of his brain for as long as he could remember. At last, he could see an end to that nagging burden. It was true that he had only acted because of Gregory. So be it. What was coming would be far better than standing in the same place as the years ground him down.

He considered for a final time tossing it all and taking what he had in hand to his major, posing it as a trap he had set for the killer. Gregory would be finished, but St. Cyr would still be standing. So he sat back to wait for whatever would come next.

Justine was up and dressed early. Valentin sat up and pulled the curtain behind the bedstead apart. "Maybe this would be a day to stay home," he said.

"It's not that bad," she told him. She sat on the edge of the mattress to lace her shoes. "Will it make you feel better if I call when I get to the house?"

"It would make me feel better if you stayed here," he said. "It might make you feel better, too." He reached for her, but she pulled away with a flash of eyes. "This was your idea, remember? Now I have to go." She kissed his cheek and backed out before he could make another lunge.

Ten minutes later, he heard the front door close. When he got to the kitchen, he found fruit, bread, and a hunk of cold sausage on a covered plate and coffee steaming in the pot. He nibbled and sipped and stared out the window, trying to keep his mind on the business of the day and off the woman in a convent in Terrebonne.

It was no use. From the first moment she had crossed his mind, he knew she wouldn't let him alone. He had spent the night tossing and turning. At one point, he got up and stepped onto the front gallery. With the rain riding on the edge of the wind, it was like standing at the prow of a ship on a stormy sea. He retreated to the kitchen, poured himself a short glass of rye and returned to the night before. After an hour, he crawled back into bed and was able to sleep.

But with dawn, the stirrings began anew. Twenty-three years. What were the chances? Impossible or next to it. Still, what if...? And so his mind swung from one side to another. He ate a few more bites from the plate and roamed the house for what seemed like half the morning. He might have kept going that way but for the sudden squawking of the telephone. The urge to ignore it crossed his mind. What had the black wire brought him save for bad news? But the way it shrilled caught his ear and he went to the foyer and lifted the receiver.

For the second time in two days, he heard the voice of Ray Lee Townes and wondered if that clever Pinkerton had somehow eavesdropped on his thoughts. "Ray Lee," he said. "What is it?"

"Sheriff Lasser just telephoned," Townes said.

Valentin said, "Yes?"

"Your Captain Picot called him this morning. Claiming that the woman at the convent might be a person they believe disappeared from New Orleans in eighteen-ninety-one."

Valentin slid down the wall to the floor and laid a hand over his eyes, trying to get a grip on what was spinning in his brain.

"Mr. Valentin?"

"I'm here."

"I know this is going to sound strange. I called because...you remember when you told me about your..."

"Yes," Valentin said. "I've been thinking about it, too. It just doesn't seem possible. I'm going to have to go and see for myself."

"When?"

"Today."

Townes said, "The weather's bad. It could get worse. You might not be able to get through."

"I'm coming, anyway."

"When?"

Valentin stood up. "This afternoon. You can tell the sheriff."

"Maybe you should wait. They're talking about moving the women into town until the storm passes. We'll know for sure by noon. I can telephone you back."

Valentin said, "I can wait two hours. Then I'll start out. I just can't stay here. You understand that."

"I suppose I do," Townes said. "All right, then. Do this. Stop at Des Allemands. Go to the telegraph office. It will be on the main street. I'll send a message there. So you don't come for nothing."

Valentin agreed to the Pinkerton's suggestion, thanked him, and broke the connection. He sat for another ten minutes, then got to his feet and paged through the telephone book to find the number for the state weather station.

~

Sheriff Lasser had begun traveling the parish before dawn with Corporal Marks at the wheel. His first concern was the collection of small bridges and crossings that spanned the wider bayous within a ten-mile radius of Houma. Beyond that were the few roads that would be impassable as the water rose.

They arrived back at the office at eight-thirty. The sedan was splattered with mud and the two officers were soaked from their forays outside the vehicle. The sheriff sat down at his desk, pulled off his wet shoes and socks, and placed them both by the furnace grate. A pair of dry socks from his bottom drawer made him feel like a new man. He had a second pair of shoes in the closet for when he needed to go out again. When he did, his first stop would be Our Lady of Sorrows.

One of the deputies brought him a cup of coffee and he had just taken a first sip when the phone rang. The same officer took the call and stepped into his doorway to say, "New Orleans Police on the line, sir."

The sheriff lifted the handset and said, "Sheriff Lasser."

"This is Captain Picot of the New Orleans Police. We spoke a few days ago."

"Yes, Captain. How can I help you?"

Picot was brisk. "I'm calling in regard to that woman in the convent. I've come across some information that indicates she could be a missing person from our jurisdiction."

"Is that right? Missing since when?"

The captain hedged just long enough for the sheriff to prick his ears. "Oh, twenty-odd years."

Lasser moved directly from surprise to suspicion, though he kept that out of his voice. "How did you track her after all this time?"

"One of my people remembered the case," Picot said so smoothly that the sheriff knew it was a lie. "He looked into the files. A good bit fits."

Sheriff Lasser took another sip of his coffee. *A good bit of what?* No one knew anything about the woman. She could be one of hundreds who had gone missing around that time. This city copper thought he was a yokel, a bayou dunce who was too slow to pick up the clumsy gambit. He decided to play along.

"So," he said. "How do you want to handle it?"

"If you could keep her in sight until I can get a couple of my officers to carry her back here. We've been looking for people who knew her. See if someone can make an identification."

It was so thin that the sheriff would have laughed had it not also been so suspect. Still playing dumb, he said, "Well, I'm going out there this afternoon to see if we need to evacuate."

"Evacuate to where?" Picot said, again too quickly.

"Back here to Houma. We have a school that can house them for a few days. But only if they agree. I can't force them to do anything. I wouldn't try."

Picot said, "That's fine. As long as we don't lose sight of the woman."

The sheriff had to bite his tongue to keep from snapping back that he knew how to do his damn job. Let the bastard think he needed the advice. "That won't happen. The sisters are watching out for her. And so am I."

"Then I'll send a couple of my men out there as soon as the weather clears," Picot said. "Do you have any idea when that will be?"

"Maybe tomorrow evening. That's a guess. These storms don't behave."

"I'll plan on Thursday, then."

"All right, Captain."

The connection died. Lasser stared at the telephone for a few seconds before rising to fetch his second pair of boots from the closet. As he tied the laces, he called out to Marks to track down Ray Lee Townes. After he spoke to the Pinkerton, he told Marks he was driving to the convent and walked out into the rain.

Justine had just reached Annunciation Street when the downpour started in earnest, driving so hard against the windowpanes that she wondered if she would get back home at the end of the day. The storm had everyone indoors. Annette was staying home from school. Thomas and Tante Dolores lingered in the kitchen after breakfast, drinking coffee and talking quietly as the rain came down and the thunder echoed.

"For now, no one's going anywhere," Mr. Alberton said before secluding himself in his library.

An hour later, when Valentin heard the telephone jangle, he hesitated. He did not want Townes calling to tell him that the roads in Terrebonne were impassable. And yet he always wanted to know things sooner rather than later. What he heard was Justine's voice and a stream of static. She explained about the streetcars and that she didn't know how she'd get home at the end of the day. "I might be here for the night," she finished. "You can't drive in this."

Valentin was about to explain that he was going to do just that, then stopped. She would try to talk him out of it. She would worry her day away. She'd be just as angry if he didn't tell her. So he didn't.

"If the cars aren't running, we'll find a way to get you home." The connection was getting worse. "I'll find you later."

He hung up and made another call before the lines were gone. McKinney was at his desk. "Sitting here drinking coffee," the detective said. "No going out for a while." The static was now a faint hiss.

Valentin related what Townes had told him and his plan.

"You sure you want to do that?" McKinney said.

"I'm going. I'll try to call you later. My first stop will be the telegraph office in Des Allemands. Leave a message there, if you need to reach me for anything. Then I'll be at the parish sheriff's."

McKinney said, "I don't think our friend will be at work today."

Valentin said he hoped that was true, thanked him, and hung up. In the bedroom, he put on a chambray shirt and a cord jacket he hadn't worn in years. He found his broad-brimmed hat on the shelf above, his high-topped shoes in a corner of the closet, and an old pair of de Nimes trousers in the bottom drawer of the dresser. While he was there, he drew out his pistol, stiletto, and sap.

He dressed as the rain rattled on the roof. It had occurred to him to call the sheriff's office, then decided it would just bring another opportunity for someone to get in his way. As he was readying to leave, the lights flicked off for a few seconds and then back on. Odds were that at some point the power would go out. And what good would he do sitting stuck in a dark house?

Lesseps Street was mostly empty. He saw a truck crossing the intersection at Roman, but no other automobiles were in sight. That would make things a little easier. He set the choke and retarded the ignition and then stepped around to start the machine. When the engine twice coughed and died, he feared that his day was falling apart before it began. At the third round, the four cylinders rattled and gurgled and settled into an idle.

He hopped into the cab and pushed in the choke handle, then sat drumming his fingers on the wooden wheel. Steering what were on rough roads, working the gearshift, and keeping a constant hand on the windshield wiper handles would make for a busy trip. He pressed the accelerator handle. The headlamps brightened as the Ford rolled out, though they would be scant good in heavy rain.

He made his way south to Chartres, then west to St. Ferdinand and the bottom of Canal. A dozen pedestrians, crouched under umbrellas, watched him pass with looks of surprise. He had guessed correctly that a ferry captain wasn't going to allow a little wind and rain to keep him at dock and drove on, joined by one truck and one jitney. The chop caused the roadster to sway on its high tires and Valentin realized that a strong enough gust could send him over the side. He gave a murmur of relief when the gate came down and he rolled off on the Algiers side.

There were few trucks and fewer cars on River Road. The rain slowed to a moderate drizzle and in the respite he could relax his arm for ten seconds at a time before grabbing the wiper handle again. As he rounded a curve at St. Mary's Cemetery and pointed due southwest, he turned his head to see the skyline of New Orleans losing itself in gray. Far along the macadam beneath his tires was the town of Houma, Our Lady of Sorrows, and the lost woman who went by the name Evangeline.

Sheriff Lasser parked at the front gate, slid out of the Baker, and passed beneath the iron angel. The brim of his hat was low over his forehead as he trotted along the pebbled path to the reception building. The desk was unoccupied. He used the telephone to call the Mother Superior's office.

He was waiting in the lobby of the dormitory when Sister Rosalie appeared. She guided him to the far corner. As the rain gusted across the grounds outside the windows, he told her about the call from New Orleans and the police captain's interest in Evangeline.

"Where is she right now?" Lasser asked.

"On her floor," the sister said. "Everyone's been restricted to the building until this passes."

"You'll need to keep an extra close eye on her," the sheriff said. "I don't know what these people are up to. But it doesn't feel right."

"Does this captain know who she is?"

"I'm not sure. I still don't trust him."

Sister Rosalie nodded in a pensive way, then said, "She's been remembering things."

"Oh?"

"She says she had a husband. And children."

"I hope she remembers more." He donned his hat. "I'm going to see Mother Superior now."

"Will you be evacuating us?"

"Right now, it looks like the worst is swinging around to the south."

Sister Rosalie gave her rosary an absent caress. "Could it be true? That our Evangeline is..."

"I don't know what's true, sister."

The nun came up with a quiet smile. "After all this time and the intrigue, I think you can call me Rosalie."

The sheriff said, "That will take some getting used to." He gave her a nod of thanks and walked out into the rain.

With both Mr. and Mrs. Alberton in the house, Tante Dolores went about finding chores for Justine that would not disturb them. The women climbed the steps to the second floor with Dolores huffing ahead on her short legs. She opened the door to Beatrice's room.

"Ain't no reason to do anyt'ing." Her accent came from deep in the bayou. "She don't be in the house more than onst every couple weeks. So just change out the sheets. Them *clean* sheets." Her lip curled. "Makes madam happy, so..."

236

To this point, Tante Dolores hadn't spared an extra word to Justine, giving her orders and then walking away. This morning, she didn't leave the room, but sat down on the chair next to the door while the new maid went about stripping the bed. As she worked, Justine felt the dark eyes tracing her every move.

"So what all you know 'bout Miss Emelie?" the older woman said.

It wasn't really a question. Justine stopped and looked at the small, handsome woman. "Ma'am?"

"I don' miss much 'round here," Tante Dolores said. She tilted her head in the direction of Annette's room, then surprised Justine further by cracking a sly smile. "I know the jabbermout' been talkin' to you."

Justine said, "Yes, ma'am. She has."

"They sayin' Emelie been *kidnapped* or some such." Her tone was sarcastic.

Justine left the sheets folded on the bed and came around to the footboard. "What do you think happened, Tante Dolores?"

The question brought a sharp shake of a head and Justine thought the housekeeper was finished. Then she said, "I t'ink it ain't true. She done run off. And they know why. Oh, yes."

"Oh." Justine tried for a wide-eyed gaze and lowered her voice. "Do you, ma'am?"

Tante Dolores regarded her for a few seconds, then switched back to her old self. "Even if I did, it wouldn't be for me to say. I suppose we'll find out soon enough." Her face went blank as she pushed herself to her feet. "You take your time up here. Don't want madam findin' more things for you to do." She let herself out.

The Old Spanish Trail was made up of sections of clay, gravel, and dirt, and all of it was slick and peppered with potholes, some of which resembled small ponds. Valentin watched the speedometer.

The Ford was making at best thirty miles an hour. The rain had not increased, though the clouds over the gulf were an angry gray. After he passed through Paradis, the road curved almost due south and he drove on toward the darkness. Des Allemands was ahead and he was ready to get out of the machine for a few minutes. Or for as long as it took to get the message that he could keep going.

Gregory stood at the attic window from where he had designed his campaign against the loathsome and wicked men and women of the red light district. Now he mulled the most recent turn. He knew as soon as Picot explained his ploy that it wouldn't work. Even over a telephone line invaded with noise, he could tell the captain was unnerved, but the man's hunger to destroy St. Cyr was so strong it overcame all else. Gregory wondered what could be so terrible as to drive the man to such perilous lengths.

Whatever the case, Captain J. Picot had shown himself to be stupid, first by entering into a pact with a crafty murderer and then by believing he could get away with betraying such a cunning partner.

The scheme Picot announced was never meant to succeed. Gregory had guessed from the first moment that Picot had a whole other intention. Somewhere in that foolish brain was the notion to have him captured or killed.

But Gregory had been steps ahead of him, just as he had been with St. Cyr and the New Orleans police. The captain had made a monumental mistake by telling him about the woman in Terrebonne. He said the Creole detective didn't know about her. Gregory doubted this. His gut told him that St. Cyr was far too cunning. Which worked in his favor.

When it was over, St. Cyr would surely be erased and Tom Anderson and Storyville would come apart. Picot would end up on the scrap heap, too. After Gregory broke them all, he would leave the old woman's corpse somewhere as a final testament and fade back into the veil of invisibility at the house with the attic that overlooked Prytania Street.

It was time to move. He had kept the workman's clothes he had stolen from Henry in a bundle and now rolled the boots into the trousers and jacket. He took a look around the attic that had been his private lair, the aerie from where he had swooped down to Storyville. So much had happened so quickly and now he was about to end it with a flourish that would have people talking for years. Hadn't he always known he was special? Why hadn't anyone else seen? Why had it taken all that spilled blood to make them understand?

He carried that thought down the attic stairs and into his bedroom at the end of the hall. From the window, he could spy the automobile parked around the side of the house, a forest green Locomobile Model 48, tall and sturdy, with a six-cylinder engine that would push it through a tidal wave. A bit of rain would not faze it one bit. His father rarely allowed him to drive it because of that incident with the Winton which was not his fault, but try telling the old man that.

With the clothes under his arm, he left the room to stand at the top of the stairwell. His father would be in his study, poring over his legal papers. His mother would be fussing at the help over something or other. He had an excuse prepared if one of them crossed his path. He thought it might be amusing to kill his parents before he drove off. He imagined the looks on their faces. Ha-ha. But that was not part of the plan.

He descended the stairs and then into the basement, the sound lost in the thunder and drumming rain. He stood by the workbench that his father never used and changed clothes, then pushed the hurricane door open and poked his head out. The street was clear.

In a half-minute, he had trotted to the machine, set the spark, cranked the engine, and driven off.

Sheriff Lasser was changing back to the socks he had left to dry when Corporal Marks told him the Pinkerton was on the line again.

Townes began by reminding him about the detective St. Cyr. "That woman at the convent? There's a chance she's his mother."

Lasser sat down. "Is that true?"

"He doesn't know. She disappeared over twenty years ago. It was during the Sicilian troubles. And I guess he's hopeful."

"Is that all?

"That's all he said. But he's on his way down there."

"On his way when?"

"Today. Right now."

"In this weather?"

"Unless he's changed his mind. I told him I was going to talk to you. He'll stop at the telegraph office in Des Allemands. If you don't want him to come, I can send a message."

"And he'll turn around?"

"Probably not."

Sheriff Lasser took a few seconds to think it through. "Let him come, if he can make it. We need to find out what the hell is going on with that lady."

Valentin pulled around the side of the Western Union office on Railroad Avenue in Des Allemands. When he ducked through the rain and stepped inside, he found four customers and an agent who looked flustered. The telegraph would be in demand even in a sleepy hamlet, with so many telephones out. He fidgeted until the four men ahead of him had sent or received their messages, and stepped to the counter.

"I'm expecting a wire. My name's Valentin St. Cyr. It would have been sent today."

The agent flipped a finger through a file box. "Nothing yet."

"I'll wait," Valentin said.

The agent gestured to the bench on the wall. Valentin walked instead to a window and watched the gush that ran a hundred feet into a bayou that was swelling. If the rain kept up, the water would rise higher and begin to flood the town. Getting to the other side would be impossible.

The room was silent save for the shuffling of paper. Valentin was relieved that the operator was not inclined to chatter, so he could let his thoughts drift. What if the trip was a stupid lark and the woman in the convent nothing but fiction? He had duties in New Orleans. While he dawdled in a telegraph office, Gregory would be plotting some new outrage. There was still a chance he could repair things with Sam Ross. If not, he needed to pursue other work, lest he and Justine find themselves on the street. If he turned around now, he could be back in the city ahead of the storm.

The telegraph key clattered, startling him out of his musings. After a dozen staccato strokes, the agent said, "Mr. St. Cyr? Here you are."

Valentin stepped to the counter and signed, dropped a dime for a tip, and read the type on the yellow paper. *Come if you wish STOP Sheriff agrees STOP Meet at his office STOP*

He thanked the agent and hurried outside. He cranked the Ford and drove at a creeping pace across the slick timbers of the bridge before picking up speed for the rest of the trip.

Justine roamed the upper floor, making herself scarce while creating the noises of a busy servant. She went through every room save for Annette's. The door was cracked open and peeking inside, she saw the girl napping with her arms curled around a pillow.

241

She made a quiet descent to the first floor by way of the back stairs. Tante Dolores and Thomas were back at the kitchen table, drinking coffee. She didn't want Dolores to catch her sneaking, so she put a worried look on her face, and murmured something about calling home to check on her husband, and hurried to the foyer.

She dialed the number of the house on Lesseps Street and let it ring a dozen times before dropping the handset. She wondered where he could have gone on such a dreadful day.

CHAPTER TWENTY

The rain picked up as Valentin drew nearer to Houma, though it had not yet turned into the deluge that had been worrying him. The black and angry skies remained to the south over the gulf as the storm curved like a scimitar aimed at New Orleans. If it kept swirling over the water, it would wear itself out and in another two days, the sun could be shining again.

At the moment, the gusts of wind and the hard drizzle were keeping him busy. A good thing, because he did not want to think about the convent in the middle of the bayou and the woman who had come from nowhere. He was sure he did not want his mind traveling back over the years to the little house near First and Liberty, and the family who lived there: a Sicilian father, Creole mother, and three children.

Before that happened, he came up on a crossroads. The Spanish Trail would continue to Lafayette while New Orleans Road jagged south to the gulf. As he entered the hamlet of Raceland, he noticed one other lonely automobile ahead of him, a Locomobile touring car, forest green save for the splatters of mud from radiator to boot.

He stopped at a roadside sign announcing Houma another fifteen miles distant. After spending a minute listening to the rain drumming on the canvas and staring at the muddy road ahead, he put the Ford into gear.

~

Ray Lee Townes knew that other Pinkertons out of the Morgan City and Baton Rouge offices and even more in New Orleans preferred big automobiles with tufted leather upholstery and flashy brass work. This was a clear signal to criminals that a private copper was around. To Townes, it was a clear signal that the driver was earning money in addition to the paycheck he was drawing every Friday. He chose to drive a black Model T because there were dozens on the roads and he could easily get lost among them.

He had stayed the night in a hotel in Thibodaux to wait out the storm. In the morning, a bellboy came knocking with a message from Sheriff Lasser in Terrebonne Parish. After he got off the lobby phone with Lasser, he called St. Cyr in New Orleans. There was no talking the Creole detective out of making the drive south. And Ray Lee didn't blame him; if it was his family in question, he would have done the same.

He rode the elevator back to his room. He took the time to clean his old Liege revolver, then slid it into its holster, and finished packing. He checked out and carried his satchel and weapon through the rain to the Ford.

The sixteen-mile drive to Houma took forty-five minutes. Main Street was all but deserted when he pulled around and parked behind the sheriff's office. Inside, he found Lasser at his desk. The two men shook hands and a deputy appeared with a cup of coffee for the visitor.

"So St. Cyr's on his way?" the sheriff said.

"He is."

"When can we expect him?"

"I'd say within the hour."

"I hope he's prepared for a disappointment."

"I don't think that matters," Townes said. "He just wants to see for himself."

"That part, I understand." The sheriff swiveled in his chair and gazed out the window. Then he turned back.

"Have you had lunch? Corporal?" he called out. "Need you to go over to Petrie's."

Justine had just hung up the phone when Tante Dolores stepped into the front room and gave a silent jerk of her head. The housekeeper wanted her out of sight. She hurried up the stairs to the second floor. This time, she found Annette's bedroom door closed. At the other end of the hall was the door to the attic, the one place in the house that she had not visited. Valentin had been invited. She had not.

Years before, on a lark, he had shown her how to pick a lock using almost any sharp tool. She now made her quiet way to the door and pulled a hairpin from her curls. After a quick ten seconds, she felt a soft click and turned the doorknob, then stopped. If the family had wanted her on the top floor, Tante Dolores would have taken her there or given her a key; if she was caught, it would be trouble for her and Valentin both. She'd likely be sent packing and they might never untangle the puzzle. But she couldn't just stand there, so after a casual glance over her shoulder, she opened the door, put a foot on the first step, and closed it behind her.

The rain drizzling on the roof echoed in the empty space and covered the sound of her ascent. Still she moved slowly and when she reached the top step, she saw shadows broken by the faint gray light from the east window. A wall with a locked door had been constructed on the other half of the attic.

She moved into the cozy bedroom had been fashioned beneath the mansard beams, with an iron-framed bed at its center. A fading Oriental rug covered the floor, with a floor lamp in each corner and a smaller one on the bedside table.

Justine crossed to the chifferobe and opened it. Emelie owned a small selection of dresses compared to Annette and they all appeared dated, much what she expected for the daughter of a servant. The wardrobe included four pairs of plain shoes. How it must have galled her to see the other girls in the house, the *American* girls, with all their finery.

Justine examined the one small set of shelves with a row of books and assorted knick-knacks. She saw nothing out of the ordinary, not a single item that pointed to anything new. After scanning the odd-shaped room for another minute, she moved to the door on the wooden wall at the other side.

A bit of jiggling with the hairpin opened the lock. In the dim light inside the room, she could make out an assembly of steamer trunks, boxes and crates, and a few random pieces of furniture. Treading softly, she passed among the stored objects until she came upon four boxes that had been stacked in the farthest angled corner. Three were marked: "dishes," "linens," and "books." The fourth had no markings. When she opened it, she found two thick photograph albums. She pulled the first one out and paged through it. So here was the family in portrait: father, mother, Beatrice, and Annette.

She placed the album aside and was drawing the second one from the box when a manila envelope fell from inside the cover. She turned it to the light. A fine hand had written *Belle Baptiste* in one corner. Her thoughts scattered in a half-dozen directions and she felt an eerie prickle run up her spine.

She used her thumbnail to slice the flap loose. She drew out a thick sheaf of papers and a smaller, pink-tinted envelope. Several were letters from the same law firm where Valentin was employed and had to do with a change to a will. The remaining one was a letter referring to the filing of a birth certificate. She recalled seeing

246

such a document before and wracked her brain until she remembered one of the girls at Miss Antonia's getting pregnant and the madam arranging to have her lawyer draw up papers giving the child status.

A notion of what she might have in her hands came nibbling at the edge of her thoughts. How she wished she could run downstairs and telephone Valentin. But she was there, not he, and so she opened the rose envelope.

Inside, she found three photographs of an infant in newborn's bedclothes, lying in a bassinette. The child was adorable, with a head of dark curls, button eyes, and latte skin. Justine turned the photograph over and read the inscription, made in a feminine hand: *Emelie Baptiste-Alberton - July 2nd, 1898.*

When Gregory arrived in Houma, he saw a selection of citizens in raincoats and hats making forays onto the banquettes as the wind blew and the rain fell. All were in a rush, which suited him. He did not want questions about his business there. Nor did he wish to give anyone time to take in his features. So when he saw an older gentleman braving the weather in a olive slicker, he pulled over and dropped the canvas flap. The fellow peered in at him.

Gregory said, "I know you're in a rush, sir. Could you direct me to the convent?"

"You mean Our Lady of Sorrows?"

"That's the one," Gregory said.

The man pointed in a hasty motion. "Go down that way, take your left on Barrow Street, then follow Bayou Dularge. You see the Virgin Mary, that's the road. Not the actual Virgin. A statue. You see her, that would be damn sight." Cackling, he headed off.

Gregory buttoned the flap and pulled into the street.

~

Valentin entered Houma, steered the Ford along Main Street, and pulled over when he spied the frame building with the flag in front and a stout sign that read TERREBONNE PARISH SHERIFF'S DEPARTMENT and JOHN LASSER, SHERIFF beneath it in smaller letters. As he made his way up the walk, he saw a figure in the window and recognized Ray Lee Townes.

The door opened and the Pinkerton waved him inside. They shook hands and Valentin took off his coat and hung it from one of the pegs on the wall. "How was it?" Townes said.

Valentin gestured to his damp clothes. "I wish I had a sedan," he said. He hadn't seen Townes in eight years. He didn't look so different. A bit wider and grayer, but who escaped that?

"I see you still have your beard," Valentin said, to which Townes replied, "And you still don't have yours."

He looked past him. Valentin turned to see a tall and solid man standing in the next doorway. "Sheriff Lasser," he said.

The three men sat around the sheriff's desk. Townes watched with amusement as the peace officer and the Storyville detective took measure of each other. Valentin was not surprised that even lounging in a chair, Lasser radiated a quiet authority. Lawmen who didn't have small armies of officers to count on tended to the type who struck fear by their very presence. Lasser would likely be wary of any of the New Orleans crowd, all the more so a detective who had made his reputation in Storyville. But he looked mostly curious as they exchanged some mild chatter.

That lasted until he said, "So what about this Picot character?"

Valentin kept it brief, working around any mention of the years of bad blood between him and the captain. "He found his place and he's working it. Nothing you could call scruples. He gets arrests, though. Piles up the numbers."

"On the take?"

"Oh, yes," Valentin said. "More than his share, though."

"So what's his interest in this woman?"

"I'm going to guess that it would be me," Valentin said. "To see what damage he can do."

"He hates you that much?"

Valentin smiled in grim way. "That's only the beginning."

Justine put everything back the way she had found it and descended the attic stairs. As she leaned her ear to the door, she was startled into a silent sharp breath by the sense that someone was lurking on the other side. She held herself still and waited while the seconds dragged. She felt the air change and bent to peek through the keyhole. The long hallway was empty. She sat down on a step and waited another three minutes before looking again. Nothing. She turned the knob with a gentle hand and pushed the door open a few inches wider. No sound came from the hall. After closing the lock, she hurried to the back stairwell and stood there until her heart slowed and she could think.

Captain Picot arrived at his office in a funk that had been building since the moment he had finished the call with Gregory. Through the next hour, his agitation increased as he grasped how much control he had surrendered. He had only done it because St. Cyr had started him down the path. Once again, the damned Creole had forced his hand without even knowing it. Worse, he could do nothing to stop Gregory if that madman decided to trick him and go off on some bloody jag. For all he knew, that madman had already dropped letters for the chief and the editor of *The Times-Picayune,* revealing how he had entered into a bloody secret pact with Captain J. Picot.

He climbed the steps in such a state that by the time he reached the second floor lobby, he was red-faced and sweating and his stomach was sour. He waited until he could step into an elevator alone and kept a stone face and tight lips when the Negro operator wished him a pleasant good morning.

When he arrived at his office, he called Cassidy in to explain that he was expecting a very important call. He dismissed the clerk, closed himself behind his door, and stood by the window, trying to guess where under those gray skies that lunatic might be.

Gregory drove along the muddy road with the thin tires slipping this way and that until he saw the Virgin Mary appear out of the drizzle, a ghost in stained white. The sight unnerved him and he slowed to make the turn onto an even narrower road, passing through a tunnel of trees that posed like gargoyles ready with their claws to clutch and devour the puny machine and him with it.

A half mile on, he caught sight of the walls. When he reached the convent, he pulled up at the near corner and shut off the engine, then surveyed the surroundings before climbing down and picking his way to the front gate.

The archway was plastered an eggshell color, except for the dark wooden crosses on either side and the iron angel set above the keystone. The eyes of the figure, though cold metal, held him for a few seconds. A rope hung from an opening in the stone. He pulled it and the bell on the other end pealed. When no one appeared, he pulled the rope a second time. Then he pushed one side of the door of heavy cypress open.

The grounds were empty and silent, except for the rain on the leaves above and the stones at his feet. As he walked to the small square building that was directly ahead, the door opened and a nun stepped outside onto the gallery. Gregory stopped and tipped his hat.

"Good afternoon," he said. "I'm looking for the lady called Evangeline."

Sister Rosalie was on the floor tending to Sister Bernadine, now in her sixth decade in the order, the last twenty years at Our Lady of Sorrows. The elderly woman's health had been failing and Rosalie expected that they would soon be carrying her body to the little cemetery just beyond the east gate. Likely the same one where she would leave her mortal remains when she went to join God.

Bernadine was going on about the time she had traveled to Rome and had seen the Pope. *The year of seventy-six*, she whispered. Rosalie, having heard the tale at least twenty times, gazed down the row of beds to see Evangeline with her Bible and rosary beads, her face infused with that strange light.

"Sister Rosalie?" A novitiate with apple cheeks and merry eyes had called to her. Rosalie could not think of her name. She bent to the sister's ear to tell her that a man had come from New Orleans to see Evangeline.

The sister stood up. "What man?"

"He says his name is St. Cyr. And that he might be a relative of hers."

Sister Rosalie had the younger woman — she had recalled that her name was Sarah — escort her across the grounds, the two of them all but hidden under an umbrella. They returned to the reception area, Sarah by the front door and Rosalie in through the back. The senior nun peeked out from the office as the novitiate did as she had been told, explaining to the visitor that they were rousing Evangeline and would he please have a seat while those preparations were being made?

251

Rosalie listened to the voice of the man who called himself St. Cyr. It held a high, nervous note that made her uneasy. When she caught quick sight of him through the gap in the doorway, she perceived a gentleman who looked out of place in workman's clothes. She heard the chair creak as he shifted his weight. Sister Sarah told him she would be back shortly and hurried out.

Sister Rosalie and the novitiate stood beneath the dripping eaves of the laundry building. When Rosalie told Sister Sarah what she was about to do, the younger woman came up with a stunned look and said, "You can't!" Then: "Why?"

"It's the only way, that's why," Rosalie said. "I have to know who he is."

Sister Sarah was frightened and Sister Rosalie said, "Don't worry. You'll be safe."

"But what about you?" Sister Sarah said.

"I'll be fine." She grasped the novitiate's hand. "Now I want you to go to Mother Superior and use the telephone to call Sheriff Lasser. If he's not in his office, have them find him. Tell him about this man. Do you understand?" Sister Sarah nodded, half-dazed. Rosalie kept her voice firm. "Sister? Go on, now. Go."

The young nun took the umbrella and hurried away. Sister Rosalie stood wondering if she had lost her mind. What she was about to do was for Evangeline's sake and she knew God would understand.

The sheriff had ordered an extra sandwich. The Creole detective took a few bites, then folded it in the waxed paper. He was beginning to feel butterflies. He drank some of Sheriff Lasser's strong coffee and waited. The sheriff was talking about calling the convent and letting one of the sisters know they were on the way when the corporal stepped into the door, pointed to the telephone, and said, "You'll want to take this, sir."

Lasser picked up the handset and as he listened, stared at Valentin in a fixed way. He rose to his feet in a sudden motion. "She *what?*" He put the phone down and went to the corner for the slicker that was hanging on the stand. As he pulled it on, he addressed the Creole detective. "Well, sir, it seems you're in two places at the same time this afternoon."

"Beg your pardon?" Valentin said.

"There's a gentleman at Our Lady of Sorrows claiming to be you," he said.

Valentin said, "Gregory."

Townes said, "The one who's—"

"Good lord," Lasser said. "What's he doing out here?"

"He's after her," Valentin said. "Evangeline."

"You think he's going to try and kill her now?" Townes said.

"Or take her," Valentin said. He was reeling. How had the murdering bastard located her when he had just now managed it?

Lasser pulled on a wide-brimmed hat, then glanced at Valentin, and said, "I hope you're armed, sir."

When the novitiate in her blue habit and the older woman in a gray frock entered the room, Gregory rose to his feet.

"Mr. St. Cyr?" the novitiate said. "This is Evangeline."

Gregory's first thought was that instead of him deceiving Picot, he was the one being tricked. But that was not possible; the captain didn't have the wiles. The woman who greeted him was too young to be the mother of a forty-year-old man. She didn't look to be much older than that herself. Her eyes were bright and her face was serene, but not in the lost and dreamy way he had come to know from his time in the hospital. This one was alert to the moment; and she was pretending to be someone who was likely hidden somewhere in the convent.

His thoughts raced to the decision to go along with the charade and try to work it to his advantage. With his most sorrowful face, he said, "I heard from a friend in the police department that you were staying at the convent. Some years ago, I lost my mother." Here he offered a somber sigh. "I had hopes that you might be her."

The woman nodded gravely. Behind her, the white-faced novitiate looked ready to bolt. "But I'm afraid I made the trip for nothing," Gregory went on.

The woman in the gray dress said, "I'm sorry," in a voice so low he could barely hear it.

Gregory turned to the novitiate. "I'd like to speak to one of the sisters," he said. In a clever stroke, he tapped the pocket of his shirt. "I brought a gift for the convent."

Sister Sarah was unsure of what to do next. Then a silent signal passed and she said, "Will you be all right?"

"I'll be fine." Again, the voice was barely above a whisper. Glancing back, the novitiate hurried out the door.

Sister Rosalie had always depended on God for calm and she did so now, as the man who claimed to be St. Cyr sat gazing at her with eyes of glass. She did not judge her fellow men and women, but after so many years, felt she could see into their hearts. She knew which of the sisters were the truly godly and she was not so proud as to count herself among them. She knew that Sheriff Lasser was a decent man. And she knew that this fellow's brittle stare announced a heart without pity. His rotting soul wafted off him like a foul odor.

So she was not surprised when he laughed, stood up, and in one smooth motion drew a knife from his pocket and placed it against her throat. He grasped her arm with his free hand.

"You're going with me," he said. "Don't refuse. Or I'll butcher the first person who walks through that door."

Sister Rosalie took a moment to genuflect before rising to her feet.

CHAPTER TWENTY-ONE

Tante Dolores had called up the stairs that she had lunch ready. Justine walked into the kitchen and took a seat at the table, staring in a blank way at her bowl of chicken and rice. Presently, Annette appeared, poured a glass of water from the pitcher and sat down. She treated Justine to a sidelong glance, but said nothing. When Tante Dolores went to place a bowl in front of her, she swept the delicious peppery aromas aside with a wave of her hand.

"What's wrong with you, young miss?" Dolores said. "You don't feel good?"

"I feel fine," Annette said and shrugged. "Just not very hungry right now."

Tante Dolores peered at Justine's bowl. "Look like no one's hungry." She stopped to regard the two younger women with her brow stitched.

As Justine picked up her spoon, she felt Annette's eyes on her again. She decided that she wasn't about to play games and met the gaze full on. A moment passed and Annette's mouth curved in a sly smile.

Sheriff Lasser stared through the windshield while Townes worked the wiper handle. In the back seat, Valentin kept his mind off what was transpiring by checking his pistol. A second police sedan carrying two deputies was following behind.

"Tracks in the mud," the sheriff said as they rolled beneath the dark trees that hung over Bayou Dularge. He slowed when they came up on the statue of the Virgin and still the tires lost their grip when he made the turn onto the narrow trail leading to Our Lady of Sorrows.

Townes leaned to the glass and pointed. "You see there? Parked at the side wall." It was a green Locomobile.

"You know it, Sheriff?" Valentin said.

"It's not from around here," the sheriff said. "That's a city man's machine. A rich city man's."

He pulled up at the gate. With few gestures and fewer words, Lasser directed the two officers in the other sedan to spread out to points on both sides of the convent. He turned to Townes and said, "I need you on the back gate." The Pinkerton drew his revolver, trotted to the north end of the wall, and disappeared around the corner. "We're going in," Lasser said to Valentin. "But no weapons unless he forces our hands." He noticed that the detective was staring at the iron angel standing guard over the gate. "What is it?"

"Nothing." Valentin gave a slight shake of his head. "I'm ready."

The sheriff pushed the gate open and the two men slipped inside to see a gaggle of nuns on the gallery of the reception building. At their center was the Mother Superior. As soon as Sheriff Lasser and Valentin drew within earshot, she called out, "He's taken her!"

"Taken who?" the sheriff said. "Evangeline?"

"No, Sister Rosalie."

The two men had reached the bottom of the steps. The Mother Superior's pale cheeks were flushed and her eyes were wide with worry. "That man came here saying he might be one of Evangeline's relatives. She changed out of her habit and pretended to be her. Sister Sarah came to fetch me and call you. When we got back here, they were both gone."

"Could they still be on the grounds?" the sheriff said.

The sisters murmured like anxious birds. Valentin had been looking down and noticed the scattering of the pebbles on the path. Two people in a hurry. "Sheriff?" he said and pointed.

"Side gate." The sheriff started off.

"Wait," the detective said. "What about...?"

Lasser stopped. "Where's Evangeline?"

"She's locked in a room with two of the sisters," the Mother Superior said. "No one can get to her."

"Then please move the sisters inside."

Following the scattered stones, he and Valentin passed through the side gate. Outside, the forest stretched tangled and green, the earth spongy beneath their feet. Valentin waited for the policeman to reach for his weapon before he drew his Iver Johnson. They began a slow creep along the east wall of the convent, covering the fifty paces with eyes on the ground, following footprints. Every few yards, Lasser would point to a new indentation.

When they reached the corner, the sheriff gave a wave and Ray Lee Townes, who had been standing by the back gate, joined them.

"Anything?" Lasser said.

"Nothing," Townes said.

Keeping his voice low, the sheriff said, "He took one of the nuns. Now we need to track him." He nodded to a break in the trees. "That's the only path. When we get through, we'll have to split up." He started walking, the revolver hanging at his side.

Valentin said, "What's back in there?"

"What you see, for about a mile." He pointed to the northeast. "Lake Du Cade is out that way. So he's got water to cross whichever way he goes. That doesn't mean we have him cornered. With all this foliage, he could still slip past."

They moved in silence for a hundred feet and arrived at a clearing. The sheriff and the Pinkerton peered through the tangle of trees and vines. Valentin surveyed the ground for a few seconds. Bending down, he said, "They came this way."

When the blade flashed and Sister Rosalie felt the tip at her throat, her mind went still. If these were to be her last moments on earth, she wanted whatever violence that would be visited on her to come with peace, her final agony before reaching paradise.

The man had grabbed her bicep and lifted her from the chair. She could sense the tension around him like an electrical charge. An instinct told her to avoid his dead gaze. "I want Evangeline," he said. "Where is she?"

Sister Rosalie braced herself and shook her head, then winced as the blade broke the skin. A tiny rivulet of blood ran down her throat to the collar of the frock.

He hissed at her. "I'm not joking."

She said, "I'm sorry, no."

"Do you know who I am?" She shook her head again. "I'm Gregory."

Sister Rosalie sensed that this was supposed to frighten her. She couldn't think of anything else to say, and in a crazy instant thought of blurting *We've had popes by that name.* Instead, she said, "I'm afraid I don't know you."

"You don't know—" Now he seemed confounded. A few tense seconds passed and he said, "All right. We're leaving." He dropped the blade to her ribcage and steered her through the front door. "How do we get out without being seen?" he said. Rosalie made a gesture.

They passed through the east gate and followed the wall to the gap in the thick underbrush. "Here," he said and shoved her ahead of him along the footpath. The forest closed around them. After a few minutes of steady hiking, they reached a clearing. Gregory came around to her side and turned his head this way and that, looking through the foliage. The sister took the distracted moment to reach to her neck, hook a finger on the thin gold chain that held her cross, and snap it. Chain and cross dropped through her frock and to the soggy earth at her feet.

Gregory made a sudden move and she thought he had seen what she'd done. But he was only resuming his position behind her. He jabbed the knife over her shoulder and toward a break in the trees and said, "That way."

Valentin straightened and held up a gold cross on a broken chain. "It's only been on the ground a few minutes," he said.

Lasser said, "Here's where we split." He pointed to his right. "Mr. Valentin, a hundred yards through there and then turn due north." He put one hand on Townes' shoulder and gestured left with the other. "You do the same through that way."

Valentin's shoes were sturdy, but they weren't cobbled for slogging through a swamp and after a half-mile, he realized he might just as well have gone barefoot. The rain dropping from the leaves was a blessing, as the close air had him sweating. The forest ahead looked exactly like what was over his shoulder. Maybe because he was walking in a small circle.

He weaved through the trees for another fifty yards and picked out more light ahead, while the green to his sides remained dense. That would mean it was the same for Gregory, so he moved more carefully, taking slower steps.

Within a few minutes, he was seeing patches of the flat water of Lake Du Cade. He wondered if anyone had considered the possibility of a pirogue. What if he stepped out of the trees to see

Gregory halfway across and rowing away? And where would the sister from the convent be? Above the surface or somewhere else?

The last few yards to the muddy, root-tangled bank were the hardest and he couldn't keep from raising noise, a joke of a big city sharp floundering about the backwoods. He stepped onto the bare wet ground and leaned a hand against the trunk of a cypress that angled over the water to catch his breath.

"We meet again."

He stepped back and turned around. Thirty feet away stood the man whom he had only glimpsed in the dark of a Storyville alley, again with a woman before him, and again with a knife to her throat. The madam's eyes had been wild with terror; this captive gazed at him with a studied calm, as if unfazed, even with her gray frock splattered with rain and drops of blood.

In the light of day, Valentin saw that Gregory looked different, an odd-shaped young man, round in the middle, with a small head on which pinched eyes and a spike of a nose were planted. His mouth was too wide and his lips too thin and adorned by a sorry excuse for a mustache. Had he been wearing anything but a cruel smirk, he would have been simply homely. But he was ugly to the eye, and Valentin thought of how ghastly that face must have appeared to those poor women in their last terrible seconds.

If Gregory had any idea of a tableau repeating, he showed no sign. Nor did he appear bothered that this time there was no dark maze where he could make an escape. Behind him lay an expanse of green water that was home to alligators and water moccasins. He had only one card to play, in the form of the holy sister who stood between him and the Creole detective.

"What do you think will happen now?" Valentin said.

"Now?" Gregory gave a short laugh. "Now you'll allow me to go back the way I came. With this woman. She's not who I came for."

Now the cruel smile returned. "She's not Evangeline."

Valentin said, "And after that? I've seen you and so has she. The police have your machine. You can't get away."

Gregory studied him. "You've been a worthy foe so far."

"You're not my foe," Valentin said. "You're a killer of helpless women. And that's all you are." He had caught a tiny movement on the periphery of his vision and took a step forward and to his right. Gregory came on alert and posed the blade at a new angle.

Valentin said, "How are you faring, Sister?"

Rosalie said, "God is with me."

"You hear that?" Valentin said. "You hear what she said?" It wasn't much of a gambit, but he needed the seconds. The motion off to Gregory's left was gaining shape. "You harm her, you go to hell."

Gregory stretched his rubbery lips wider. "Oh, I suspect I'll go there anyway. Just not today."

Valentin took another step and it appeared to dawn on Gregory that something was wrong. He started to turn and the blade wavered. At that exact instant, a shot cracked and he spun around and pitched to one side, freeing the sister's arm as he dropped to one knee in the shallow water at the shoreline. Valentin took two long, quick strides and pulled Sister Rosalie to safety.

Sheriff Lasser was standing with his arm extended, smoke drifting from the barrel of his Navy .45. His gaze broadcast such a fierce light that the sister gaped at him as if he was a stranger.

Gregory swayed on the one knee, his eyes bright with pain as he gripped his bloody shoulder. The bullet had chewed the fabric of his coat before passing through the flesh and out again. Ray Lee stepped up with his pistol drawn to snatch the knife from the ground. Sheriff Lasser holstered his weapon and edged along the bank. He pulled his hard stare off Gregory and circled around to Sister Rosalie's side.

"Have you been harmed?" he said.

"I'm all right," the sister said. "The wound isn't deep."

Gregory had managed to sway to his feet. "Why did you come here?" Lasser said. "Why did you come to my parish?"

"For Evangeline."

"How did you find her?"

Gregory now fixed his eyes on Valentin. "I had help. From a friend. A police officer in New Orleans."

Valentin felt a churning in his stomach. Was it ever going to end? "What's your real name?" he said.

Gregory addressed the sheriff. "Are you arresting me?"

"Man asked you to state your name," Lasser said.

"If you see my doctor, he'll explain everything. Dr. Rochelle. In New Orleans."

Townes laughed. "Your *doctor*? What the hell's he talking about?"

Valentin was watching Gregory's face. "He's talking about getting away with it."

Again, Gregory said, "I want to see Dr. Rochelle." Now he sounded like a petulant child.

Sheriff Lasser listened, his expression turning distant. The others waited. Gregory was opening his mouth to complain some more when the sheriff said, "Mr. Townes, please escort Sister Rosalie back to the convent and have her wound treated."

Sister Rosalie blinked. "Sheriff?"

"It's all right, Sister. Go with Mr. Townes."

Sister Rosalie moved toward the trees with Ray Lee following behind. The sheriff said, "Mr. Townes?" The Pinkerton hung back as the sister walked ahead. "Not a word," Lasser said. Townes gave a nod and continued trailing the nun into the woods. The sheriff waited until the sounds of their progress had faded to silence before turning back to the prisoner. "A hospital? Is that your intention?"

262

Gregory said, "Well, that's where I belong. The doctor will tell you. He's been treating me for years." He whispered as if shamed over the admission. "Can we go now? I'm hurt." His cheeks were white and his green eyes twitching.

Lasser regarded him for a few seconds more, then said, "Mr. St. Cyr? You can return to the convent as well, sir."

"What?" Gregory said. "What's this?"

Valentin gave him a last look before starting back into the woods. Behind him, he heard the high voice going thin with panic. "Wait! Hold on, now. Where's he going? I want Dr. Rochelle. I *demand* to see him."

As the Creole detective made his way deeper into the woods, he heard the sheriff say, "You shouldn't have come here."

Valentin caught up with Townes and his charge a few hundred yards along the path. The woman who only minutes before had brushed close to a grisly death was concerned for the sheriff.

"Where is he?" she asked. "Is he all right?"

Townes mumbled something about Lasser staying behind so as not to endanger her further, but it was clear from her narrow gaze that she didn't believe him. She went quiet, tramping along and thinking her own thoughts until the white walls of the convent came into view.

The women who devoted their lives to silence and obedience turned rowdy when Valentin and Ray Lee opened the gates for Sister Rosalie. A dozen of the nuns swept forward to surround their sister, a flock of shouting and weeping monochrome birds. Their excitement lasted until the Mother Superior clapped her hands and reminded them that their sister needed to get to the infirmary. As Rosalie was hustled away, she gazed back at Valentin and Ray Lee Townes with a tragic shadow upon her good face.

The two men retreated to the shelter of the small gallery at the front of the reception area. The rain had ebbed and they stood watching the gate for the sheriff. Townes said, "You know where a man might get a drink in this place?"

Valentin laughed shortly. "I'm guessing they've got a wine cellar somewhere. The Mother Superior will have the key. If you want to ask her for it."

Townes said, "No, thanks. I can wait." He and Valentin studied the rain dropping from the trees. "You think we should go back and check on him?"

Valentin said, "I think we should leave it be." The Pinkerton didn't ask again.

Twenty minutes later, Lasser stepped through the front gate. He was alone. Standing directly beneath the iron angel, he beckoned to Valentin and Townes and the detectives left the gallery to join him. He ordered one of the junior officers waiting by the road to drive the Locomobile back to town. Then he and the two private detectives climbed into the Baker.

When they arrived in Houma, Lasser parked the vehicle and they climbed out. Before they went into the building, he stopped and said, "He tried to escape. He ran into the water and went under. That's the last I saw of him."

He waited to see if Valentin and Townes had anything to say. When neither man spoke, he opened the door for them.

CHAPTER TWENTY-TWO

Valentin had lived most of his life in New Orleans. On only three occasions had he wandered away for any length of time, the first two for a couple years, the last for a few months. In all those travels, he had stayed mostly to cities, where he knew how to operate and could stay hidden. Even so, he knew small towns and the deep country well enough to understand that they had their own ways of dealing with crime and punishment.

Sheriff Lasser had shaken hands with Valentin and Ray Lee Townes and explained that they would be contacted if needed. He thanked them for their time, proceeded to his office, and closed the door. Outside, Townes said, "You ready for that drink? There's a place back by the tracks."

Valentin said, "You start. I'll be there in an hour."

The Pinkerton treated him with a wise look. "Are you going back to the convent?"

"I'll see you in an hour," Valentin said.

When Valentin arrived at Our Lady of Sorrows, he asked to see the Mother Superior and was escorted to her office. That sober but not unkind woman greeted him with fervent thanks for helping to rescue Sister Rosalie.

"How is she?" he asked.

"She's fine. She looks like a wounded soldier." She regarded the visitor, her brow stitching. "Who was that man?"

265

"Someone we've been after in New Orleans," Valentin said. "A murder suspect." When her eyes widened, he tapped his temple to indicate a broken mind. "One of those cases."

"What happened to him?"

"He tried to escape Sheriff Lasser out on the bayou. He went into the water and likely drowned."

"I don't understand what he wanted here."

"He wanted to find Evangeline. It's very complicated. I'm not quite sure about all of it myself." He could tell the Mother Superior was perplexed, but she did not probe further. Valentin shifted in his chair. "But that's why I'm here," he said." I'd like to speak with her, if I may."

She studied his face, looking for something. Then she said, "I'll call for Sister Rosalie. It will be her decision."

When Sister Rosalie came to collect Evangeline, the older woman was startled by the bandages. When she said there had been an accident, she could tell Evangeline didn't believe her. She had always been a terrible liar. Her mother had always known and would lay a finger to her lips.

The Mother Superior had sent Valentin to the dining hall to wait. The sister broke into a smile when she saw one of her protectors standing at the window and watching the clearing sky. Her throat was swathed in a cotton bandage that peeked above the neckline of her habit. Other than that, she appeared in good spirits. Along with her was a woman dressed in a plain blue frock.

The nun beckoned to him and Valentin approached, feeling his nerves beginning to jump.

"Evangeline," Sister Rosalie said. "This is Mr. Valentin."

"Did you say Valentin?"

"Yes, ma'am."

The older woman regarded him in the most curious way, her head tilted to one side and mouth holding a shadow of a smile. Valentin stood back so as not to disquiet her, and watching the sister, who did most of the talking. He did not trust the swirling notion that she was in some odd way familiar.

She asked where he had come from. When he explained, she said, "I lived there once." She glanced at Sister Rosalie, who said, "You had a house."

"Yes. A house. I had a husband. And children."

Valentin pushed down an urge to press her. *Where did you live? What were their names? Do you know me at all?* If she was a stranger, there was nothing he could do to make it otherwise. But if she wasn't...

"What about you?" Evangeline was asking. "Do you have a wife?"

"I do," Valentin said. "No children. Not yet."

"Not yet." Evangeline smiled. "Maybe someday. Children are a blessing." Her face was serene. The nun and the detective waited for more. She said, "Well, we all have things to do." It was not a dismissal, more a statement of fact.

Valentin pondered for a few moments, then turned to Sister Rosalie. "It's time for me to get on my way back to New Orleans. But first I need a moment of your time."

When he stood up, Evangeline broke away from whatever thoughts were holding her, smiled a lovely smile, and said, "Thank you for coming to see me." She clasped Valentin's hand in hers.

The nun and the detective stepped outside to find the last fat drops off the trees pattering on the white stones. They walked to the front gate. "I'm worried about Sheriff Lasser," she said.

"The sheriff is fine," Valentin said.

"I'm not talking about his health."

"You think he needs to speak to a priest?"

"I think he needs to speak to God. About whatever happened out on the lake."

Valentin gazed off into the green forest, thinking about the solid strength of some women. From those of flesh and blood, like the sisters in the convent and his wife and Evangeline, to the iron angel that stood guard over the front gate. "I have something to ask," he said.

Sister Rosalie waited for him to continue, though he had a sense that she knew what he was going to say.

Captain Picot had become more agitated as the morning progressed. He was now certain that he had made a horrible mistake by choosing to ignore his cop instincts and joining a crazed murderer in a scheme to bring down St. Cyr and at the same time deal Storyville a fatal blow.

Now he saw with sudden clarity that it would never have worked. His career could be in its death throes even as he stood there — and his very life in danger, too. If St. Cyr discovered his treachery, what would stop him from ending their business at long last by putting him in his grave?

When midafternoon came and went with no call, he felt the fear welling in his gut with a sickening weight. He had two choices: to wait for lightning to strike or to move. He made a call to headquarters and then beckoned Cassidy into his office to tell him that he was leaving the building and would be absent for the next two or three days. He had cleared it with the major. He explained that his business was of a confidential nature, but he would be calling. Otherwise, he would not be near a telephone. If there was a dire emergency, the clerk could post a notice in the Personals section of the newspaper addressed to "The Captain."

Picot felt Cassidy's baffled stare as he collected a handful of papers and made a quick and quiet exit. He walked to the rear of the building, climbed into his automobile, and motored due north out of the city to the hamlet of Spanish Fort. He parked the machine beneath the lake house that was mostly hidden from the road and leaned the old boards that he had stacked there against both sides, blocking it from view.

The house been vacated when he had run a criminal of means out of the city. Somehow the deed had fallen into his hands and he had kept it as a hiding place, should a need arise. At times, he had thought this a foolish worry. Now he was glad for the refuge. Though it would not save him. He could not hide there for long. Soon he would have to make a decision to stand and fight or run.

Valentin found the little box of a saloon along the tracks and the Pinkerton at a corner table inside. He ordered a whiskey and the two men sat sipping in silence.

"That Picot," Townes said.

"What about him?"

"He's going to be shitting in his britches about now. What the hell was he thinking? Going in cahoots with that fucking..." He jerked a thumb in the direction of the bayou.

"I'll ask when I see him," Valentin said.

The Pinkerton's mouth twisted. "And then what?"

"*Then what* will be up to him."

Valentin asked the bartender if he could use the telephone and laid enough money down for three calls. The barkeep brought the set and he first called the Parish Precinct and got Detective McKinney on the line.

"Good afternoon, sir." The officer knew better than to speak a name. Valentin could hear tension in his voice. "What's the news?"

"I don't think we'll be seeing that fellow again."

McKinney didn't speak for a few seconds. Then he said, "So it's over."

"No, it's not," Valentin said. "There's still the matter of your captain. He was in on it."

"I knew it," McKinney said. "That's why he left."

"What are you talking about?"

"He left the building and didn't tell anyone where he was going. He just told his clerk he wouldn't be back for a few days."

"I want to find him before he disappears," Valentin said.

"I'll see what I can do."

Valentin thanked him and broke the connection. He next reached Justine at the Albertons'. "You survived the weather," he said.

"Where are you?" she said. The connection was rough. "I've been calling the house."

"I'm in Terrebonne," he said and waited for an eruption.

What he heard was a long silence. Finally, she said, "Does this have to do with Gregory?"

"It does." He paused. "I'll tell you when I get back."

"What about the woman?"

"I'll tell you about her, too." He paused. "Has anything happened there?"

"Oh, yes," she said. By the tone of her voice, he understood she couldn't say more.

"I'll be there in two hours," he said. "And I'll come for you."

"Please," she said.

Justine climbed the stairs to the second floor. Annette's door was standing halfway open and she could see the girl standing by one of her windows. "Miss?" she said.

Annette didn't turn around. "Come in."

Justine stepped into the room. Before she could speak, Annette said, "You have a husband."

"I do, yes," Justine said.

"Is he a good husband?"

"He is."

"He doesn't stray?"

"He wouldn't." Justine paused to smile. "He knows better."

"But you don't take him for granted."

"Never."

Annette considered the street for a few moments. "It's wrong."

"What is?"

"To dismiss people. To treat them like they don't matter. Don't belong."

Justine remained silent, waiting. When Annette didn't continue, she said, "Do you want to tell me about Emelie?"

Annette turned her head slightly. "You mean my sister?" she said. "Close the door, please."

The first part of the drive back to New Orleans passed without incident. Valentin would have preferred a downpour to keep his thoughts off the last moments at the lake and Picot and Evangeline. While the roads were muddy enough to hold his attention, they weren't bad enough to give his musings peace.

After Des Allemands, the patches turned to a steady drizzle and he was working the wiper handle again. He could see clouds moving on his right as if to intercept him, hurrying to play their part as background for what would happen once he crossed the river.

Justine opened the door, readying herself to leave. Annette's pretty face was tragic. "What will you do?"

"About what?"

"Will you be back tomorrow?"

"If I'm needed."

Annette's eyes shifted. "You're not a maid, are you?"

"Is my work that bad?"

Annette laughed and shook her head. Her expression deepened and she looked away. A tear welled in her eye.

Justine said, "My last name is St. Cyr." She spelled it out. "On Lesseps Street. The number is in the book. If you want to reach me. Or if someone else does."

Annette dabbed her cheek. "Maybe you'll be back tomorrow."

"Yes, maybe," Justine said. She stepped into the hallway. Annette closed the door.

Justine went to find Tante Dolores on the back gallery and ask if she could leave if her husband could brave the streets to collect her.

Dolores eyed her for a few seconds before saying, "Yes, go on whilst you can. No tellin' what's goin' to happen 'round here." She was back to her wily self, leaving Justine to wonder what she was supposed to read from her words. There would be no getting her to reveal more. She reminded Justine of the voodoo women she had known growing up on the bayou. Though Tante Dolores couldn't match their cunning. Valentin would scoff at such talk. Justine refused to dismiss their powers. She had seen them at work.

Valentin was beginning to think of the storm, distant but still visible, as his traveling companion. Or perhaps another villain looking for a fight. Of course, he knew better. He was no Quixote. So he bent his head to whatever angry god had sent this latest hindrance and drove on until he reached the river. This time, he had to wait the better part of an hour before he caught sight of the ferry leaving the New Orleans side and sloughing his way.

As he drove on, he heard one of the deckhands telling the man in the car next to his that this would be the last run of the day. The river was getting too choppy. The ramp buckled as he drove onto the pier. As he navigated streets littered with fallen branches, it occurred to him that Justine wouldn't know when he was outside.

He hadn't given her enough credit. As he crept past the house, he saw movement in one window. When he pulled into the alley behind the house, now a shallow stream of muddy water, she came off the back gallery and crossed the garden to the gate.

She climbed into the cab, her face bright with relief at seeing him, and he was struck anew by how lovely she was. The feeling had come from nowhere. No, not true; the murdering madman and the mysterious woman in the bayou convent had done their parts, shaking his core. He leaned close and kissed her with passion.

She pulled back and opened her eyes wide. "You should go off more often," she said.

When they reached the house, the rain was performing a quiet dance on the roof. Valentin decided that calling Mr. Tom and McKinney could wait. In fact, the whole world could wait.

He started the hot water running in the bathtub, pulled off his still-damp clothes, and eased down, letting the steam wrap around him. In the kitchen, Justine pulled what was left of the chicken from the icebox and started a low flame under a pot of water. Once the rice was simmering, she reached for the bottle of Raleigh Rye, poured two glasses half-full and carried them to the bathroom. She sat down on the small chair and placed one of the glasses on the rim of the tub. "So," she said. "Tell me."

He sat up and began with the plan that Picot and Gregory had come together to devise and how it had gone badly from the start, both of them consumed by their manias. He moved on to

Terrebonne Parish and Sister Rosalie and the chase through the bayou to the bank of the lake where it had ended. Finally, he described the quiet moments with Evangeline that followed. She didn't question him until he had finished and leaned back.

"Well?" she said. "Is she?"

"I don't know who she is," he said.

It was her turn. She told him that Emelie was a child born of George Alberton and Belle Baptiste, that she had seen the proof, and that Annette had related the rest of the story. Alberton, his wife, and Belle had kept it a secret. But as Emelie grew older, she began to suspect something, and finally got her mother to confess the truth. When she turned sixteen, she began hinting that she wanted him to declare her as his blood.

"And give her all the privileges of his name," Valentin said.

"Correct," Justine said. "He refused, so she began behaving badly. She went with Paul and let him have his way with her and then made sure her mother and father found out. Instead of doing the sensible thing and making peace, Alberton used it against her. And her mother.

"How?"

"He had Belle tell Emelie she would lose her position. Emelie would be on the street as well. He threatened his own daughter."

"So she ran off."

"It wasn't the first time. This time, she stayed away. She and Paul have a room somewhere. They started with the telephone calls. As a way to threaten her father. But it was all a farce. And there's Beatrice. The other daughter."

"What about her?"

"She's marrying well. The fiancé's father is president of the largest bank in Baton Rouge. Can you imagine the word getting out that she has a colored half-sister?"

Valentin didn't tell her that he was amazed by how she had worked through the puzzle — as if he would have expected anything less.

She said, "So why did he hire a detective in the first place? If he wanted this kept quiet, I mean."

Valentin sipped his whiskey and thought about it. "He never asked me to bring her home. Only to find her."

"So he could get to her."

He splashed handfuls of water of his face. "I missed that, too."

"Well, you had the other case on your mind," Justine said. After a moment, she said, "Why didn't he just stand up for her? Who would have cared? This is New Orleans."

Valentin said, "I stopped trying to understand these people long ago." He pulled the brass chain to drain the water. "I'm done here."

Valentin told the King of Storyville that he needn't worry about Gregory anymore and that the District could go back to business as usual. Anderson didn't sound as pleased by this news as he had expected and Valentin wondered if he secretly wished for the demise of his little empire and the peace that would bring.

"So when can we sit down and talk?" the old man asked.

"Not tomorrow," Valentin said. "The next day. Right now, I need a favor from you."

He found Justine in the kitchen, standing at the stove with a wooden spoon in her hand and a brooding gaze fixed somewhere beyond the dark window. When he stepped close and kissed her cheek, she smiled. Then she noticed the look in his eyes. "What is it?" she said.

"I'm going back to Terrebonne tomorrow. And I want you to come with me."

CHAPTER TWENTY-THREE

When morning arrived with the sky a clear azure with only high streaks of cloud, Justine called Tante Dolores to explain that she was not coming to work. The housekeeper responded with the kind of *mmms* and *ahhs* that told her this was no surprise to her. Valentin took a turn with the telephone to call Sister Rosalie at the convent and make sure there were no problems with their arrangement.

They ate breakfast and then drove to Anderson's house on Marengo Street, where they left the Ford and took the King of Storyville's blue Maxwell. At the front door, Mister Tom kissed Justine's cheek and shook Valentin's hand and wished them well on their journey.

Captain Picot slipped into the Western Union office on Poydras Street and used the booth in the back corner to call the section. When Cassidy came on the line, he asked for any news or messages. The clerk was vexed by the captain's strange behavior. He was not yet a detective, but he had the wits to sense something even more out of kilter with that odd egg.

It was business as usual in the department and he gave Picot his report in a few quick sentences. There had been no breaks in any of their major cases. Calls had come from upstairs regarding minor matters. No one had inquired further about the captain's absence.

When he finished, the captain said, "I'll call later today. Or maybe not until tomorrow." The line went dead.

Cassidy settled the handset in the cradle. Detective McKinney was at his desk, his head bent and hand scrawling a report. The clerk spent a half-minute agonizing, then rose and crossed the room.

McKinney looked up. "Officer?"

"Could I have a minute of your time, sir?" The detective gestured to a chair. Cassidy said, "No, I mean in private."

This time, the river crossing was smooth and they sped south. The day before, Valentin had driven into an angry tunnel the color of dark slate. Now the road ahead was awash in swaths of buttery light and the breeze was a cool swirl.

They talked about this and that as the miles rolled by, steering clear of the business at hand. Once they had passed through Des Allemands, Valentin fell silent, gripping the big wooden wheel and watching the road ahead. Justine held a hand into the wind and left him to his thoughts.

When they reached Houma, he drove at a slow pace along Main Street, then turned onto Barrow Street and Bayou Dularge Road, and passed beneath the overhang of trees. Now that they were so close, he was driving at an almost hesitant pace.

They arrived at the statue of the Virgin and he steered the Maxwell down the narrow road. It had been a long time since Justine had been in the country and she gazed through the trees until the white walls of the convent appeared. Valentin pulled onto the gravel, stopped, and turned off the engine, leaving the forest silent save for the rustling of the leaves.

Justine waited for him to move, passing her gaze over the heavy door and settling on the iron angel at the top of the arch. For a moment, she imagined that the eyes were staring straight at her husband. She laughed, rousing him. "Are we going in?" she said.

"Yes," he said. "They're waiting."

~

They watched from the gallery as Sister Rosalie and Evangeline crossed the grounds. During the drive, Valentin had been reminding himself that the older woman might have had a change of heart. Now he saw her approaching with the nun, who held a satchel in each hand. They descended the steps and Valentin stepped forward to take the bags.

"Here we are," Sister Rosalie said.

Evangeline regarded Valentin with the same curiosity, then looked past him to Justine. "Is this your wife?"

"Yes, ma'am."

"I'm pleased to meet you," Justine said.

Valentin said, "We have a car outside."

"Yes, yes," the sister said. "We're all ready."

As he led the three women through the gate, it occurred to Valentin that Evangeline had not stepped outside the grounds in a month. He glanced back to see her proceeding with elegant calm, murmuring to Sister Rosalie on one side and to Justine on the other. He helped his passengers into the Maxwell, then cranked the engine and climbed up behind the wheel.

"We're traveling to New Orleans?" Evangeline said.

Justine said, "Yes, ma'am."

"I lived there once."

"That was a long time ago," Sister Rosalie said.

Evangeline began to respond, then caught herself. "It's a pretty day for a drive." As they pulled away, she gazed back at the convent gate. Then she turned around and settled in the seat.

Detective McKinney took Cassidy down the back stairs to an interrogation room that was set out of the way and intended for suspects and witnesses of such standing that the brass wanted them hidden from probing eyes. The room was furnished with an oak table and comfortable chairs, glass ashtrays, and brass spittoons. Heavy drapes covered the single window. The walls had been painted a gentle shade of beige.

The detective closed the door and motioned Cassidy to a chair. The clerk began without preamble, starting with Captain Picot's requests for information from the records room and the newspaper morgue, to the officer's terse words about his absence and the orders regarding phone calls.

"You still have no idea where he's gone?" McKinney said.

"He didn't tell me. Just said it was a personal matter. That the major approved it." Cassidy shifted in his chair. "He telephoned a few minutes ago. Asking if I had anything to report. The call only lasted a minute. It's just strange, sir."

McKinney folded his hands before him. "I want you to think like a detective. Go back to the call. Did you hear anything in the background? Any special noises?"

Cassidy fidgeted in distraction. "I'm not sure. I don't think so."

"Close your eyes." The clerk did as he was told. "Did you hear traffic? How about horns? Ship horns, I mean." Cassidy shook his head. "Birds? A crowd of people?" The clerk started to shake his head again, then stopped and opened his eyes. "What is it?" McKinney said.

"Music."

"Music?" McKinney said. "What kind? A marching band. Jass? Or a piano like in a saloon? What?"

"No..." The clerk bit his lip, then said, "Like they have at the circus. Or on a merry-go-round. The organ. The, uh..."

"Calliope?"

Cassidy gave a quick nod. "Yes. Like that."

McKinney mulled the information. "God damn," he said.

"Detective?"

McKinney said, "You did great work today. Great *police* work. Now I need you to keep quiet about it. Don't tell anyone until it's over."

Cassidy was giddy with pleasure, but baffled. "Until what's over?"

The detective didn't reply. Instead, he said, "Go back to your desk and attend to your work. If the captain calls again, pay attention to everything you hear. Then come find me. Understand?"

"Yes, sir."

McKinney tilted this head. "Go on, then."

The clerk made a happy exit, his face flushed. Once the door closed, the detective crossed to the corner, picked up the telephone, and dialed the number from memory. After eight rings, he hung up. He opened the curtains a few inches and stared out at the street, his thoughts churning over what would happen when he finally reached Mr. Valentin.

The sun had dried the slick roads and the ride from Terrebonne went more quickly. Valentin concentrated on driving while the women chatted. Now and then, his mind wandered to the odd happenstance of having a pious nun who had only the day before been the hostage of a murderer, a one-time Storyville sporting girl, and a mysterious woman who lived without memories, all in the same vehicle. Who knew what the three of them were thinking as they motored toward the city? What they shared was the common sense to keep their conversation on everyday matters.

When they arrived at the ferry dock, Evangeline looked out at the river and said, "the Mississippi," in a long breath, as if savoring the name. As they passed east through the city, she studied the streets with a faint wonder.

They arrived at the house on Lesseps Street and Valentin helped the ladies down. Inside, Justine showed their guests to the bathroom, then went to the kitchen to start coffee and lay out a plate of tea cakes from the bakery. She and Valentin had decided to let Sister Rosalie and Evangeline have the house while they stayed at the Crescent, the closest decent hotel. But when they explained this, Sister Rosalie said that she preferred that they stay with Evangeline as their guest while she took a room in the rectory at Immaculate Conception. One of the nuns was a nurse who could tend to the dressing on her wound.

"If it's not any trouble," Evangeline said after the nun had gone off to use the telephone.

"No, please, that would be grand," Justine said.

Sister Rosalie returned and the women moved to the table. Valentin did not take part, though he traded inquisitive glances with their elder guest. After they finished their coffee, Justine asked if the women would help her with dinner.

Evangeline's eyes lit up and said, "Yes, please. It's been so long."

Valentin was sent to the corner market two blocks over with a shopping list. When he returned with a sack in each hand, he stopped in the kitchen doorway and watched his wife and their guests work and chat. It was a comforting scene and at first he couldn't quite put his finger on why it felt foreign to him. Then he realized that he was observing the common ritual of a family gathering. Something he had lost long ago in the darker shadows of his childhood.

He placed the bags on the sideboard. Justine leaned close to kiss his cheek. He took off his coat and went into the cabinet for a

281

bottle of wine and four glasses. After he filled the glasses, he retreated to the table.

The meal was cordial and the women's conversation more like soft music. When dinner was finished and the wine bottles empty, Valentin got up to clear the plates. Sister Rosalie announced that she was tired and asked if he could please carry her to the church. They said their good-nights. He picked up her satchel and escorted her out the door to the Maxwell.

As they drove away, she said, "I believe she's happy to be at your home."

"I hope that's true."

The sister paused to regard him. "So? What do you think?"

"About what?"

Her mouth tilted. "About Evangeline. And who she might be."

"I don't know, Sister. I'm not thinking about it right now."

Sister Rosalie nodded as if she had expected this reply. She didn't speak again until they rounded the corner at North Roman Street. "What happened yesterday..."

Valentin said, "Yes?"

"We should not have left the sheriff alone with him. We should have stayed. I failed my duty to God. He spared me and I failed Him."

Valentin thought about it. "Isn't this what confession is for?"

"It is," she said. "That doesn't change anything."

Valentin drove on for a few silent moments. "I fell away from the church, Sister," he said. "I don't remember the last time I went to Mass. So I can't say anything about it. We did what the sheriff asked. What he thought was best."

The sister let another street go by. "Fell away why?"

"I was beckoned in other directions," Valentin said. "And I went."

He readied himself to hear some homily about everyone being

tempted to stray from God. But the sister studied his face for a few moments, then nodded and watched the passing traffic.

An older nun was waiting when they pulled up at Immaculate Conception. Valentin climbed down and walked around to open the passenger door and help Sister Rosalie. "I'll call here tomorrow," he said.

Sister Rosalie held his hand for a moment. "He's here for you," she said. "When you're ready." She turned away and the two nuns walked around the side of the building.

Valentin drove on to Marengo Street. The King of Storyville had already gone to bed. Edward said the old man was having his first good sleep in a week. Valentin left the Maxwell and drove the Ford back across town. Moving from the grand touring car to the roadster was like stepping from a yacht into a pirogue. As he parked, he reminded himself that he was lucky to be driving anything.

He unlocked the front door to the sound of the voices from the kitchen. He was on his way there when the telephone chirped.

Justine heard Valentin coming through the door. When he didn't appear, she stepped to the foyer to see him standing with the handset to his ear, staring at the floor. He was so fixed on what he was hearing that he didn't notice her and she slipped away again.

He appeared in the kitchen, still looking distracted, though he managed a smile. "How are you faring?" he asked Evangeline.

"I'm well." She treated him to a searching look. "But you're not. What is it?"

"I'm fine, ma'am." He turned to Justine. "There's something I have to do. I have to go out again," he said.

"Now?"

"It won't take long. I'm sorry," he said to Evangeline.

She stared him for another intense moment, her smile fading. "Please be careful," she said.

On the drive north along Elysian Fields, he mulled what McKinney had told him about Picot dropping from sight. It was all he needed to know. Gregory hadn't been telling a story. Somehow, he and Picot had conspired with each other. The captain had told him what he'd learned about the woman in the Terrebonne Parish convent and a possible connection to a certain private detective. Whether Picot directed him or Gregory came to his own decision, he made the fatal decision to travel there. To do what? Kidnap Evangeline? Murder her? That two unstable minds had hatched the crazy plot confounded him; he wasn't that important. Now McKinney had discovered that the conspirator who was still alive might be holed up somewhere along Lake Pontchartrain, no more than a mile away.

Valentin turned onto Edinburg Avenue as the last of the daylight slipped over the horizon. When he drew near Spanish Fort, the shadows were already deep and he could see the glitter of lights from the amusements at the north end of the park. After a few minutes, a Studebaker runabout stopped behind him. The music from the merry-go-round that had given Picot away had ended for the day, but Valentin could see the gay lights of the amusement ride glittering in the dark.

The detectives met between their automobiles. McKinney didn't waste time on a greeting. "Most of the summer homes don't have telephones yet. There's a Western Union office up on Columbia, by the pier. You can hear the music from the merry-go-round from there."

"Good thing he didn't think of that." Valentin said.

"I'm guessing that he's in a panic," McKinney said.

"You know he could be miles away by now. He has a machine, doesn't he?"

McKinney produced a mirthless smile. "A red six-cylinder Premier. One year old. On a captain's salary. It's a big joke inside the department."

"So he won't be parading it around."

"I don't think he's that stupid."

They began the three-block walk along Preaux, following the bayou to Columbia. The lake houses stretched in both directions from the pier. Now that the schools had reopened for the fall, most of the homes had been vacated, leaving only a handful still occupied.

They reached the corner. The pier was just across the way. "If you go east, I'll go west," McKinney said. "Check for lights in windows. How about we meet back here in a half-hour?"

Valentin gave a nod and a wave and walked off.

Detective McKinney made his way along the narrow dirt road that began at the pier and wound west. He passed a half-dozen houses, slowing his steps and casting what would appear a casual eye at each structure. None of the first six showed lights from inside, nor were there any automobiles parked beside or beneath those homes raised on pilings. Only one dwelling showed lamplight and he saw the silhouettes of two women framed in the window. After walking for ten minutes, he stopped. Next came an empty stretch of a hundred paces before the houses began again and all of them were dark. So he turned around.

He arrived back at the pier and stood gazing out at the calm water. The moon was hazing over, yet still reflecting little points of light off the peaks of the waves. The night had gone quiet. He heard footsteps approaching.

St. Cyr's face showed nothing as he said, "I found him."

As they walked eastward on a path that kept them mostly out of sight, the Creole detective described the dim glow of a lamp through a slat of a shutter. The house had been silent as he approached and circled to the side. The other windows were shuttered as well. He thought he heard the sound of someone moving about, but couldn't be sure.

"It was all dark below the deck. I went under and found out why." He made a steeple of his fingers. "Boards leaned against a nineteen-thirteen Premier. Ruby red."

Now McKinney stopped. "Which house?"

Valentin pointed to the third one along, a tidy clapboard bungalow with a deck that stretched halfway to the shoreline, half of it screened. In silence, they moved to the side of the house and then beneath the deck.

McKinney peered through the boards and whispered, "That's it, goddamn it."

While the policeman stepped back out to watch the house, Valentin made slow work of lifting three of the boards and then one side of the bonnet. Feeling his way, he found the magneto wire and pulled it loose. It was hardly possible that Picot could escape them, but if he somehow managed that, he wouldn't be driving away.

Valentin dropped the wire into his pocket. He and McKinney climbed wooden steps to the door of the screened part of the deck. The policeman stared at Valentin for a few pensive seconds, then leaned close to whisper, "Whatever you decide to do in there, I won't stop it."

Valentin raised his bent head. McKinney opened the screened door. He caught a breath and followed. They inched their way across the deck and took sides at the back door. McKinney drew his police revolver.

For Valentin, the next half-minute dragged out like a long road, with a grim question hanging like a cloud. Picot had mounted a last desperate campaign to destroy him. He had likely also dreamed of taking down Anderson and Storyville with him. That two more innocent women might have died in this crusade didn't signify. And what had he hoped to gain? A delicious kind of revenge? A triumph over a foe? Escape from a blood curse that only he perceived? The case of the murdered jass players had happened almost seven years in the past. It seemed to Valentin such a long time ago.

He knew there was no point in asking these questions. Nothing would change. Now he wondered if he possessed the will to step inside the house and put a bullet into that same man's heart. If the small body of water in Terrebonne Parish could hide Gregory's remains, the one just a few yards distant would never give up the body of J. Picot. The threat he posed would be forever vanquished.

McKinney was watching and waiting. He reached into his pocket and laid fingers on the butt of the Iver Johnson. Would the world would be a better place with Picot gone, as it was with Gregory at the bottom of Lake Du Cade? Valentin felt something settling on his shoulders and taking on weight. He imagined the door opening, the look on Picot's face, and the final seconds.

Picot was replaced by Evangeline, just out of the frame, her eyes deep pools of worry, saying, *Please, don't do this. Don't.* He pushed the image away, drew his revolver and whispered, "Ready."

McKinney produced a skeleton key like the one all coppers carried, fit it into the keyhole, and turned. The lock slipped back. He laid a hand on the knob and gave it a slow twist. Valentin was about to say, *Wait!* when McKinney shoved the door open, slid inside in a single fluid motion, and scrambled a hand to the light

287

switch. Valentin leveled his revolver as the lamp lit the room with a hot yellow glare.

Justine and Evangeline spent the hours talking in gentle circles. Much of it was the older woman asking questions. That was after they had washed and dried the dishes and returned to the table and the wine.

Evangeline touched her temple. "Did the sister tell you about me?"

"She told Valentin," Justine said. "He told me."

"I can remember bits and pieces. More as time goes on." She smiled. "But you know it's not such a tragedy. I don't recall all the bad things."

Or all the good ones, Justine mused. The older woman asked about her upbringing, where she had lived, how she had met Mr. Valentin. Justine laid out the story, steering around the ugly and sordid parts. All the while, she was watching Evangeline in search of a clue. There was nothing striking about her features that matched Valentin's. And yet something resided in her stillness that reminded her of him. Both observed the world with a creature calm, alert and relaxed at the same time.

As the night wore on, Evangeline began casting fretful glances in the direction of the front door. Presently, she said, "It's late, isn't it? When will he be back?" When Justine asked if she was tired and ready to sleep, she said, "I'll stay up, if you don't mind."

It was winding toward eleven o'clock when the rattling of an engine echoed along Lesseps Street. Justine rose from her chair and Evangeline sat up and gave a small sigh. They both left the kitchen for the foyer. When the key rattled in the lock, Justine stayed where she was and let the older woman step forward. Evangeline's face was infused with a light so kind that it made her want to weep.

"You're home," Evangeline said.

Justine poured her husband a glass of wine. She and Evangeline finished the few sips left in their glasses while he relaxed. The older woman looked on him in a fond way and then placed her glass on the table and said, "It's time. I'm tired."

Justine saw her to bed and when she returned, she had changed into the silk shawl that Valentin had bought for her back at the beginning, a design of peacocks on flowered branches. Her feet were bare and with her hair pulled into two braids and her eyes bright in the darkness, he wondered if she had ever looked as lovely. Of course she had, time and again over the years, in random moments that always made him go weak and reminded him that he was where he belonged.

She sat down again. Valentin had refilled their glasses. He spent a still moment, then took her through the previous two hours, beginning when he and McKinney met and up to the instant when the policeman pushed the door wide and threw the light switch.

"I had my weapon drawn," he told her. "But in that last second, I knew I couldn't do it." He placed his fist beneath his chin. "If he had been in there, I might be dead. But he wasn't." He described the empty front room and their search of the rest of the lake house. The kitchen cupboards were bare. The ice chest was empty. The bed had been stripped.

"But his automobile was under the house."

Valentin produced a blank smile. "Oh, yes." He reached into his pocket for the magneto wire. "I fixed it so he couldn't drive it. But it didn't matter. He was already gone. That model would be too easy to spot. So he left it behind."

"And now what?"

"Now, I don't know," Valentin said. "It depends on if he comes back. I have a feeling that he won't. Not for a long time. We'll see."

He took a sip of wine. "Do you have something to tell me?"

"I do," Justine said. "I was—"

She stopped at the sharp rapping on the front door. "Were you expecting someone this late?" she said.

He shook his head and rose from the chair. His revolver was still in his coat pocket. She followed him to the foyer. He peeked through the small curtain to see two figures standing on the opposite banquette, draped in the night mist. "Come look," he said.

Justine moved to his side and stared. "Emelie," she said.

When Valentin opened the door and they moved onto the gallery, Emelie stepped off the banquette. They saw that she was dressed in a common shift with a pullover sweater draped across her shoulders. Her companion — it would be Paul — hung back, huddled in an overcoat and with his slouch hat pulled low.

Emelie called, "Miss Justine?"

The two women met in the middle of the quiet street and spoke in low voices. It was over in less than a minute. Justine put a gentle hand on Emelie's shoulder. Then she and Valentin watched the young girl and her beau fade into the night. Lesseps Street lay in somber silence once again.

"Come back inside," Valentin said.

He went to the kitchen to fetch their wine glasses. When he stepped into the living room, Justine was at the window.

"You told me that you always pay more attention to why people do things to solve your cases," she said. "So that's what I did. It's not so hard. She's sixteen. She learned that he's her father. She wanted his name. And he said no. So she went away." Her hand made a bird in flight.

"What will she do now?"

"She'll be stubborn," Justine said. "As stubborn he is. She won't surrender. She'll announce it to the world if he doesn't give in." A smile tilted her mouth. "I told her that perhaps I could help her." He laughed and she gave him a quizzical look. "What?"

"You're a devious woman," he said.

"Oh," she said. "I already knew that. I captured you, didn't I?"

They didn't speak again until Valentin said, "We can end this day now."

Justine said, "That would suit me fine."

He offered her his hand.

Chapter Twenty-Four

The sun broke through the wisps of clouds just after dawn, the river and the lake stopped rising, and the few tiny puddles between the cobblestones gave up their last sparkling droplets. A perked ear might have caught the general sigh of relief that rose from the streets that the feared storm had not come ashore, but had lingered over the gulf and then died a quiet death. Those citizens back of town had more reason to relax. There had been no bloody violence, no bodies left ravaged, indeed not so much as a drunkard hauled off to Parish Prison.

This same morning, a letter marked *Confidential* had been delivered to police headquarters. It was addressed to Chief Reynolds and had come from Captain J. Picot.

In the letter, captain explained that due to an emergency, he was compelled to leave the city for an unknown period of time and was thereby resigning his commission, effective immediately. He apologized for the sudden notice and hoped that it would not cause the department undue trouble. Instructions for his remaining salary to be sent to an account at First National Bank were included.

After the chief got over his surprise, he puzzled over the letter and then heaved the deepest sigh of all. A long-running pain was finally gone. Who cared about the circumstances? He tucked the letter away and went about fabricating an excuse for Picot's sudden departure and starting his search for a replacement.

~

Valentin sat down for breakfast with the ladies. At one point, he got up to answer the telephone. After he made some calls of his own, he returned to tell them that he had business to take care of in town, but would be back in time for lunch and then to squire them to whatever corner of the city they pleased. At the front door, he whispered to Justine that he was going to the law offices and might have to leave the Ford there. She could see the crestfallen look in his eyes when he said this.

Before he attended to that, he drove to Anderson's Café and found Each and McKinney waiting with the King of Storyville. They were drinking coffee from the silver urn, laced with brandy. Once Valentin got settled, Anderson said, "Well?"

"Gregory's dead," Valentin said.

"You know this for a fact?"

"As close as I can say."

"Who was he?" Each said.

"I don't know," Valentin said.

"We'll find out as soon as someone files a missing person report," McKinney said. "We're also tracking down the owner of the Locomobile. So whichever comes first." Anderson stroked his mustache with a thoughtful fingertip. "Captain Picot has left the police force," McKinney went on. "And the city. To parts unknown."

The King of Storyville stared at the detective, then began to smile.

After a jovial hour, Valentin shook hands all around and drove out St. Charles Avenue. Inside, he announced himself. Sam Ross appeared and led him to a conference room.

"About Emelie," the detective began. "You can tell Mr. Alberton that she's safe. We don't know where she is. But we do know who she is." Ross frowned at him, puzzled. "Tell him that. And tell him he doesn't have much of a choice. He'll understand.

We can go from there. You know how to reach me."

The attorney considered and said, "All right, then."

"If I'm still working for you."

"We'll see about that. We can talk next week."

"That's fine," Valentin said. "By the way, has Alberton asked for the Ford to be returned?"

Ross gave an absent shrug. "He hasn't said anything to me."

Valentin said, "Good. Then I'm driving it back home."

Justine prepared a simple lunch, packed it in a basket, and Valentin carried her and Evangeline to Audubon Park. As in all the other public parks in the city, people of color were officially restricted. But because this was New Orleans, the law was porous, and he escorted them without concern.

The women strolled the trail along the lagoon as he followed behind. Now that all the dark drama was over, he enjoyed the world being quiet again. The afternoon was pleasant, with a patchy sun and soft breeze. Soon it would turn cool and the rest of the leaves would fall. The weeks of September 1914 would fade into the past.

They were sitting on one of the benches with the colas Valentin had bought at the stand and enjoying the antics of a young mother with two children who ran in frantic circles, pulling kites. Watching them, Evangeline said, "I took my children to play."

"Oh?" Justine said. "When was that?"

"Long ago." She closed her eyes for a moment, then opened them. "Yes. I remember the sunlight on the grass. And their voices. Their happy voices." She said nothing further, her gaze dreamy.

Justine turned to see Valentin wearing an expression that made her want to wrap him in her arms.

The moment passed. He looked up and said, "We should be getting on."

~

The sun had gone down and the faint stars were joined by a pale half-moon. Valentin was standing on the back gallery when Evangeline stepped outside. When she moved close to him to gaze up at the indigo sky, he realized it was the first time that they'd been alone.

"It's clear now," she said. "And I thought it would be terrible. A night without end." Valentin didn't speak, feeling her presence enclose him. Or maybe that was only his imagination. "I'm glad the storm passed," she went on. "And that everyone is all right."

Valentin nodded. *Yes, everyone that I care about.* A quiet moment came and went and he spoke the words that had been stirring ever since she had arrived. "Miss Evangeline. I...I mean we would...like you to stay with us."

She drew her eyes from the stars. "But I'd be such a burden."

"You wouldn't," he said. "Justine wants you here. I want you here. This would be your home. For as long as you want to stay."

She laughed, a gentle sound. "But I'm a stranger. You don't know who I am. *I* don't know who I am."

He bowed his head to whisper the words he could not speak aloud. She treated him to a patient look, then placed a hand beneath his chin and raised his face to her steady eyes. "What did you say?"

"Please," he said. "Will you stay?"

The seconds lingered until she smiled at him and said, "I will."

THE END

ABOUT THE AUTHOR

David Fulmer is the author of seven critically-acclaimed and award-winning novels. He has been nominated for a Shamus Award for Best Novel, a LA Times Book Prize, a Barry Award, and a Falcon Award, and has won a Benjamin Franklin Award, an AudioFile Earphones Award, and the Shamus Award for Best First Novel. He has been nominated to numerous "Best of" lists, including Atlanta Magazine's "Best of the Shelf" and New York Magazine's "Best Novels You've Never Read" and his books have received superlative reviews from publications including *The New York Times, Publishers Weekly, The Washington Post, The Boston Globe, Library Journal*, and *The Christian Science Monitor*. In addition to audiobook releases, his novels have been translated into Italian, Japanese, French, and Turkish. His novel *Will You Meet Me in Heaven?* was released in 2014. The rights to all five of his Storyville mysteries were recently optioned for television.

CPSIA information can be obtained at www.ICGtesting.com
Printed in the USA
LVOW08s2008230616

493770LV00003B/18/P